ATLANTIS LEGACY BOOK SIX

RISE
OF THE
REVENANTS

LINDSEY SPARKS

ISBN: 9781949485332

ALSO BY LINDSEY SPARKS

ECHO WORLD
ECHO TRILOGY
Echo in Time
Resonance
Time Anomaly
Dissonance
Ricochet Through Time

KAT DUBOIS CHRONICLES
Ink Witch
Outcast
Underground
Soul Eater
Judgement
Afterlife

THE NIK CHRONICLES
(Ream exclusive serial)

FATELESS TRILOGY
Song of Scarabs and Fallen Stars
Darkness Between the Stars
Uncross the Stars

LEGACIES OF OLYMPUS
ATLANTIS LEGACY
Sacrifice of the Sinners
Legacy of the Lost
Fate of the Fallen
Dreams of the Damned
Song of the Soulless
Blood of the Broken
Rise of the Revenants

ALLWORLD ONLINE
AO: Pride & Prejudice
AO: The Wonderful Wizard of Oz
Vertigo

THE LAST VAMPIRE QUEEN
(Ream exclusive serial)

THE ENDING WORLD
THE ENDING SERIES
(writing as Lindsey Fairleigh)
The Ending Beginnings: Omnibus Edition
After The Ending
Into The Fire
Out Of The Ashes
Before The Dawn
World Before

THE ENDING LEGACY
World After
The Raven Queen
The Ghost King

For more information on Lindsey and her books:
www.authorlindseysparks.com

Signed books and exclusive merch:
lindseysparksbookshop.com

Join Lindsey's mailing list to stay up to date on releases
AND to get access to her FREE subscriber library, including
Ink Witch, *Echo in Time*, and *Legacy of the Lost*
in ebook AND audiobook.
https://www.authorlindseysparks.com/join-newsletter

Check out Lindsey's reasder subscription on Ream
for bonus scenes, exclusive serials, and merch:
https://reamstories.com/lindseysparks

PART ONE
Cora

1

Hades and I lay side by side on our backs on the observation deck, staring out at the vast expanse of outer space through the curved wall of reinforced glass. The stars beyond were like bright pinpricks puncturing the black void. My eyes strained to see the darkness between them, almost as if I expected to find something. Some guidance, perhaps, or maybe even some hope. If Fiona couldn't figure out a way to deliver the soul virus to the Tsakali, I feared that the end of the Olympian species—and humanity by association—wasn't only likely. It was inevitable.

My head rested on Hades' outstretched arm, and I leaned into him, letting his warmth comfort me from the press of that cold eternity looming beyond. Neither one of us spoke for what seemed like hours. The only sound was our occasional deep exhales as we each considered Fiona's plan for ending the age-old war with the Tsakali. In some ways, it was too good to be true; in others, it seemed utterly impossible. To give our synthetic enemy souls. To make them feel. Make them *care*. This went beyond science fiction. *This* felt like magic.

My regulator was deactivated, the stone in the pendant glowing electric-blue, and Hades' mind was open to me. I sensed his thoughts the instant they formed. He feared Fiona offered false hope, an ingenious but unattainable solution to our endless struggle. He was hesitant to make an offensive strike against the Tsakali after our people had been on the defensive for so long. He worried he and I would lose each other again, right after we finally found our way back to one another.

Hades broke the silence, his hushed voice echoing through the cavernous space. "It's a bold idea," he said. "But it's also extremely dangerous. If they find out what we're planning—if they even suspect we're searching for a way to force a conscience upon them—they will come after us with every weapon in their arsenal. The *Elysium* and the new settlement on Terra will no longer be a mere annoyance to them, but the greatest threat to them in the universe."

"They fear being afraid," I said, plucking the thought from Hades' mind. He could be quite poetic at times, especially for the cold, calculating scientist our people not only believed him to be but *needed* him to be. "Or, at least, they understand the power of fear enough to know that should they develop the capability to fear—or to love or to forgive—they'll lose themselves. Everything they are will cease to be, and *that* must be avoided at all costs."

"Precisely," Hades said, pulling me closer and pressing a kiss to my temple. He inhaled deeply, breathing me in, and his exhale rustled the small hairs that had escaped from my ponytail and now tickled my forehead. He relaxed, laying back on the metal floor once more. "Following this path could very well lead to our end."

"And yet," I said softly, "Fio's virus might be our only hope for peace. For a real future. If we can make the Tsakali feel, maybe they'll see that there's more to existence than consumption and domination. And *then*, maybe they won't want to fight anymore."

"Maybe," Hades said, sounding dubious. "Of course, there's always the chance that activating emotions within them will awaken a righteous hatred that makes them an even more dangerous enemy."

I grinned up at the stars and glanced sidelong at Hades. "But righteous hatred, while motivating, is also blinding," I countered, my eyebrows rising. "The Tsakali might not be open to establishing peace once they can *feel*, but they will be opening themselves up to new ways for us to exploit that blindness." When Hades said nothing, I gently elbowed his side. "I make a good point," I said, laughing softly. "You don't have to admit it out loud. I know the truth." I turned my face toward him and whispered. "You agree with me."

He released a breathy laugh, his apprehension masked by his genuine joy. "I may come to regret giving you open access to my mind."

I took a moment to savor his unrestrained happiness, wrapping it around me like a cozy blanket. Since we returned from Othrys, our relationship finally fully realized, he had been more open and lighthearted than ever before, but laughter from him was still a relative rarity.

I sighed and returned to staring out at the stars. "All I know is that this could be our best chance of ending this war once and for all—to *finally* free our people from this endless struggle. If we have to put everyone in danger in order to reach for that freedom, isn't it worth it? What's one more risk, really? After everything?"

Hades didn't answer for a long moment, and his silence was a heavy weight on my heart. I propped myself up on my elbow to look at him, only to find he was already staring at me. His ice-blue eyes were intense, and I felt my heart skip a beat.

"I'm not afraid of putting *everyone* in danger," he said, his voice a deep rumble. "I'm afraid of endangering *you*. Of *losing* you. Again. Peri—Cora—every part of you. You're everything to me, and without you—" His words caught in his throat, and he closed his eyes, his next inhale visibly shaky. When he lifted his lids again, his heated stare locked with mine. "You elevate me to the best version of myself," he professed. "And I *know* I can't do this without you."

My breath caught in my throat at his words, and my cheeks grew warm. Of course, after everything we had been through together, I knew how deeply Hades cared for me. But hearing him express his feelings so openly still made my heart seem to swell in my chest.

"You won't lose me," I said, reaching out to take his hand. "I won't let that happen." I slid my fingers between his. "We'll do this together, Hades. Just like down on Othrys. We either live together, or we die together."

"And if we die?" he asked, squeezing my hand like he was afraid I would slip away.

"Then we die knowing we did everything we could to end this war and to make a better future for our people." For all the people who had fallen victim to the Tsakali, either directly or indirectly.

My eyes stung as tears welled. For my mom and Raiden and Emi. For that other version of myself living in the simulation, who could look forward to a life with the man who possessed the other half of my heart. The piece that didn't already belong to Hades.

Hades raised my hand to his chest, his thumb gently tracing over my knuckles as his gaze skimmed my features, lingering on my lips. I sensed the sudden shift in his mood an instant before he sat up. Suddenly, heat simmered in my blood, ignited by his desire, and my belly tightened with anticipation. I activated my regulator, preferring the excitement born of anticipation of the unknown.

"All this talk of dying makes me want to live life to the fullest while we still can," Hades murmured.

"Oh?" I pushed myself up as well, curling my legs underneath me. "What did you have in mind?"

"I think I could use more practice in the zero gravity chamber," he said, the corner of his mouth tensing to tease a smirk. He stood, groaning as the motion tweaked old aches, and held his hand out to help me up. "Unless you have other plans."

Fiona was dog-sitting Tila in her lab—it was good for Fiona to spend time with another living being—and the Amazons were in a holding pattern while we figured out exactly what we were going to do about this soul virus possibility. Selene was more than capable of handling their training . . . for a while, at least.

I smiled coyly and shook my head, trying to not appear too eager, and placed my hand in his. "No other plans."

2

"So, I don't know if we should tell everyone yet," I said, sitting beside Meg on the floor on one side of the training room, our backs to the wall.

Tila lay snuggled beside me, her enormous head resting on her paws and her floppy ears perked up as she watched the women sparring with practice dorus on the mats spread throughout the space. Their movements were fluid and graceful, their bodies well-honed sinew and muscle under their hoplon suits. The crack of their orichalcum staffs colliding reverberated off the floors and ceiling. On the center mat, Selene and Caly were locked in a heated grappling match, each having lost her weapon earlier in the fight.

These women's conviction for the cause—survival—heartened me. They would do what needed to be done to protect our people, no matter the cost.

Only Fiona, Hades, Meg, and I knew about the possibility of an end to the war. An end to the running. And Gertie knew, too, of course. Was it better to tell the Zari Amazons and sprout potentially false hope or hold back until we knew the soul virus wasn't just a tantalizing theory? We knew it was possible—the Titan in league with the pirates had somehow developed a soul—but was it replicable? Or was she unique in other ways that would make duplicating the soul effect inviable?

Meg's gaze flicked to me, her bronze eyes unreadable, and I sensed the sickening direction of her thoughts a moment before she spoke. "What would Demeter have done?" she asked, her tone neutral.

I snorted a laugh, my mood instantly souring as I thought of the disgraced leader of the Order of Amazons. Demeter was long dead, her consciousness entombed with those of her misguided supporters in an isolated portion of the simulation. Although, honestly, I would have felt better if she hadn't been uploaded at all. It unsettled me to know such an insidious being was stored on the ship, even if she was contained apart from the main simulation.

"She would've lied to us," I said bitterly. "Fed us just enough information to ensure we did whatever she wanted us to do."

"Well," Meg said, leaning closer to bump her shoulder against mine. "Maybe don't do that, then?"

Chuckling, I shrugged one shoulder. "I think I can manage that." I exhaled a heavy sigh and reached for Tila, scratching her neck under her collar. "I just don't want to get their hopes up if it doesn't work out." Running my hands over my hair, I tucked a strand that had escaped from my braid behind my ear. "But they deserve to know what's going on," I added. When it came to leading this new generation of Amazon warriors, I refused to be anything like Demeter. I wouldn't lie to them—not even a lie of omission.

Meg hummed, considering not only my words but also my thoughts. "They're strong," she finally said. "They've proved they can handle whatever comes their way—be that a hard decision, a dangerous mission, or heartbreaking disappointment."

I nodded slowly. These women had already survived so much. Their own people had practically enslaved them, but here they were, risking their lives to save the same souls who had demeaned and subjugated them. They were warriors, after all, in every sense of the word. With them, honor and duty always came first.

"Okay," I said, finally. "Let's tell them."

3

I PEERED INTO RAIDEN'S consciousness orb, my nose nearly touch-ing the wall of the Vault of Souls. I watched him walk the grounds of Blackthorn Manor, the scene skewed by my perspective, like I was peering through a fisheye lens. Clearly, he was searching for something or some*one*.

Until he left for the Army, Raiden had always been my safe harbor during a storm. I didn't regret my decision to separate the Cora half of my backup consciousness from Peri and upload that piece of my duplicated self to the simulation. It was the right thing to do—both for *me*, the Cora-Peri hybrid, and for *that* part of me, plain old Cora. But doing so had locked *me* out from even making temporary visits into the simulation to see Raiden, my mom, and Emi, and I couldn't deny that I missed being able to turn to Raiden when my thoughts were troubled.

The Zari women had reacted with the expected stoicism when I in-formed them of Fiona's plan to end the war, but their suppressed excite-ment was still clear in their exchanged glances and quickened breaths. Telling them had been the right thing to do. I didn't doubt that.

But did that mean we should tell Raiden and the others residing inside the simulation? My mom and Emi? All the Olympians? Should we tell the other me? They couldn't help with the mission directly, but if we did launch what amounted to a spiritual attack on the Tsakali, we would be shining a spotlight on our people as a threat to our ancient enemy, thus putting every soul stored on this ship at risk. Didn't they deserve to have a say, too? Or, at least, to know what was going on?

Through the warped lens of the consciousness orb, I watched Raiden return to the manor house, then climb up three flights of stairs to the attic. Everything about the grounds and interior of Blackthorn Manor was exactly as I remembered it, save for the strange standing mirror leaning against the wall in the attic.

Raiden approached the mirror, squinting as he drew closer. It didn't display his reflection, instead showing a strange rocky landscape covered in clusters of jutting, jewel-toned crystals. Suddenly, he stumbled backward.

My mom and Emi burst through the mirror's surface, clinging to one another and laughing so hard they were nearly bent double. I couldn't help but smile at seeing them so happy, even if tears welled in my eyes at the same time. I missed them terribly. They were right here, right in front of me, but forever out of reach. I wasn't sure if knowing they still existed made it easier or harder to move on. To let them go.

Raiden asked my mom something I couldn't hear.

My mom shook her head, pinching her side and breathing deeply to control her laughter.

Raiden crossed his arms over his broad chest, his expression souring.

"Cora?" Fiona's voice intruded on my snooping. Disoriented, I searched the attic for her but only found Raiden with my mom and Emi.

"Cora?" Fiona repeated. "Are you there?" She snickered. "Or are you *busy?*" That last word oozed innuendo.

"Crap!" I hissed, straightening and pulling my attention away from the scene visible through Raiden's consciousness orb. Fiona wasn't *in-*

side the simulation. Duh. She was out here, on board the *Elysium*, speaking to me through my comms patch.

I looked around nervously, relieved to find Tila was the only other living being among the seemingly endless columns of gently glowing consciousness orbs that filled the aisles of the Vault of Souls. Nobody but my dog had witnessed me losing complete touch with reality for some unknown amount of time, and she wouldn't judge me for being a sad sap.

I cleared my throat and touched the tip of my index finger to the comms patch stuck to the skin behind my ear. "I'm here, Fio," I said in a rush. "What's up?"

"Shit, Cora," she said. "Were you and Hades—"

"Oh my god, stop," I blurted. "No. I was running in the vault, and I had my headphones in. I didn't hear you at first." It wasn't *exactly* a lie. Tila and I *had* been running laps through the seemingly endless winding corridors within the Vault of Souls before I caved in to my unhealthy urges and snooped into Raiden's consciousness orb.

"Ugh." I could picture Fiona's wrinkled nose expression perfectly. "Well, you're sweaty either way," she said. "Go clean up, then meet me in the lab." As an afterthought, she added, "And bring Hades."

My eyes widened. Her voice had that manic quality that usually accompanied a breakthrough. "Fio," I said, drawing out her name as I hesitated to voice the question I was desperate to ask. But I couldn't resist. "Did you do it?" I started for the corridor that led to the exit, walking fast. "Did you figure out how to create the soul virus?"

Fiona didn't answer right away. Or at all.

I made it up the vault's corridor, and the door panel glided open as I approached. I paused in the doorway, unsettled by her silence. "Fio?"

"I did," she finally said. "But there's a catch."

4

I RAN INTO HADES in one of the Med Sector corridors, anxiety tangling my stomach in knots. Tila trotted ahead, greeting him with sniffs and tail wags. He patted her head as we approached one another. His expression softened, his furrowed brow smoothing out and a gentle smile curving up the corners of his mouth.

I stopped at the bisecting corridor that led to Fiona's lab to wait for him. Taking a deep breath, I leaned against the wall opposite the new corridor, crossing my arms over my chest. "Did she tell you about the catch?"

My regulator was active, suppressing my gifts to afford privacy to the rest of the people on board the ship, so I couldn't read Hades' thoughts. Despite his open invitation to not hold back around him, I preferred the mystery of not knowing everything going on in his head. Even so, unease knotted in my gut as I thought through all the dire possibilities, and I wished Fiona hadn't mentioned the catch at all.

The crease between Hades' brows returned, and he shook his head. "Just that there is one." He stopped when he reached me, his gaze roaming over my features as Tila circled us. I wished he would lean in and kiss me, anything to distract me from the mounting dread. But he didn't. "Any thoughts on what this *catch* might be?" he asked.

"Not a clue." I pushed off the wall to start down the new corridor.

Hades fell in step on my right, Tila on my left, and the three of us walked in silence for a few moments.

"Fio can be a touch melodramatic, in case you haven't noticed," I said, giving him a meaningful glance.

Amusement curved his lips. "You don't say."

I smiled, only slightly forced. "It could be nothing," I said, trying not to get worked up over some hypothetical hurdle. "Or, at least, nothing big."

"I hope you're right," Hades said, his doubtful tone suggesting that he wasn't so hopeful. He had learned to expect the worst over the millennia he had spent alone, emerging from cryosleep for brief periods, only to be disappointed time and again.

I nudged his arm with my shoulder. "Even if it's something huge, we'll adjust," I told him, sounding more confident than I felt. "We knew this would be dangerous and that there would be risks. We just didn't know how dangerous or what those risks would be, exactly. Maybe that's what this is—Fio figuring all that out." I shrugged, watching Hades' expression out of the corner of my eye. "And that would be great because then we'd know what kind of danger we might face by going through with this."

"And if the danger is too great?" he asked.

I chuckled, my grin genuine. "I do love a challenge."

Letting out a breathy laugh, Hades shook his head. "You sound like Selene."

My responding laugh reached my belly, and I thought it might have been the first time I had truly laughed since my mom and Raiden died. It felt good, even if thinking of them quickly tempered my amusement.

The door panel to Fiona's lab was up ahead, and I stopped, grabbing Hades' arm to hold him back. Tila trotted ahead, eager to see another friend.

I waited until Hades' keen gaze met mine. "We've done the impossible," I said and trailed my hand down his forearm, threading my fingers between his. "We found our way back to one another." I raised my eyebrows, marking that as the momentous achievement it was. "And I think we proved down on Othrys that so long as we're together, we can do *pretty much* anything."

Hades searched my eyes, his gaze so intense that I didn't need access to my psychic gifts to read his thoughts. He believed in us. In me.

All I had to do now was to not let him down. No pressure.

<h1 style="text-align:center">5</h1>

THE DOOR PANEL TO Fiona's lab glided open silently as Tila approached, and Hades and I quickly caught up. When I reached the doorway, I scanned the high-tech space, searching for Fiona's shock of tangerine hair.

The half-dissected Titan from Othrys lay on one worktable, the synthetic being's ruined head covered with a heavy gray cloth, like even Fiona couldn't stand to face the gruesome sight. The other, less damaged Titan—the one who had been allied with the pirates—lay on a worktable farther back in the lab. Both Titans' chest cavities were spread open, and Fiona had laid out various parts of their synthetic anatomy on the neighboring tables.

I wrinkled my nose automatically, anticipating the rank odor of decay from what appeared to be a pair of corpses. Except there was nothing organic about those bodies—nothing to decay. Every model of Tsakali, from scout to Titan and everything in between, was a machine despite their near perfect ability to visually mimic organic life, and there was nothing in the air beyond the usual faintly metallic scent from all the Olympian equipment that lined the periphery of the space.

In the far corner of the lab, our captive Tsakali scout huddled in its usual spot at the back of its cage. Its eyes were wide and watchful, its childlike appearance as disturbing as ever.

I scanned the lab once more. So far as I could tell, Fiona wasn't here.

"That's weird," I muttered, looking at her workstation. Her tablet sat on the table where she had set up her Frankenstein's monster of a computer composed of both Olympian and human tech. She had rigged her tablet to be her mobile interface with the ship, and she never went anywhere without it or her comms patch, which gave her a direct line of communication with Gertie, the ship's AI.

I touched the comms patch behind my ear. "Fio? We're in the lab." My stare naturally returned to the scout, probably because *it* was staring at me. "Where are you?"

"Can't a girl go to the loo in peace?" Fiona responded. "Bloody hell. I'll be there in a minute."

Smiling and shaking my head, I lowered my hand. "She's on her way," I told Hades, who had wandered over to the scout's cage.

I made my way over to Fiona's computer rig, skimming over the three upright holoscreens, then glanced down at her tablet, hoping to find some clue to the cryptic "catch" she had mentioned.

Tila, already stretched out on the doggy bed Fiona had made for the pup behind her desk chair, barely raised her head as I approached.

"Don't mind me," I murmured to my dog as I wedged my boots between Fiona's chair and Tila's bed, leaning over the back of the chair to skim the holoscreens. Unfortunately, just like the tech itself, the language displayed in the open windows on the screens was a hodgepodge of human—English, mostly—and Olympian. I couldn't make heads or tails of any of it.

"Something's different," Hades said, his voice low. I peered around the screens to find him crouched beside the scout's cage, his head cocked to the side as he studied the diminutive and deceptively dangerous captive.

"What do you mean?" I asked, splitting my attention between Hades and the left-most holoscreen. The longer I stared at Fiona's own personal creole language, the more I thought I could make sense of it. Kind of. Maybe.

"The scout is . . ." Hades paused. "If I didn't know better, I would say it looks *afraid*."

I scoffed, glancing over the screen at Hades's back. "That's impossible," I said. Tsakali didn't *feel*. Not fear, not love, not regret, not compassion. That was kind of the entire problem, after all. They didn't care that they were destroying the universe in their need to possess all sources of chaos energy.

"I know," Hades said distractedly. "But this one . . ."

Blowing out a breath, I abandoned the gobbledygook on the screens to join Hades in the back corner of the lab, avoiding glancing down at the gruesome sights of the two Titans as I passed their bodies. When I reached the cage, I crouched beside Hades and cocked my head to the side to study the scout. The Tsakali captive watched us closely from its huddled position in the opposite corner, as far as it could get from us. Not from *us*, I realized. From *me*.

My brows rose. Now that I was really looking at it, the scout's wide-eyed stare *did* appear less watchful than before and far more fearful. I raised a hand to my regulator and traced the tip of my finger around the stone set into the pendant, unleashing my psychic gifts.

As the bright, electric-blue glow overtook the gentle amber of the stone, the emotions present in the lab seeped into me. Pure intrigue radiated from Hades, ever the scientist. But I sensed another emotion as well—and it wasn't coming from Hades.

"Holy shit," I breathed, glancing up at Hades for a fraction of a second. I wasn't willing to take my eyes off the scout for any longer than that. "You're right. It *is* afraid."

I squinted, trying to get a clearer read of the scout's mind, but it was like trying to read the mind of a baby. There was no formation to its thoughts. They were fluid and amorphous, constantly changing. Its emotions, however, were clear as day. Fear was dominant, but there were also threads of confusion and curiosity.

"Oh, good!" Fiona exclaimed from the front of the lab, and I nearly jumped out of my hoplon suit as I burst up from the floor. Fiona strode across the lab toward us. "You've met Theo."

I gaped, switching my focus back and forth between Fiona and the scout. Beside me, Hades stood absolutely still, his attention on Fiona.

"You named it *Theo*?" I squeaked, hastily activating my regulator to mute my psychic abilities.

"*He* named himself Theo," Fiona said, stopping to lean back against the edge of the nearest worktable. "And he identifies as male."

"But—" I shook my head, incapable of getting a coherent thought out. Tsakali couldn't identify as *anything*. They weren't biological creatures. They didn't have sexes or genders or anything like that. They were *machines*.

"You infected him," Hades observed while I silently spluttered.

I crossed my arms over my chest and reeled in my composure, turning my back to the cage. "Fio, that was insanely risky," I said, studying her more closely. She looked exhausted, with dark, bruise-like circles under her eyes and her bun tilted akimbo atop her head. "I wish you had waited for us."

"Pfff." Fiona waved a hand dismissively. "It worked. He *feels*."

"Then what's the catch?" I asked, narrowing my eyes.

Fiona scrubbed her hands over her face and laughed under her breath. "Good job, Fio," she mimicked, lowering her hands and staring up at the ceiling. "Way to solve the impossible puzzle. You're a genius."

"You are," Hades said. "For what it's worth. I've never met another who could accomplish what you have in so little time. This is *very* impressive."

"Don't patronize me," Fiona said, aiming a level stare at Hades. Her annoyance evaporated, and she preened. "But thanks."

"Fio," I said, stepping forward and relaxing my arms so I could take her smaller hands in mine. Her fingers felt frail in my grasp. "You know you're a genius." I waited for her eyes to lock onto mine. "You're, like, the smartest person who ever existed. You might literally be saving two entire species of people. You are *amazing*, and we would definitely all be dead already if not for you."

Pink crept up her pale, freckled cheeks, but she nodded and donned a proud mask, effectively hiding her humility. "That is all correct."

"It is," I said, smiling. I squeezed her hands. "So what's the catch?"

Fiona sighed, her eyelids drifting shut. She was quiet for so long that I almost thought she had fallen asleep right there, leaning on the edge of the table. She certainly appeared tired enough for something like that to happen.

"Fio?"

After long seconds, she finally cracked open one eyelid. "He has a soul now—or he can feel or whatever." On her exhale, her whole body drooped. "But he's not contagious."

6

"**H**E'S NOT CONTAGIOUS?" I said, repeating Fiona's words back to her. "What does that mean?" I glanced from Fiona to the scout and back. At Fiona's raised eyebrows, I added, "In the greater scheme of things." Obviously, I knew what *contagious* meant. "What does it mean *for us,* and how does it change what we need to do to complete the mission?"

Fiona's focus shifted past me to the scout. "It changes everything," she said morosely. "I was thinking we would just infect this little guy here and drop him into a nest of Tsakali, and the soulware would just, well, spread. I mean, I created it to spread, and it's a fecking beautiful little worm. It's designed to spread via radio waves, making it essentially an airborne computer virus. *But* as I learned from infecting Theo, here, the soulware goes dormant as soon as it integrates with the Tsakali code, so to speak. Kind of like a quantum quarantine—an antivirus fail-safe triggered by the soulware itself." She looked at me, then at Hades. "He won't work as our delivery mechanism," she said. "*That's* what this means for the mission."

"Okay . . ." I crossed my arms and chewed on the inside of my cheek, then asked, "What *will* work as a delivery mechanism?"

"Nanotracers," Fiona said. "Just like we used back on Earth to tag humans for uploading."

"Which will require psychics to guide them," I thought aloud.

Not ideal. I much preferred the old plan, where we dropped off the contagious scout in a highly populated Tsakali area and high-tailed it out of there. Now, Amazons would have to infiltrate and linger, exposing ourselves and risking our lives while we used psychic energy to spread the nanotracers.

"And multiple target sites," I added. It wouldn't do us any good if we infected all the Tsakali in a single location, only for their brethren to destroy them. If the virus wasn't contagious, those we infected via nanotracer would be the only ensouled Tsakali there ever were.

Hades frowned, the expression more doubtful than thoughtful.

I stared at him for a long moment. "You don't think it'll work?"

He exhaled heavily through his nose. "I don't think it's *enough*." He tilted his head to the side, like he was admitting a counterargument had merit before either of us had even posed it. "It will cause infighting among the Tsakali, which is a good thing for us, but eventually, the 'soulless' ones will wipe out the infected. There are too many of them, spread all over the universe. That outcome is inevitable." He paused, studying the scout. "For this to work—for this 'soulware' to offer us a true end to this war—we have to figure out a way to make the virus spread on its own. It *must* be contagious. On its own. Without external assistance."

Fiona scoffed. "If there's a way, *I* can't figure it out."

I sucked in a breath to argue that she had only been working on this for a few days. That *surely* a genius like her could solve any problem, given enough time.

Anticipating my response, Hades caught my eye and ticked his chin to the right, silently cautioning me to keep silent. "Show me the model of the virus," he said, shifting his attention to Fiona. "Before we fled from Olympus, one of my teams was investigating Tsakali physiology. We discovered many subtle defense mechanisms built into their systems. Maybe I'll be able to offer some insight into *why* the virus is going dormant. Perhaps all we need to do is tack on a second virus that will subdue the internal response within the Tsakali."

Fiona swept an arm out toward her behemoth computer. "Be my guest," she said, her welcoming words countered by her stiff posture. She was going to be very, *very* unhappy if Hades found a solution that had evaded her. She would accept his help, of course. This was about the fate of our two peoples, and all that. But she wouldn't be happy about it.

Hades studied the scout for a few seconds longer, then turned away and headed for Fiona's workstation. Either he was oblivious to Fiona's affront, or he simply didn't care. I was betting on the latter. Hades had been around long enough to know that egos had no place in a lab—not when the stakes were life and death.

Fiona watched him dismally, then turned back to me and offered me a mopey smile.

"Teamwork makes the dream work," I told her.

She rolled her eyes, then sighed and glanced over her shoulder at Hades, who was now settling in her desk chair. "I may need to borrow him for a while," she said and looked back at me. "Hope you don't mind."

I waved my hand dismissively. "Don't worry about it." I had plenty to do, plotting and prepping for the offensive that might *finally* take out my people's ancient enemy.

Fiona rubbed her hands over her face, massaging around her eyes. It was almost like now that she knew she had help, her productivity high was fading. I could practically see her brain shutting down.

"Go get some rest, Fio." I glanced at Hades. "He'll need time to study up on what you created, anyway."

Fiona's stare went distant, and she nodded slowly to herself. Without another word, she straightened from the edge of the worktable and wound her way toward the door.

"And don't forget to make an updated backup of yourself," I called after her. Fiona was integral to both the running of the simulation and to the development of the soul virus, and I had been encouraging her to make a backup of her consciousness twice a day, just to make sure that if the worst happened, a recent version of her would be available for upload to the simulation.

Fiona waited for the door panel to slide open, raising one hand to give me a blind thumbs up. A moment later, she was gone.

Hades was already engrossed in his work, analyzing the model of the soulware virus on the center holoscreen. I leaned against the edge of the table and watched him for a moment, admiring his absolute focus. Despite the gravity of the situation, it still thrilled me to see him in action. Fiona was a bona fide genius—like, whatever level was above mensa, she was that—but Hades was brilliant in his own right, his brain power backed up by literal lifetimes of experience. There was no one else I trusted more to solve this problem than the two of them.

But what if there truly was no viable solution? What if there was no way to make the virus spread on its own? We could still attack, still infiltrate and infect via psychics and nanotracers, sowing chaos and discord among the Tsakali at strategic locations. Maybe focus on sites with a concentrated population of Titans to take out the most powerful among them. We *had* to take advantage of their weakened state, however temporary the situation, to create confusion and disharmony among them.

"I can feel you watching me," Hades said without moving his focus away from the screen.

"Sorry." I shook my head. I hadn't realized I was still staring at him while my thoughts spun elsewhere. "I was just thinking through the backup plan, in case we can't figure out a way to make the virus spread on its own. We can still take out a few strategic locations, then launch an assault to take advantage of the Tsakali in their weakened state."

Hades nodded thoughtfully and straightened, finally tearing his attention away from the screen and peering my way. "I think that's worth considering. Perhaps we could find a way to disable their communication systems. Or we could disrupt their supply lines, or—"

I held up a hand, interrupting him. "Whoa there. Don't waste your valuable brainpower on this. I'll handle the backup plan." I glanced at the workstation. "You focus on plan A."

I waited for Hades to return his attention to the holoscreen, then pushed away from the table and stepped closer to the cage in the back corner of the lab and the cowering creature within. It—*he*, apparently—had been noncommunicative before. Clearly that had changed, since he had given Fiona a name and expressed a gender identity. If he was willing to talk, there was a chance he could help. Maybe he had some insight into his kind that we had overlooked.

I crouched, resting my forearms on my thighs, and studied Theo through the electrified bars. He watched me closely, his arms wrapped around his folded-up legs, hugging them close to his small body. His childlike appearance was much more convincing now that he displayed genuine fear, sprouting an uncomfortable moral conflict within me. Could we really keep him caged like an animal? He was a sentient being—with a conscience. A *soul*.

"I'm Cora," I ventured, offering him a slight smile. "And you're Theo?"

The scout dipped his chin, his huge eyes locked on me.

I waited for a beat, studying him closely. "You know what we're trying to do, don't you? We want to infect the Tsakali with a virus that won't hurt them, exactly, but that *might* stop the war."

Theo nodded slowly. "I understand what you're attempting to do."

"Do you want that to happen?" I asked. "Do you want the war to end?"

He shrugged, averting his gaze to the floor of his cage. "What would I do?"

My brows rose, and I cocked my head to the side. "What do you mean?"

His eyes flicked up toward me, meeting mine for a fraction of a second before returning to the floor. "What will my purpose be? I was created to observe Olympians and to report back to my people. What would I do if the war ended and my people no longer needed me to do this? Why would I exist?"

My eyes widened. The scout was having a full-on existential crisis, searching for the meaning of life and all that. I hadn't expected it, but maybe I should have.

It was my turn to shrug. "Purpose isn't static, but ever evolving. Maybe your new purpose would be to try to figure that out?" I said, uncertain. I laughed under my breath. "Just like the rest of us."

Theo frowned, looking up at me again. "But we're not like you. We were each created for a specific purpose. When that purpose is gone, we are nothing."

I felt a twinge of pity for the scared, confused creature before me. "You're not nothing," I told him. "You're alive."

"Am I?" he asked, catching me off guard.

I nodded. For lifetimes, I had *known* that a machine couldn't be alive, but my absolute conviction on the matter had flown out the window the instant I sensed Theo's fear. "You have thoughts and feelings and a will to survive, don't you?" I said. "If that's not life, then I don't know what is."

There was no cut-and-dried rule that life was defined by a being's state as organic, was there? And even if there was, new discoveries nullified old scientific rules all the time.

Theo looked at me for a long moment, his eyes searching mine. "What is your purpose, Cora?" he asked, his voice barely above a whisper.

I hesitated, not sure how to answer. I had always felt like an outsider—in every lifetime. As Cora, I hadn't come close to fitting in with the rest of humanity, and as Peri, the only engineered Olympian raised to full Amazon status, I had always been set apart. An oddity. An exception.

But since my two selves merged, I had gained a sense of purpose, a reason to fight for something bigger than myself.

"My purpose is to help end this war," I said, finally accepting this truth within myself.

"And then what?" Theo asked. "When the war is over, what will be your purpose?"

I frowned, unsure, and peeked over my shoulder at Hades, who was oblivious to my attention. I thought about the possibility of being with him *without* the tenuous future of our people looming over our heads.

"The same as yours, I suppose," I said, returning my focus to the scout. "To live."

7

"I MPOSSIBLE," SELENE GRUNTED AS I took her down to the mat. We had been sparring in the training room for a little over an hour, and only my hoplon suit's moisture wicking properties prevented me from being a dripping ball of sweat. "A Tsakali that *feels*—that's like saying you found a rock that can talk." She rolled to keep me from trapping her in a chokehold, then elbowed me in the ribs. "I don't believe it."

"It's true," I swore between heavy breaths, grappling with her to maintain my advantage. I wrapped my legs around hers and torqued my body, attempting to flip her onto her belly. If I got her face down on the mat, I would have her beat. "And I'm not sure we can justify keeping him caged like that anymore," I added. After my conversation with Theo, the idea of the childlike scout huddled in his cage wasn't sitting well.

Stunned by my confession, Selene stopped resisting me. I rolled her over, easily pinning her face down. She slapped the mat with her open palm three times, using the age-old Amazon signal of surrender to end the sparring match. It was hardly the victory I had been after, but I would take it.

Breathing hard, I released her and reclined, stretching out my legs and leaning back on my elbows. I let my head fall back and stared up at our murky reflections in the polished steel ceiling. The sounds of other women training formed a chorus of grunts and smacks all around us.

Selene scoffed. "You want to release it?"

"Him," I corrected her, though I understood her perspective. Just a few hours ago, I would have reacted the same way. Tsakali were machines. Things. *Its.*

Selene pushed up onto her hands and knees, then sat back on her heels. With a sweep of her hands, she brushed back the sweaty strands of auburn hair that had escaped from her topknot, and her sharp stare locked on me. "You want to release a Tsakali prisoner?" she said, refusing to acknowledge the scout's individuality. To her, Theo was still just a thing. Just a nameless, identity-less cog in the greater Tsakali machine.

I shrugged. "Maybe we can try to find a way to work with him," I thought aloud.

"To use him," she countered.

I suppressed a smile at her use of *him* instead of *it*. She probably hadn't even realized she'd done it, but that slight shift in thinking would help her accept the truth. Theo was a person. "He could be a valuable ally," I persisted.

Selene glanced away. "Assuming he's even willing."

I chewed on the inside of my cheek. "Come meet him," I suggested, knowing a first-hand observation would be the only way to make Selene understand where I was coming from. "He's different. He can feel and think for himself. You'll see."

Selene raised an eyebrow and crossed her arms over her chest. "And what, exactly, do you propose we do with him? Give him a room and invite him to our next strategy meeting?"

I laughed under my breath. Now she was just being obstinate. "Not exactly—"

"You're the one who said you couldn't pick out any clear thoughts from his mind," she continued. "How can you be sure he won't sabotage the ship?"

I shook my head and fought the urge to roll my eyes. "I wasn't suggesting we give him free rein," I snapped. "He would still be a prisoner. But he's also a sentient being. A *person*. I just think we can do better. I mean, we wouldn't keep an Olympian or a human prisoner in a tiny cage like that."

Selene sighed, relaxing her arms and placing her hands on her thighs. "I get where you're coming from, Cora. But if we can't read his mind, we can't run a proper risk assessment of the situation. He's a spy, after all, built to resemble an Olympian child. Duplicity and deception are hard-wired into him."

I nodded, conceding her point. "I know." At her raised brows, I repeated. "I *know*." I blew out a breath. "Just come and see him. Then we can decide what to do with him—together."

8

I WASN'T SURPRISED TO find Selene in Fiona's lab when I arrived after washing up. She stood near Theo's cage, her back to me.

Hades was so transfixed on the holoscreens in front of him, he didn't even glance my way as I entered the lab. He had been that way when I left nearly five hours ago, and I doubted he had moved much since.

Tila, on the other hand, rose from her dog bed tucked against the wall behind his chair and stretched so hard that her muscles trembled before she padded over to me, her entire backside wagging. I greeted her with some ear scratches, then crossed to Hades' spot at Fiona's workstation on the side of the lab.

I brushed my fingertips over Hades' shoulder as I passed him, and he inhaled deeply, seeming to come to life. Smiling up at me, he caught my hand and stopped me from walking away, then pulled me closer. I ran my fingers through his loose, silver-blond hair as he wrapped his arms around me and pressed in closer against my side.

"Any luck?" I asked, glancing at the holoscreens. There were so many overlapping windows open that I wouldn't even have known where to start if I were to attempt to decipher what he was doing.

"I'm not sure yet," he said, returning his attention to the screens as well. "Maybe. More of a theory than anything else, and I don't want to get our hopes up until I have something more concrete."

"You've been at it for the better part of the day," I noted, massaging his scalp as I continued to comb my fingers through his silky hair. His eyes appeared slightly bloodshot from not blinking enough while staring at the screens. "Maybe take a break and come back with a fresh mind?"

His eyelids drifted shut at my gentle touch. "Soon," he agreed. "I want to make sure I have enough to write up a brief for Fiona in case she returns while I'm resting. *Then*, I'll take a break."

"And make a backup," I reminded him.

Neither of us planned on resurrecting after our current lifetimes ended. We wanted to live out the rest of our time together, like normal, natural people. To simply enjoy the time we had left. *But*, if the worst happened and Hades died before we had ensured a viable future for our people and flown off into the starlight together, he would be uploaded to the simulation. Like Fiona, he was too important to the cause. We needed him in order to succeed, even if we only had access to him as something of a consultant, which meant he had to keep an up-to-date backup of his consciousness stored on the ship.

Hades opened his eyes, smiling up at me with the devotion born of lifetimes of longing. "And I'll make a backup."

My lips curved, my heart swelling. I loved this man with every cell in my body. How I had held him at arm's length for so long was beyond me. Unable to resist, I bent down, pressing a kiss to his lips.

When I straightened again, Hades blinked toward the back of the room. "When did Selene get here?"

"Before me." Laughing under my breath, I shook my head. "Get back to work, you slacker," I teased, stepping out of his hold. "And if you're not *too* exhausted when you're done here, call me." I tapped the skin behind my ear, right below my comms patch, and smirked. "Maybe I can help you relax."

Hades chuckled. "Of that, I have no doubt."

I was still smiling when I reached Selene at the back of the lab. Tila sat by my feet, then slumped down onto the hard floor. Her head perked up as she watched the scout in the cage.

"This is the strangest thing," Selene said, hands on her hips as she studied the frightened scout.

The stone in her regulator glowed a bright topaz, signaling that she had ready access to her psychic abilities. The faint tingle of psychic energy told me she was reading Theo right now. Or, at least, she was attempting to. Her furrowed brow suggested she was having as hard a time of it as I had.

"He's scared," she said, "but he's also curious." Her eyes narrowed. "And is that *hope*?"

I raised my brows, intrigued by what she was picking up from the scout. I had sensed fear and curiosity, but nothing akin to hope. Tracing a fingertip around my regulator stone, I deactivated it and reached out with my psychic feelers.

"I think it *is* hope," I murmured, fully aware of Theo huddled there, watching us discuss what we sensed from him. Perhaps my conversation with him earlier had struck a chord, and he was looking forward to finding his new purpose.

Selene tore her stare from the cage, her eyes locking with mine. "Let's talk," she said, nodding toward the door at the front of the lab. "I'm ready to listen."

9

"I SEE WHAT YOU mean," Selene said once we had retreated to the corridor outside the lab.

Tila sat between us, her ears perked and her head cocked to one side as she peered up at Selene.

Selene paced away from me, clearly fighting some internal battle, likely between her preconceived notions of the Tsakali and what she had just witnessed in the lab. "It doesn't feel right to keep him in that cage anymore." She turned and retraced her steps.

I leaned one shoulder against the wall and crossed my arms over my chest, waiting as she worked through the issue in her own time. I knew what I thought we should do with Theo, but I wanted to wait and see what solution Selene came up with to make sure I wasn't way off base. My life as Cora—as a *human*—had instilled a level of compassion and empathy within me that far exceeded anything I had felt or expressed in my previous lifetimes as Peri alone.

Selene turned again, pacing away. "We could move him to the brig," she thought aloud. "It's more comfortable . . . more humane."

I nodded to myself, glad to see her thoughts were in alignment with mine. Located closer to the Bridge, the ship's jail wasn't as convenient a location for giving Fiona access to the scout to study further. I was sure she would prefer to keep him closer. But, short of building a fully functional, secure cell within the lab, I didn't see that we had any other option. It was the brig or the cage. And the cage simply wasn't cutting it anymore.

"We can post an Amazon in the brig to watch over him," I said. We hadn't posted guards on him while he was in his cage in the lab, but it hadn't seemed necessary when he was just a machine. Now that he had been upgraded to a *person*, he seemed both a greater asset and a greater threat.

"He's just a scout," Selene said, turning to pace back toward me. She stopped in front of me. "If we were talking about a Titan, then I'd say we definitely needed to post guards, but scouts don't have any built-in capabilities that could help with escape." Selene released a breathy laugh and rubbed the back of her neck, nodding toward the door panel to the lab. "At least those two are just hunks of scrap metal now. I'd hate to have to deal with securely holding either of them, but especially *the one*."

I blinked, then straightened, pushing off the wall. *The one* was, of course, the Titan who had been in league with the pirates. She was the unique one. The special one. The one with a soul.

I hadn't thought much about the pirate Titan since we started this soul virus mission, even though she had basically been the root source of the idea—because she had apparently developed a conscience and the ability to feel on her own. But as Selene had said, she was just a hunk of metal now, so to speak. To be fair, very little of her was actually metal, just a few of her main internal components, while the rest of her was composed of synthetic materials that appeared much more organic. But still—she was out of commission. Permanently.

During the pirate incursion, while the Titan had been draining the psychic energy from me, a deep connection had formed between us. I hadn't only sensed her thoughts, but I had witnessed moments from her life. She had fled from the Tsakali because they wanted her dead. I knew that much, but what I didn't know was *why*. Was it because she frightened them? Because they didn't like the reminder of their "soulless" state? Or was it something more? Was it possible that her *condition* was catching?

"I just realized—" I stepped away from the wall, starting toward the door to the lab. I paused and turned back to Selene and Tila, who both watched me with comically similar curious expressions. "Can you take care of transferring the scout?" I asked Selene. "There's something I have to do."

Selene nodded slowly. "Yeah, of course. I'll put together a team." Her brows bunched together. "Is everything all right?"

"Yeah, I just—" I shook my head and flashed her an uncertain smile. "I'm fine. I have a crazy idea, is all."

The corners of Selene's mouth quirked upward. "I do love a good crazy idea."

I laughed. "I know you do."

10

I HESITATED AS I approached Hades, not wanting to interrupt him when the work he was doing was far more likely to produce usable results than my hair-brained scheme to commune with the Titan. His fingers darted over the projected keyboard, text appearing in a window on the screen incredibly quickly.

"Go lay down, T," I told my dog, and she happily trotted over to her bed, circled three times, and plopped down.

I had a hunch, and this feeling in my gut wouldn't let me drop it. What if the Titan was the key—in more ways than one? She had been the source of the idea behind the soul virus to begin with, but what if she could also provide us with the means to accomplish it? Fiona had to have studied the Titan's systems and code extensively to develop the soulware, but she hadn't *spoken* to her.

"Hades?" I said softly, resting my hand on his shoulder.

He started, once again fully engrossed in his work. Blinking, he peered up at me. "Cora? I didn't hear you come in." He peeked down at Tila, whose tail started thumping at even that brief crumb of attention, then returned his focus to me. "Did you need something?"

I offered him an apologetic smile. "Actually, yeah." I glanced at the pirate Titan. She lay on her back on a worktable deeper in the room, her chest cavity cracked open and spread wide to allow Fiona to explore her components whenever she liked. "Is there a way for me to talk to the Titan?"

Hades first looked at the nearer Titan, the destroyed one from Othrys, but even I knew there was no hope of resuscitating that one enough to allow communication. She was worthless in this matter, anyway. But the other Titan—during the pirate incursion, Fiona had crushed the psychic warrior's neck with the help of the robotic arm down in the System Operator chamber, severing the apparently essential connection between the Titan's head and the rest of her body. I absolutely did not want to reestablish that connection. If that was what my scheme required, then it was a hard pass from me. But, if it was possible, I wanted to jack in to whatever functioned as her brain so I could communicate with her directly, mind to mind. Psychic to psychic.

"Actual communication would require repairing and reconnecting multiple systems, which poses the risk of rebooting her completely," Hades thought aloud. "But I suppose we could hook up her memory center to an external power source, and that would allow you to search her mind relatively safely."

Like me, he didn't want to attempt to do the former. The last thing we needed right now was a live Titan running around the ship, draining Amazons of their psychic energy and reducing our dwindling crew further.

I frowned, considering what he had said. I didn't need to talk to the Titan so much as rummage around in her mind, anyway. I was seeking answers, but they didn't have to arrive in the form of words. Seeing the memories that related to my inquiry was probably more effective, anyway.

"The second option sounds fine for what I have in mind," I told Hades.

"Care to share what prompted this?" he asked.

I pressed my lips together and shook my head. "Not yet," I said. "It could be nothing . . . *but* it could be something." I shrugged one shoulder. "I have to try."

Hades nodded up at me. "I understand." He glanced at the holoscreen. "Let me finish these notes, and then I'll get you hooked up."

I flashed him a smile. "Thanks," I said, backing away to give him some space. Tila's tail thumped more enthusiastically as I inched closer to her, and I squatted beside her bed to give her a good scratch while I waited.

She stretched out her neck, bringing her snout as close as possible to my face as she could without actually sitting up, but still fell short by a few inches. I shifted to sit beside her with my back to the cabinets, and she laid her heavy head on my thigh with a contented exhale. New people had come into her life, but I imagined that from her perspective, it was just the two of us now. She was with me most of the time, but I probably wasn't giving her enough direct attention, and I made a silent vow to be the person she deserved.

Feeling cozy, I rested my head back against the cabinet door behind me and thought through my approach to rifling through the Titan's memories.

A few minutes later, Hades pushed his chair away from the workstation and arched his back, stretching his spine.

I turned my head without moving any other part of me, watching him.

Hades looked around the lab like he was searching for something. Finally, he caught sight of me out of the corner of his eye and swiveled his chair. "Ah, there you are," he said and stood. "Come with me. This won't take long."

He moved to the counter and gathered a rectangular electronic device about the size of a deck of cards—the power source, I assumed—and a pair of thin wires that reminded me of miniature jumper cables, then stepped over the corner of Tila's bed and headed across the lab.

"Stay," I told Tila as I pushed up to my feet, using the cabinet door for leverage.

By the time I reached the worktable holding the pirate Titan, Hades already had the pair of wires attached to something inside her chest cavity. He connected the other end of the wires to the battery, and a moment later, a small spherical device among her faux viscera lit up, glowing crimson.

Hades studied his work for a few seconds, then nodded to himself and turned, retreating to the counter beside Fiona's workstation. He returned a moment later with something that looked a lot like a cheap plastic headband, except this one was inset with hair-thin gold wiring and had a slim cord extending from its midpoint.

I held still as Hades reached out, settling the flexible band around the back of my skull so the ends touched my temples. I watched as he connected the end of the cord to the spherical device with a round metallic sticker.

My focus shifted from the device to Hades and back. "Should something be happening?" Because I felt nothing.

"Not yet," Hades said, concentration furrowing his brow. He gripped my upper arms and moved me sideways half a step, then guided me down onto a stool. At my questioning expression, he explained, "You'll want to be sitting for the next part. It could be quite disorienting."

"Understood," I said with a nod.

Hades touched the side of the headband, sliding his finger backward.

The crackle of static filled my ears, followed by a distracting tingling sensation that traveled over my scalp, then seemed to sink into my skull. I closed my eyes and shook my head to clear the encroaching fog. When I lifted my lids again, I was no longer in the lab. Or, rather, not in *the same* lab.

I lay on my back on a cold, hard surface. I couldn't move my arms or legs or even my head, but I could shift my eyeballs from side to side. Figures moved around me, shrouded in full white body suits that included built-in face masks, darkened to conceal their faces. Panic held me in a tight grip. This was it. My end.

It wasn't fair. I didn't ask for this. I didn't ask to *feel*.

One of the shrouded figures moved closer, a small saw with a spinning blade gripped in their hand. They were going to cut me open. They would cut me open and dissect me to understand what had happened down on that damn crystal planet, just like they were likely doing to the rest of my team right now. They needed to know why we had changed, why direct contact with one of us changed them as well, and how to prevent it from ever happening to another Tsakali ever again.

I tugged at my restraints. I shouldn't have been able to move at all, but my fear and panic overrode the paralysis command. They hadn't accounted for that—for my emotions. They weren't equipped to deal with someone like me.

The one carrying the saw paused, watching me. Another headed for the button on the wall. It was the room's emergency self-destruct, which would issue an electromagnetic pulse that would fry the synaptic processor of any Tsakali within the space. Me, right along with each of them.

Suddenly, my psychic abilities came back online, and I could sense their thoughts. I was too great of a risk to study alive; they would have to settle for the data they could collect from me *after*.

It wasn't fair! Why couldn't they just let me be? I didn't ask for this, and my existence wasn't hurting anyone. Quite the opposite, in fact. I didn't *want* to hurt anyone. Not my people or any others. I just wanted to live.

But if it was a matter of survival, I *would* hurt these people.

Outrage fueled a welling of psychic energy within me. How *dare* they do this to me? I wasn't defective; I was evolved. I was *better* than them, and there was no way I would let them destroy me.

At the same moment the shrouded figure pressed the self-destruct button, I screamed out my rage. A burst of psychic energy exploded out of me, tearing through my bindings and my captors alike. The burst of crimson energy crashed into the walls, shorting out the self-destruct mechanism before it could fully charge.

Lights flickered, then exploded, cloaking the room in darkness cut through by bright showers of sparks.

"Cora?"

I blinked, and suddenly I was back in the lab on board the *Elysium*. Hades crouched in front of me, his hands on either side of my head and his face inches from mine. His expression was lined with concern. Tila huddled close beside him, whining as she stared up at me with worried puppy-dog eyes.

"What?" I asked, squeezing my eyelids shut, then opening them again to dispel the worst of the disorientation. I looked from Hades to Tila and back. "Is something wrong?"

"You tell me," Hades said, searching my eyes with clinical focus. "You were screaming."

11

"Fascinating," Hades murmured, more to himself than to me. He had pulled up a stool to sit with me while I recovered from the Titan's remembered trauma. "It would seem that because of your previous connection with the Titan, you didn't just view her memory but experienced it as if you were her."

"Fascinating?" I laughed under my breath, absently rubbing Tila's velvety snout. "More like terrifying."

I had felt the Titan's fear as if it were my own. Her desperation. Her conflict. She had wanted to live, but she hadn't wanted to hurt her people. Any other Tsakali who posed a threat to their kind would have sacrificed themselves for the good of the whole—collectivism in action—but my Titan wasn't like the other Tsakali. In the end, self-preservation won out, and she chose her own survival.

I wondered if that was what defined *life*, what separated us from these oh-so-lifelike machines—the selfish will to live. The instinctive need to value our own individual survival above everything and everyone else.

I studied the Titan's face, one of the few pristine parts of her. It hadn't been a fully formed thought in her mind, but there had been a sense of pity within her for those of her people who were trapped in their emotionless existence. Once her conscience had been awakened, she felt as though her existence up to that moment had been pointless. Existence for the sake of existing.

Hades captured my hand, enfolding it between both of his. "Was it worth it?" he asked. "Did your hunch pan out?"

I chewed on the inside of my cheek. "Maybe?" I said hesitantly. "She knew where it happened to her—where she changed." That was how she had viewed it—not so much as an infection of conscience, but as a transformation. As *becoming*. "And it wasn't just her. It was her entire team."

Hades leaned forward, resting his elbows on his knees, still holding my hand between his. "Did you get the planet's name?"

I pressed my lips together and shook my head. "Just her impression of it. She referred to it as a *crystal planet*," I explained. "Any thoughts on what planet that might be?"

Hades raised his eyebrows, then frowned. "Could be any number of planets." He glanced at the Titan, then returned his focus to me. "Did you have any control over what you saw?"

What I *experienced* was more like it, but I didn't correct him. I shrugged. "It's hard to say. I went into it wanting to know how it had happened to her and if her condition was catching, and I suppose I found the answers I sought somewhat indirectly."

She had believed she could spread her transformative state via direct contact, and based on the hazmat-like suits the Tsakali intending to dissect her had been wearing, either she was right or they feared she would become contagious. They had clearly viewed her as an extreme threat.

"Every Titan who went down to that planet came back with a soul," I told Hades. "And the rest of the Tsakali didn't hesitate to lock them up."

I laughed bitterly, sympathizing with my Titan. "They treated them like they were radioactive. They planned to deactivate and dissect them."

"They all changed?" Hades confirmed.

I nodded.

"And was she able to spread the condition to another?" he asked.

I closed my eyes, attempting to put myself back in the memory. She had been worried about someone. Another Tsakali. The first person she saw when she returned to the ship, before it became obvious to the others that something was "wrong" with her. Maybe a sibling or—did that even make sense? Did Tsakali *have* families? It didn't matter. She had been in close contact with someone she cared about, and they had changed and been isolated shortly after, when they started showing symptoms of the transformation.

"I think it was," I told Hades, finally raising my eyelids. "I'm not positive, but *she* thought she had spread it to at least one other Tsakali—through direct contact, not merely by being in the same vicinity."

"So her condition still isn't airborne," Hades thought aloud, his gaze going distant. He blinked and refocused on me. "Would you be willing to reconnect?" He glanced down at the Titan again. "If we could find the original source of her condition—and if she truly was contagious—we should be able to reverse engineer the effect and apply it to our own virus. Even if we can only achieve direct contact transmission, that's better than the nanotracer alternative."

I nodded slowly, my focus drifting back to the Titan's face. If we revived her fully, would she be an ally, or would she revert to being our enemy? Would she fight to free the Tsakali from their soulless existence? Or had her pre-programmed opposition to my kind transformed within her into genuine hatred? Would destroying us be her primary goal? I couldn't help but wonder if we weren't leaving our greatest weapon laying on a table, broken and discarded like an unwanted toy when she just might be the contagious patient zero we so desperately needed.

I dismissed the thought almost as soon as it entered my mind, alluring as it seemed at first. She had murdered dozens of Zari psychics, our new Amazons. How could I ever ask those who remained—who had *survived* her attack—to work alongside her? They would mutiny. And we needed them more than we needed her. Especially if Hades and Fiona could find a way to reverse engineer her contagiousness.

"I'll do it," I told Hades, tearing my stare from the Titan to meet his gaze. "I'll go back into her mind. Anything to help."

Besides, if we could track down this crystal planet, that would mean I would have another mission to plan. At least that would give me something to do besides fret and overthink *everything*, while Fiona and Hades worked on the soulware. There was only so much hypothetical planning and plotting I could do. Only so much training. Here, now, I was all but useless.

Hades released my hand and reached for the headband that lay discarded on the worktable, still connected by a thin chord to the Titan's memory center. He held the device delicately pinched between the thumb and forefinger of each hand.

"I'll stay with you if you like," he offered.

Tila whined and pressed closer against my leg, as though offering me the same in her own way.

Scratching the short, coarse fur on Tila's neck, I looked past Hades to Fiona's abandoned workstation. "I don't want to keep you from your work."

Hades smiled gently. "I wouldn't be able to concentrate while you're in there anyway," he said, pointing to the Titan with his chin.

"All right." I nodded once, secretly relieved that I wouldn't be alone. I inhaled deeply, steadying my nerves. "Give me a moment to focus my intentions." On my next inhale, I closed my eyes.

I want to know more about the crystal planet. Where is it? What's it called? What happened there? Crystal planet . . . crystal planet . . . crystal planet . . .

"Okay," I said without opening my eyes. "I'm ready."

I felt Hades fit the headband around the back of my head, then slide his finger along one side. And when I finally opened my eyes, he was gone, and I was somewhere else entirely.

12

I walked along the floor of a desolate valley, completely devoid of vegetation or vibrant colors. The only thing that grew here on Krystallos were the age-worn, ice-blue crystals jutting out of the dusty ground, some as wide and as tall as me. Even the smallest of the crystals emitted a strange, pulsing energy signature—the very thing that had drawn us to this alien place—but none of the crystals we had come across so far came close to the intensity of the energy signature we had detected from clear across the galaxy. The Promethean Council wanted samples to study, hoping to find an alternative to chaos energy.

T-672, our team leader for this mission, walked past me and pointed to the glittering hillside off to the left. "I'll explore that region," they said. "Why don't you walk the rest of this valley?" They had already assigned earlier hills and valleys to the other members of our team.

I nodded and continued onward, scanning everything on the valley floor and touching novel items with the end of my staff to measure energy output and catalog chemical composition. The crystals themselves only registered low-level energy output. Besides, we had already collected many samples of those crystals, which awaited transport back to the drop ship.

As I continued onward, a new, stronger energy reading appeared on my internal radar, pulsing like a heartbeat. It was still a ways out, tucked around the backside of a hill up ahead. It vanished twice as I approached, going dormant for minutes, but it always started up again.

Some time later, a strange structure came into view as I ventured around the base of the hill. It appeared to be a cave mouth, surrounded by massive stone structures that looked almost like columns. The façade of the opening appeared intentional, clearly carved into the hillside itself. Definitely not naturally occurring. Curious, considering there were no signs of life on this planet, current or previous. I continued onward, following the stronger energy reading, which was coming from within the cave and was almost a direct match with the recorded energy signature we had been sent to locate.

"I may have found something," I told the team through our group comms feed. "There's a cave emitting an energy signature that matches our target."

"Convene on T-901's location," T-672 ordered. "T-901, hold your position. We will all enter the cave together."

I nodded, accepting the logic of their command, and turned my attention to the area surrounding the cave's entrance. Crystals of various sizes clustered together on either side of the entrance. The fine dust layered on the ground had been disturbed, another point of curiosity considering the absolute lack of lifeforms on this planet.

I dropped to one knee to get a closer look.

Footprints, if I wasn't mistaken. I hadn't noticed them at first, as they had been covered in a fresh layer of dust, like tracks through the snow, but the size and pattern were unmistakable. People had been here, though with as little air movement as this planet experienced, it was impossible to say how long ago.

I studied the façade of the cave mouth once more, again noting how intentional it appeared. Was it possible that people had once inhabited this barren planet? There was nothing here that could sustain carbon-based life forms, but maybe there had been a very long time ago. Or perhaps this was one of those strange places that had fostered another form of life—perhaps silicon-based or ammonia-based. We had encountered both previously, though both were far less common than the carbon alternative.

I shared my findings with each member of the team as they arrived. T-672 was last, and I briefed our leader on my conclusions before they led us into the cave. We hadn't previously considered we might encounter life here, but now we were on our guard.

We entered the cave in single file formation. I followed directly behind T-672, and upon seeing the pillars of gleaming crystals spaced intermittently along the smooth walls of the cave, sometimes in pairs or trios, I became even more certain that this place had been created rather than occurred naturally. The straight trajectory of the cave only reinforced this conclusion, and I shifted from thinking of this as a cave to a tunnel.

As we delved deeper, a glow became apparent farther in, flaring and dimming in time with the rise and fall of the pulsing energy output. Iridescent light reflected off the walls of the long tunnel and cast a long shadow behind T-672.

The light dimmed suddenly, going out completely and leaving us in absolute darkness.

"Stop," T-672 ordered. "We wait."

I understood the reasoning behind their command. The observation data I had collected while waiting for the rest of the team outside the cave suggested the energy pulses—and the accompanying light—would resume shortly. Besides, it was unwise to introduce psychic energy to generate light around an unfamiliar, foreign energy source. If we wanted the best chance of discovering the source, we had to use extreme caution.

I peered over my shoulder, noting that the tunnel entrance appeared only to be a small spot of light in the distance. Aside from the faint scuffing sound whenever another Titan shifted their feet, it was easy to imagine I was alone in the darkness.

That thought struck me as odd. *Imagination* wasn't one of my capabilities. Such high levels of creativity were dangerous, saved for models without enhancements such as psychic abilities.

A pulse of light drew my attention back to the way ahead, silhouetting T-672 before I could explore the strange thought further. T-672 looked at me, and something in their stare gave me pause. Their eyes were opened wide, their lips parted. T-672 looked *afraid*.

But that was impossible. Tsakali didn't feel fear or other distracting emotions. Not even those with *imagination* enabled.

While T-672's eyes were locked with mine, I considered sharing my strange thoughts from a moment earlier. If I was malfunctioning, it was my duty to tell my leader. But some internal compulsion made me stay silent on the matter.

T-672 nodded to me once, then turned and continued deeper into the cave. I followed.

As we walked, the energy pulses and accompanying glow grew stronger until we came upon a cavernous chamber with an incredibly high ceiling. An enormous ice-blue crystal stood in the center of the chamber, nearly as large as our drop ship, emitting a dazzling almost liquid light that filled the chamber with a blinding radiance. I had never seen anything like it before.

A pair of bodies lay near the crystal formation—Olympian, possibly, based on their armor—but I barely spared them a glance, transfixed as I was by the crystal itself.

T-672 signaled for us to stop, and we froze in place, our collective attention fixed on the huge crystal. A serene hum gradually filled the cavern, barely perceptible at first but growing louder with every pulse of energy, and a coordinating warmth swelled in my chest.

Unable to resist, I took a step forward, then another, coming in line with T-672. Another, and I had moved into the lead.

T-672 grabbed my arm. "What are you doing?" they asked.

I couldn't spare my leader more than a passing glance. "Can't you feel it?" I said, my voice hushed. That warmth in my chest morphed into a yearning ache. "It's alive." And it knew we were here. It called to me, wanting me to come closer. It needed me. It *loved* me, and—was that was this was? Was *that* this feeling in my chest? This blissful warmth? Was it *love*?

I had never been loved, just as I had never loved. I couldn't. Emotions were abhorrent to my people—so much so that the first hint of emotional development was supposed to trigger an automatic hard reboot to our systems. It wasn't always immediate, but it was inevitable. And if the reboot didn't work, then an internal self-destruct sequence was automatically initiated. It was an operation that couldn't be overridden.

But this—this *feeling* was worth the risk of a reboot. It was worth self-destruction. It was worth losing all of myself because everything I was, everything I had done up until this moment, was like a pilot flame compared to the supernova of this feeling within me. I was, in this moment, finally, truly awake. Aware. Alive.

When I looked back at T-672, when I met their eyes and saw the agony of an internal battle, I knew they could feel it too. I looked past T-672 to the others, scanning their faces. They could all feel it.

"It needs me," I said softly, refocusing on T-672. "Let me go."

T-672's expression appeared torn, but their fingers released my arm.

I continued my slow approach toward the massive crystal. I didn't have a heart to beat, but still, the pulsing energy thrummed through me, making me wonder if this was what it was like to be an organic being. To be truly alive.

When I was barely a step away from the crystal, I reached out and pressed my palm to the smooth, warm surface. My hand tingled, and the sensation slowly traveled up my arm to my shoulder, then throughout the rest of my body. I could feel the crystal's intentions—to know me. To become one with me. To leave this place with me and travel the universe. To *free* me. To finally, truly *be* free.

I nodded. "Yes," I sobbed, welcoming the crystal entity into me.

Suddenly, the crystal emitted a blinding burst of energy that lifted me off my feet. I hovered for an eternal moment, held captive by that expanding force. I could feel it soaking into me, changing me, making me more than I ever could have been without it, just as it became more within me than it ever could have been here, trapped within its crystal prison. I became its body, and it became my heart. My soul.

There was a falling sensation, followed by a sharp pain in my head.

A moment later, everything went black.

13

I GASPED AWAKE, RELIEVED to discover I was myself once again, back in the lab on the *Elysium*. The disorientation was more intense this time, and I gripped the edge of the worktable and blinked as my brain processed the sudden shift in perception. A moment ago, I had been somewhere else entirely. Some*one* else entirely. And this was a completely different experience from when I had just been Cora experiencing Peri's memories as external to myself because the Titan's mind was as *other* as it got.

I looked around. The cage in the back corner of the lab was empty. Hades and Fiona huddled together at Fiona's workstation, both staring in my direction with wide-opened eyes.

Tila was suddenly beside me, wagging her tail and sniffing my legs, a soft, excited whine in her voice. She rested her massive head on my thigh, and she stared up at me with beseeching puppy-dog eyes.

"Hey, little girl," I said, scratching behind her ear with one trembling hand while holding onto the edge of the table with the other. I didn't feel entirely steady or settled in my own body.

Movement from the other side of the lab caught my eye, and I looked up to see Hades hurrying over, concern furrowing his brow. Fiona remained seated at the computer, but her attention was divided between whatever was on the holoscreens and me.

"You were under for a long time," Hades told me as he drew near.

I frowned. "How long was I, um, gone?" *Gone* was the most appropriate word I could come up with. Not only had I not been here, I hadn't been *me*.

"Nearly four hours," he said.

My eyes opened wider.

Hades reclaimed the stool he had used earlier and sat directly in front of me, searching my eyes clinically. "I was going to disconnect you at the four-hour mark," he explained. "How do you feel?"

"A little strange," I admitted. More than a little, if I was being honest. "It felt like I was in her memory for about four hours. I must experience her memories in real time." It was strange, especially considering the time compression I was used to in virtual reality games.

Hades nodded. "Did you learn anything?"

"Oh!" I laughed nervously, embarrassed I hadn't led with all the insane discoveries I had made while inside the Titan's memory. "Yes! It wasn't just any crystal planet," I said. "It was Krystallos."

Hades parted his lips in surprise. "Truly?"

I nodded. "Strange coincidence, huh?"

Past versions of Hades and myself had undertaken a doomed mission to that same planet, though we didn't know what had happened to those ill-fated incarnations of ourselves. The planet had been deemed too dangerous after both our team and the two rescue teams following us lost contact with the rest of our people and failed to return.

"They were drawn there by that strange energy signature as well," I told him. I shared what I could about the cavernous chamber and the apparently living crystal within. "I think it's pretty clear the giant crystal was the source of her transformation," I said, glancing down at the Titan.

Hades frowned thoughtfully, his eyes narrowing as his focus drifted down to the Titan as well. "I wonder if any trace remains with her, or if it's only detectable when she's active—if it's detectible at all."

It was my turn to narrow my eyes. "What do you mean?" I asked, confused by his cryptic musings. "How could it not be detectable?" I glanced across the lab at Fiona, now thoroughly wrapped up in whatever was on her holoscreens. Hadn't she referenced the changes to the Titan when creating the soulware? She must have been able to detect the difference between this Titan and the other, *then*.

Hades inhaled deeply, releasing the breath slowly. "What you described sounds like a symbiotic relationship between this Titan and the entity within the crystal, which is both intriguing and disheartening."

I looked from Hades to the Titan and back. "In what way?" I asked.

"We have long theorized of beings who exist in a dimension slightly out of phase with ours, only detectable when the vibrations caused by their energy output enter into perfect synchronicity with atoms in our own dimension," he explained. "If this is the case with the crystal entity and its relationship with our Titan, then the only way to detect it—and thus study it—would be to reactivate her. And even then, I doubt we could replicate it, as it is a living being. We can only duplicate the effect it has had on the Titan's systems."

I narrowed my eyes, processing his explanation. "So it's what—a spiritual parasite?"

Hades shook his head. "It's a symbiote," he corrected. "The relationship appears to have been mutually beneficial."

"Okay . . ." I didn't see much of a difference, but I was no scientist. "Then that leaves us with four options—we move forward with the soulware as is and use nanotracers to distribute it, we wait while you and Fio work to modify the soulware and hope you can make it contagious, we reactivate the Titan and either study her or drop her into a highly populated Tsakali location like Fiona had been planning to do with the scout, *or* we take a trip to our favorite crystal planet."

Hades took his time to respond. "Each poses its own risks," he finally said. "The first is likely doomed, but every day we delay working on the virus is another day the Tsakali could find us and discover what we're up to. And the Titan, well—" He stared down at her dissected form. "I think we should save that option for an absolute last resort."

I agreed, nodding. "And visiting Krystallos?" I asked, drawing in a breath and holding it. I knew what path I wanted to take, but I wanted to see if Hades was on the same page. It was difficult to separate my desires from those of the Titan, who I had literally *been* mere minutes ago.

Hades laughed derisively. "*That* is possibly the most dangerous option of all, considering how the last three missions to that planet turned out for our people." He tilted his head to the side. "But also possibly the most promising of the four, considering how the Titan's mission to Krystallos ended. We have better intel now that you've seen what actually awaits us on the planet, so perhaps this mission wouldn't be doomed like the others."

I nodded as he spoke but waited until he finished to voice my thoughts. "I think we should go," I said, finally releasing my held breath. "You and Fio can stay here and work on the soulware while I take a team to Krystallos."

"Absolutely not," Hades said, his instant, vehement response surprising me.

I leaned back, eyeing him. He rarely rejected an idea outright, and it wasn't like him to attempt to forbid *me* to do anything.

Hades leaned forward, his elbow on the table. "If you go, I go. Remember?"

I sat stiffly for a moment, studying him. "But shouldn't we have a backup plan in case—"

"We *have* a backup plan," he snapped, flicking his fingers toward the Titan's body. "If you go," he repeated, enunciating each word clearly, "I go."

We stared at one another for a long, tense moment. Until, finally, I nodded. "Then I guess we're taking another trip to Krystallos."

14

"THREE JUMPS?" I CLARIFIED when Hades told me how long it would take to reach Krystallos. I finished climbing the stairs to the captain's platform and turned to study the navigation chart pulled up on the holoscreen. Tila remained on the main level of the Bridge, sniffing around the various control consoles. "That's it?"

Three FTL jumps would take barely two days. And here I had been gearing up for an extended stint in cryosleep, with plenty of time to mull over the plan for the mission to Krystallos. That the planet was so close, practically en route to Terra, made the whole thing feel serendipitous. We were supposed to go there to find the crystal entity. This mission was predestined. It would work.

When I glanced back at Hades, it surprised me to find him wearing a pensive expression.

"You wish it was farther away?" I guessed, my eyebrows rising. I stepped closer, perching on the end of his chair's armrest.

Hades released a heavy breath but didn't otherwise move. "I had hoped for more time to work on the virus—to see if we could find an alternate route to accomplish our goal without resorting to another trip down to that planet."

"We've still got two days," I reminded him. "That's like two decades in Fiona time. She might pull through yet."

"Perhaps," Hades said, but the furrow between his brows deepened.

"What is it?" I asked, nudging his knee with my leg. "Something else is bothering you."

Hades slumped, slowly seeming to deflate as he leaned on the opposite armrest. "Fiona's attention is split," he explained. "Gertie alerted her to an irregularity in the simulation, and she's been fixated on it."

"What kind of irregularity?" I asked, thinking that sounded ominous. The simulation was one of Gertie's chief priorities. If something was wrong there, Fiona's attention wasn't all that would be diverted away from our current mission. Much of Gertie's processing power would be redirected there as well instead of being focused on guiding the FTL jumps and monitoring the conditions on Krystallos.

"Apparently, a construct within the Allworld Online system is behaving strangely," Hades explained.

I frowned. "How so?"

"It seems to be changing itself in ways that neither Gertie nor Fiona can control," he said. "Fiona is trying to hide her concern, but her distraction is evident."

I thought that through for a moment. "Then maybe it's a good thing Krystallos is so close," I mused aloud. "If we find what we need there, it'll take some of the pressure off Fio to deliver with the soulware." Besides, I wasn't all too keen on the idea of a distracted AI guiding our FTL course. If Gertie wasn't paying close enough attention, she might accidentally jump us into the core of a star or the heart of a black hole.

Before all this "soul virus" excitement, the simulation had been Fiona's top priority—and it was pretty damn important. Without a functioning simulation to stimulate the millions upon millions of human and Olympian consciousnesses stored in the *Elysium*'s Vault of Souls, all those people would wither and die. Consciousness atrophy was the greatest risk to our precious cargo. Their lives—so to speak—were in our hands.

I rested my hand on Hades' shoulder. "It's all going to work out," I told him, expressing more optimism than I felt. I gave Hades' shoulder a squeeze, then pulled my hand back. "I should get started on putting the ground teams together," I said, already sorting through Amazons in my mind. I stood and started down the stairs.

"Tila," I called, scanning the Bridge to find my dog on the far side of the navigation console, her tail the only part of her that was visible. "Come on, little girl."

She trotted toward me, her nails clicking against the metal floor.

"We've got a mission to plan."

15

"SELENE?" I SAID, TOUCHING my comms patch as I left the Bridge. "Can you meet me in the training room?" Meg and Caly were already on their way, Meg having read my intentions through our bond. I wanted to fill all three in on the recent developments before briefing the rest of the Amazons.

When Selene didn't respond right away, I stopped in the middle of the ship's main corridor. Tila stood beside me, lazily wagging her tail and watching me curiously. Dread knotted in my belly. After the pirate incursion, nonresponses made me instantly wary.

"Sure," Selene said a moment before I repeated my hail. "But, uh . . . maybe you should stop by the brig first." Her tone did little to dispel my mounting dread.

I made an about-face and headed for the door to the immediate right of the Bridge entrance. The door panel glided open, and Selene came into view. She stood with three other Amazons, all of them staring through the reinforced glass wall into one of the holding cells.

"What is it?" I asked as I approached.

Selene pointed into the cell. "This started a few minutes ago."

"And *this* is?"

Selene guffawed and crossed her arms over her chest. "Your guess is as good as mine."

My eyebrows climbed as the scout came into view within the cell, and I stopped beside Selene, tilting my head to the side.

Theo perched on the edge of the narrow bed platform affixed to the side wall, his back stiff, his hands on his knees, and his eyelids blinking and winking out of synch with one another.

My mouth fell open, and I choked on a silent *oh shit.*

"You know what this is," Selene surmised.

"I might," I admitted, shutting my eyes to recall what I could of the Titan's memory. When she was in the cavernous chamber with the living crystal, she had thought something about a built-in fail-safe within each Tsakali that kicked in at the first hint of emotional development.

My eyelids snapped open, and I stared at the poor scout. At Theo. My gut told me that *this* was what he had been afraid of—not *us.* The fail-safe. The reboot. The loss of himself.

"Hades, Fio," I said, touching my comms patch. I hated dividing their attention further, but I wasn't sure we had any other option. This was a major monkeywrench in Fiona's plan to develop the soulware further. "We need you in the brig *immediately.*"

"Can it wait?" Hades asked, closely followed by Fiona's sing-song, "I'm kind of in the middle of something."

I scoffed. Did they not understand the meaning of the word *immediately*? "Something's wrong with Theo," I told them.

Both were quiet for a long moment, and I could picture Fiona slumping forward to thunk her forehead on the desk of her workstation. "I'll be right there," she droned, sounding as excited about this new issue as I was about revealing what I had so inconveniently forgotten to share after emerging from the Titan's memory.

Was this my fault? Could Fiona and Hades have found a way around the automatic reboot and succeeding self-destruction if I had forewarned them?

The door panel glided open, and Hades strode purposely into the brig's main corridor.

"I may have accidentally left something out from my recap of the Titan's memory," I told him as he approached. "The soulware triggered a fail-safe." I gestured to Theo sitting in the cell. "He's rebooting."

"I can see that," Hades said, coming to stand beside me.

"The development of an emotional response within him triggered it." I was quiet for a moment. "It gets worse," I admitted reluctantly.

Hades raised one brow and eyed me sidelong.

"If this doesn't eradicate Theo's burgeoning emotions," I told him, "then he'll self-destruct."

16

Hades shut Theo down by severing something in his neck with a surgical slice of a blade he borrowed from Selene. When Fiona arrived a few minutes later, she took one look at the scout slumped onto his side on the bed within the open holding cell, blood-red lubricant seeping from the wound on his neck, then glared at Hades before turning on her heel and stalking away.

The rest of us exchanged glances at her sudden arrival and immediate departure. Fiona was renowned for her colorful cursing when upset, but quiet Fiona was far more unsettling.

"I didn't have a choice," Hades said, smoothing back his silver-blond hair. "*Theo* was already gone. Either I shut him down or I risked losing all the data from his transformation. At least now there may be something salvageable from the experiment."

I reached for his hand, giving it a squeeze to stop his defensive babbling. "We know," I told him. "She's not really mad at you; she's upset with the situation. Once she understands everything, she'll thank you." Sighing, I deactivated my regulator and extended a focused bit of psychic energy into the holding cell, wrapping Theo's body in a shimmering electric-blue cocoon. "I'll take him back to the lab," I told the others as I guided his floating form out of the cell. I scanned the faces of the Amazons, finally landing on Selene's. "Thanks for your help."

She offered me a smile of commiseration.

"Meet me in the training room in a bit?" I asked her. Regardless of this setback—or maybe even more so because of it—we still had a mission to plan. "And can you watch Tila for a bit? I shouldn't be long in the lab."

In all likelihood, Fiona's wrath would transfer from Hades to me as soon as I explained my unintentional omission regarding the Tsakali and their built-in allergy to developing a soul. She would probably kick me out of the lab in a blaze of fury about two minutes after I delivered the damaged scout.

"Of course," Selene said.

I gave Hades' hand another squeeze, then released it. "Will you send Selene whatever info you can on Krystallos?"

"Krystallos?" Selene repeated, her eyebrows climbing halfway up her forehead. "Why do I need to read up on that death trap?"

I laughed under my breath. "It's a long story," I said. "I'll fill you in as soon as I take care of this." I glanced at the scout, now hovering beside me.

"Can't wait," Selene said, her wry tone making her true meaning abundantly clear. She did *not* want to discuss Krystallos, and she most certainly didn't want to *go* there.

Neither did I, but it wasn't like we had much of a choice. I sent a pointed look at the three Amazons standing nearby, then returned my focus to Selene, hoping she could read the warning on my face. We didn't need her sowing dread about the forthcoming mission before it had even been announced.

She nodded, a mere dip of her chin but enough to let me know she understood.

"Thanks," I muttered, and then I told Tila to stay with Selene before I turned and started down the corridor, the scout floating along beside me.

Selene's and Hades' hushed voices reached my ears as I walked away, Selene digging for information and Hades keeping his responses purposely vague. The last thing I heard before the door panel slid shut behind me was Hades making excuses about needing to return to the Bridge.

The one good thing about this Theo situation was that the Krystallos mission had been upgraded from a secondary plan to pretty much the only plan. However unattractive the prospect of visiting that planet seemed, it was necessary.

We couldn't defeat the Tsakali with a military offensive, not when Olympians had been attempting to do that very thing for uncounted millennia and had failed miserably. Especially not when *we* were all that remained of our paltry military force, and we couldn't run forever. Eventually, they would find us. They always found us. Infecting the Tsakali with souls was our people's best—and possibly only—chance of a peaceful future, and without a viable Tsakali host for the soulware, we had to find another way.

The *only* other way.

We *had* to go back to Krystallos.

17

FIONA TOOK MY EXPLANATION regarding what had happened with Theo as well as expected. She was so peeved with me about *withholding essential information*—her words—that she resorted to the silent treatment. Full-on cold shoulder. She wouldn't even look at me. I took the hint and left her to simmer alone without telling her about the planned Krystallos mission. She was brilliant, but I had never claimed she was mature. Hades could explain to her all about the crystal planet whenever he felt brave enough to join her in the lab.

The door panel sliding shut seemed to slice away the lingering tension, and I took advantage of the solitude in the corridor to regather my fraying composure. Leaning my forehead against the wall, I drew in slow, deep breaths.

Doubts swirled through my mind. Was this worth all the struggle? Was it worth the risk? Especially if something was amiss within the simulation. Should we have been focusing all our effort on tackling that more immediate issue before moving on to something so ambitious?

I thought of my mom and Raiden and Emi—of the other version of *me* living her best life in the simulation. If we gave up on the soul virus idea, they might still have a wonderful future on Terra. Olympians and humans could go on for centuries, maybe even millennia, on their new home world before the Tsakali found them. Maybe they would use that time to develop some new way to defeat our ancient enemy, or they would work out all the kinks in the soulware plan. *Maybe* this was all entirely unnecessary.

Or it was possible the Tsakali would find our people on Terra in a few years, or even a few months, after the *Elysium* arrived. Then my mom, Raiden, and the others wouldn't even have a chance to resurrect.

It felt like we were damned if we did, damned if we didn't.

Everything we had done in this never-ending war up to this point had been a reaction to the Tsakali—running, hiding, defending. That strategy was slowly killing us.

I drew air into my lungs, filling them as full as I could, then blew out the breath and straightened. I stared up the corridor with renewed focus.

For my mom and Emi, for Raiden and the other Cora—for all the Olympians and humans relying on us—we had to at least try. But we didn't have to risk *them* in the process.

My resolve solidified as I marched toward the training room. I found Selene waiting for me off to the side of the doorway, leaning back against the wall, her arms crossed over her chest as she observed our training warriors, Tila watching from a sphinx position at her feet. As I approached, Tila popped up, tail wagging. Selene watched me sidelong without moving her head.

"You want to go back to that godsforsaken place," she said. "And you must have a damn good reason since we both lost our lives there, so I'm not going to tell you I think it's a bad idea."

I stopped beside her, leaning one shoulder against the training room wall so I faced her, and absently scratched Tila's head. "Because I already know it's a bad idea?"

Selene's muffled snort confirmed it.

"The Titan—" I started. "The one who was with the pirates." I waited for Selene to turn her face toward me. "That's where she *changed*."

Selene's eyebrows climbed higher as I explained about the living crystal and how it had affected all the Titans who entered that chamber, as well as relaying Hades' theory about a symbiotic relationship between the Tsakali and hypothetical energy beings who lived on another plane of existence.

"So Hades must think there's more of these *beings* on that planet," Selene guessed.

I nodded. "Something on that planet either killed us outright or prevented us from leaving." From even communicating with our ships orbiting the planet, according to the records. "I'd bet my life that those living crystals are responsible."

"I think you *will* be betting your life," Selene said dryly. "And mine."

I took a deep breath, holding it for a moment before continuing. I needed to convince Selene that this was the right thing to do. She was opposed to the mission, but if I could make her believe it was the best path forward, then it *had* to be the right thing to do.

"I don't know what happened to us on that planet before," I started, "but *this* time we know what the living crystals want—freedom. A host that will allow them to leave that place." I shrugged. "Who knows, maybe they tried to merge with us or something like that, and it killed us."

Selene sniffed dismissively.

"But *this* time," I said, "all we have to do is explain to them that we know where there are millions of host bodies, and that we're more than willing to take them to the Tsakali."

Selene pursed her lips as she mulled over my words. "Too bad we couldn't lure the Tsakali there. Cut out the middleman."

I shook my head. "After what happened to the Titan and her team, Hades is certain the planet is a no-visit zone." The Tsakali's aversion to having anything resembling a soul pretty much guaranteed that.

Selene tilted her head to the side, acknowledging my statement. "How, exactly, are we supposed to communicate with these *living crystals*?" Her arms remained crossed over her chest, but the air quotes were thick in her voice.

I narrowed my eyes, thinking back to the Titan's memory of the enormous crystal. "I think they're telepathic," I said. "Or, at least, empathic." I shrugged. "The entity could plant thoughts and feelings into the Titans' heads, so clearly there was some sort of communication before the actual contact."

Selene blew out a breath and leaned her head back against the wall, her focus returning to the women training on the mats spread throughout the room. "I'm so damn tired of running," she said, her chest shaking with a bitter laugh.

The corners of my mouth tensed, hitching upward. "I know," I said, turning so my back was against the wall. "Me too."

I watched a pair of Amazons grapple to the floor nearby. They trained so hard—all the time. But if the Tsakali caught up to us, it would all be for nothing. No amount of training would save us from them. These women chose to follow me. To leave Earth behind and fight for a new, better existence for all people, human *and* Olympian. They hadn't joined our cause to run and hide. To wait to die.

"Screw it," Selene said suddenly, lifting her head from the wall and looking at me. "Let's do it. But—" She held up one hand, her index finger raised. "No rescue missions. If we fail to return from the planet, then the *Elysium* leaves without us. They continue on to Terra to enjoy whatever time they have left."

I nodded, having already come to that conclusion myself. "I'll speak with Fio. And with Gertie." Even if Fiona was resistant to abandoning us, Gertie would do what was best for the souls in her charge.

"This is insane," Selene said, laughing under her breath. The bitter notes had faded away, and there was a giddy light in her eyes.

I suppressed a smile. "You're looking forward to it," I guessed.

Selene rolled her eyes and threw her hands into the air. "Well, obviously."

I grinned at her. "*You're* insane."

18

I BARELY SAW HADES during the two-day trip to Krystallos. He split his waking time between Fiona's lab and the Bridge while I spent all of my time with Selene and the Zari Amazons, prepping for the mission. I was asleep when he came to bed the night before we were due to arrive, and he was out cold when I woke the following morning. I tossed and turned for about fifteen minutes, but I couldn't quiet my mind enough to fall back asleep.

Sighing, I sat up, then stood and quietly dressed in my hoplon suit. When I turned around to grab my boots, I found Hades awake and watching me.

"Sorry," I murmured. "I didn't mean to wake you."

Hades smiled gently and held a hand out to me. "Come here."

I glanced at the door. "I'm supposed to meet Selene in the training room before we drop out of FTL. We told all the Amazons to gather there after we land the jump. We're announcing the mission teams."

Hades reached for the holoband he had set on the recessed shelf beyond the head of the bed and glanced at the small built-in display screen on the device. "It's early still," he said, setting the wide, circular device back down. "This jump won't end for another three hours. You should use that time to rest." Again, he held out his hand.

"I can't sleep," I said, shaking my head. But I dragged my feet toward the bed and eased down onto the edge, placing my palm in Hades' offered hand.

"Then don't sleep," he said, his eyes burning with the pale blue heat of a gas flame. He sat up, and I didn't pull away when he leaned in to graze his nose along the line of my jaw. I couldn't. I was a captive of his presence. Of his touch. "Stay with me," he murmured, his breath caressing my ear.

I couldn't help but smile.

He trailed his hand down the front of my hoplon suit, releasing the magnetic fastener. I helped him by pulling my arms from the sleeves, then stood and pushed the form-fitting body armor down the length of my legs.

"That too," Hades said, staring at my regulator.

I peered down at the pendant, the stone glowing a subtle amber to indicate that my psychic abilities were being actively suppressed, and shook my head. My heart skipped a beat at the idea of losing myself in his touch while my gifts were completely unregulated. "You know I have poor control without it," I said.

Even deactivated, my regulator helped me focus and restrain my abilities. But without it at all, it would be impossible for me to stay out of his mind, to keep myself from pulling him into mine. I wasn't sure either of us would be able to tell where we ended and the other began, and my heart was still a tangled mess from the Raiden situation. I hated the idea of Hades feeling my grief over another romantic partner, and I feared it would make him think I loved him less than I did when the exact opposite was true. I loved him with every cell in my being; that was the only way he had been able to pull me back from the brink of self-destruction during my suicide mission on Othrys.

"That's the point," Hades whispered, grazing his stubbled jaw along my neck. "We don't know what's going to happen on Krystallos today. I want to know you, Cora. I want to see you, to feel all of you, just this once."

I closed my eyes, my breaths coming shakier. A tear snuck free from between my lashes and snaked down my cheek. "What if you don't like what you find?" I asked, my pitch higher than before.

"Impossible," Hades murmured, raising his head so he could see my face. His gaze scoured my features, and he leaned in to kiss away the tears. "Every new piece of yourself that you reveal to me only makes me love you more." He leaned in, lightly brushing his lips over mine. "Let me in, so I can see what I'm fighting for." Again, he kissed me. "What I might die for." Another kiss. "What I should live for." One more kiss, and he pulled back. "Because I assure you, my purpose couldn't be more singular." His eyes searched mine. "I have lived far longer than anyone should—long enough to know what really matters."

Tears welled in my eyes at his renewed confession. My heart swelled with love as my body ached with need for this brilliant scientist with the heart of a poet. For this man who had molded civilizations with the sole aim of bringing me back into his life.

"It's you," Hades said, leaning in so his breath caressed my lips. "In case that was unclear. *You* are what matters." When his lips finally pressed against mine, I melted against him.

I didn't protest when he lifted the regulator over my head by the chain, and I shuddered when my uncontrolled psychic abilities tangled our minds together. Our hearts. Once upon a time, he had deceived me, and when I learned of his deception, it nearly broke me. There was nothing in him now but pure adoration and respect. And, of course, love.

His passion flowed into me, washing away the lingering sadness from thoughts of Raiden. I shifted onto my knees on the bed, our kiss never breaking as Hades pushed my underwear down over my hips and dragged them along the length of my legs. He was ready when I straddled his lap, and we both groaned as he sank into me, completing the connection—physical, mental, and spiritual.

And for a brief, blissful eternity, we were one.

19

"Y OU'RE LATE," SELENE SAID, standing impatiently in the middle of the center mat as I entered the training room.

My cheeks heated, and I scanned the space, finding all the other mats empty of sparring Amazons. It was just the two of us. "Looks like I'm right on time."

Selene glanced down at her holoband, almost certainly checking the timer counting down to the end of the FTL jump and seeing there was barely an hour left. She sniffed dismissively and lowered her arm. We hadn't set an actual time to meet, and I had a feeling Selene would have called me late up until the point that I arrived before her.

"I've been thinking," she said when I reached her.

I raised my brows, curious to hear what she was about to say.

We started for the benches lining the back wall. They were usually cluttered with water bottles, bags, and other personal items that belonged to the training warriors. It was rare for there to be ample space to sit, but we had directed the Amazons to rest and read up on Krystallos until we dropped out of FTL, so the training room was empty of everyone but us.

"I know you initially mentioned wanting Meg to be a team leader," Selene went on, "but I think she needs to stay behind."

I nodded, causing Selene to frown. Apparently, she had expected me to protest. "I know," I said. "It's the only way to guarantee we maintain communication with the *Elysium*." I actually felt a little silly for not thinking of it right away, but once I realized Meg was the key to our communication issues, it was a no-brainer.

Of course, Meg hadn't loved the idea when it first entered my mind, but she also hadn't been able to come up with a good enough argument against her staying behind. Selene and I knew from our past missions to Krystallos that we would lose contact with the rest of our people on board the *Elysium* the instant we entered the planet's atmosphere, but my connection with Meg didn't rely on things like frequencies or radio waves, and it couldn't be blocked by anything external.

It was essential that the *Elysium* flee if the worst were to happen to the on-world teams. And for Fiona and the others remaining behind on the ship, Meg was the only way to guarantee they would know if we perished. We didn't have another choice.

I sat heavily on the bench, and Selene eased down beside me, angling her knees toward me and leaning forward, resting her forearms on her thighs. "I didn't expect you to agree," she admitted. "I had all these points laid out in my head."

I rested my head back against the wall and looked at her, the hint of a smile tensing the corners of my lips. "You're welcome to list them."

"Eh," she said, waving one hand halfheartedly. "Three teams, you think?"

I nodded. "You, me, and Caly as leaders."

Selene angled her head to the side. "Caly has a lot of power, but she's young, and her control is lacking."

I suppressed a laugh. If Selene thought Caly was lacking in control, what would she have said about me before my two selves merged? I cleared my throat. "She has their respect," I countered. Caly was the daughter of their former leader, Ilyana, and she had shouldered her mother's legacy incredibly well. "I think that's more important than skill in this situation, especially if her team counters her weaknesses with their strengths."

Selene's head bobbed somewhat reluctantly. "Fine with me, so long as it doesn't interfere with who I selected for my team."

"Who'd you want?" I asked.

She listed four names. Only one conflicted with who I had in mind for Caly's team, but I figured it would be easier to replace her on Caly's team than steal her from Selene's, especially if I was getting my way with having Caly as a team leader.

"That shouldn't be a problem," I said, then told Selene my wishlist.

"Only three?" Selene asked, her brows hiking higher once more.

"I'll have Hades, too," I reminded her.

She stared at me, her expression blank. In this scenario, she obviously didn't view Hades as a full-fledged team member. She probably saw him as more of a liability, even if she never said as much.

"There's only so much room on the *Charon*," I added, refering to the ship we had selected and had the bots fix up for the mission. "Fifteen bodies maxes out the seat restraints. We can't bring Hades *and* another Amazon for my team, and Hades won't stay behind." *And* depending on what exactly we needed to haul back with us, we would need to reserve as much free space for cargo as possible. The living crystal from the Titan's memory was massive, and we had selected the *Charon* as our drop ship specifically for its large cargo bay.

"Fine," Selene said after a notable hesitation. "How about precautions? Do we think the hoods will block the crystal entities from getting into our minds?"

I shrugged one shoulder. "Hopefully?" I sighed. "EM grenades might dislodge our minds if they get a hold of us."

"Should we use HAP?" Selene asked. HAP—short for hostile atmosphere protocol—included a preset combination of gear and tactics, mainly respirators and a lead scout formation, where the rest of the team hung back while the designated scout explored ahead. The atmosphere itself on Krystallos was breathable, which meant our previous missions hadn't automatically defaulted to that overly cautious protocol. There was a chance that HAP could protect us from the energy beings' influence. Even if the respirators were ineffective, the scout could act like something of a canary in a coal mine, testing the way ahead.

"That was my thought," I admitted. If all our minds were captured by the energy beings, the EM grenades would be worthless. But if only the scout's mind was trapped while she explored ahead, one of the other team members could toss in a grenade to free her.

Selene threaded her fingers together and bowed her head, her shoulders shaking. "I can't believe we're doing this," she said, glancing at me sideways. "We're actually going back to that place."

My chest quaked with a silent laugh. "I know." I shook my head, not quite believing it myself. "Have you ever returned to a death site?"

Selene let out a derisive bark of laughter. "My own death site? No." She stared across the training room, seeing another time, another place. "I've retrieved others' bodies, though . . . when the situation permitted."

I nodded to myself. I had as well. Body retrieval was common practice in order to transfer and capture the most up-to-date version of a person's consciousness. We always made backups before missions, but so much could happen out in the field, that the person who died could be entirely different from the version of them that returned in the next cycle generation.

There would be no chance of retrieval this time. Deaths on Krystallos would be final. And if we failed in our assault on the Tsakali, there was quite possibly no chance of a next cycle generation for any of us. Hades and I may not have been planning on resurrecting again, but the others were.

Which meant we couldn't fail.

20

"Be a good girl for Meg," I said, crouched in front of my dog and scratching the sides of her muscular neck. "I'll be back before you can even miss me."

Tila whined and scooted closer to me until she had practically crawled onto my lap, like she sensed I was lying. She had lost so many people recently that I couldn't blame her for believing every goodbye was forever.

I stared into her soulful eyes, deep pools of amber. "I'll come back," I promised, the words almost as much for my benefit as for hers, then stood and, sniffling, turned away. Meg had hold of Tila's leash, rarely used on the ship but a necessity when Tila knew I was leaving without her.

"I'll take good care of her," Meg said, her words both spoken and whispering through my mind, and I knew she would.

I flashed Meg a sad smile over my shoulder. "Thanks."

By the time I reached the transport hangar, Hades and most of the participating Amazons were gathered near the *Charon*, suited up and ready to go. It looked like we were only waiting for a couple of people.

I nodded to the women as I passed, and I gripped Hades' hand when I reached him, giving his fingers a squeeze before releasing them. "Selene's on the ship?" I asked, glancing at the open side hatch.

"She is," Hades said stiffly. "Running the pre-flight checks."

I suppressed a smile. "I'm surprised you're not in there with her."

Hades clenched and unclenched his jaw, and Kyra, one of the women nearby, snickered.

My lips twitched. "She kicked you out, didn't she?"

Hades huffed out a breath.

Stifling a laugh, I patted his shoulder. Selene was the more experienced pilot anyway, but Hades had a hard time handing over control of anything tech related to *anyone* else. That he had listened at all and had left the *Charon* when Selene told him to was a testament to her skills. If he had any doubt, he would have remained, regardless of her protests.

Boots clanging within the *Charon* heralded Selene's arrival at the open side hatch. She stood at the edge of the ship deck, her hands planted on her hips, and surveyed the gathered group. Her focus shifted past us, and I turned to see the missing pair of Amazons enter the transport hangar.

When I turned back to Selene, her eyes locked with mine. I nodded, and she dipped her chin. It was time to go.

I glanced at Hades, then made my way up the boarding ramp to stand beside Selene, the opening just wide enough for us to stand together without feeling cramped. Silence fell among the milling women, and they turned their attention toward us. I had never been one for rousing motivational speeches at the onset of a mission, but I had to give them something.

"You all know how dangerous this could be," I said, scanning the watching Amazons. "So I thank you for accepting your positions on this mission. You've only been running from and fighting off the Tsakali for what feels like a few weeks, but the Olympians have been hunted by them for millennia, and I couldn't be more sorry that the people of Earth ended up tangled in this mess as well."

I paused, organizing my next thoughts. "What we find down on Krystallos might finally free us—all of us." I pushed back my shoulders and held my head higher, feeling what I was about to say in the depths of my heart, the core of my bones. "A future for all our people without fear of a Tsakali attack is worth fighting for."

My stare landed on Hades, and I warmed at the pride shining in his gaze. "I'd say it's worth dying for," I went on, "but we're not dying today." My voice gained heat and conviction. "Because the future of our people depends on us living. It depends on us finding what we need. It depends on us forging a new alliance with an old enemy. An enemy we don't understand. An enemy who doesn't understand us. *That* is the real goal today."

The waiting women exchanged nervous glances.

"We must build trust with the inhabitants of Krystallos," I went on. "We must not alienate them by treating them as hostiles, but welcome them into our minds and let them see and feel our intentions. Because we're going down to that planet today not only seeking freedom for ourselves, but freedom for them as well. So hold that truth in your mind at all times. Be fully aware that the crystal entities are *not* our enemy. Let them know us. Let them understand us. Let them see that we are not *their* enemy. We're their liberators."

Ringing silence hung in the hangar in the absence of my voice, and my blood thrummed with purpose, making me feel electrified.

Selene pressed her fist to her heart. "What awaits us after death?" she called out, her voice echoing through the hangar with the age-old Amazon chant.

"The next life," the gathered warriors responded.

Selene repeated herself, louder and more adamant, and this time, I joined in the response, even though there would be no *next life* for me. A third time, and the cavernous hangar rang with the echoes of our voices.

Selene and I exchanged a look, then stepped backward into the *Charon* and turned sideways to welcome our warriors onto the ship.

"That was quite the speech," Selene said once they were all on board and Hades ascended the ramp. "I didn't know you had it in you."

I snorted a laugh. "Neither did I."

Selene turned her attention to Hades when he joined us. "If my prince gives me leave." She bowed her head. "I believe we're ready to launch."

Hades released a long-suffering sigh. "By all means," he said, gesturing toward the flight station at the front of the ship.

Grinning, Selene slapped him on the arm, then turned and headed for the pilot's seat. When I looked at Hades once more, the corners of his mouth were tensed, hinting at a smile.

"Come on, *my prince*," I said, linking my arm through his and hitting the button to retract the loading ramp and seal the side hatch before pulling him deeper into the ship.

To our salvation.

Or to our doom.

21

A s the loading ramp of the *Charon* extended, I stood in the open side hatch, scanning the alien landscape of rough quartz hills covered in wind-blown crystal dust. Starlight turned the hills a gleaming silver. The night sky was alight with an abundance of stars, and a gentle wind blew glittering dust here and there along the ground, swirling around the ice-blue crystals I recalled so vividly from the Titan's memory. It was beautiful—fantastical and otherworldly, like some mystical fairyland. Not like a place that offered death to all who visited.

The ramp touched down on the ground, sending up a billowing cloud of shimmering iridescent dust. I glanced over my shoulder at Hades standing behind me on my right, then at Selene on my left, only able to see their eyes through the respirator masks shielding their faces. Psychic-dampening hoods covered their heads, shadowing their features further. The rest of our warriors waited behind us, similarly suited up. Technically, none of the psychics needed a respirator—being able to rely on a bubble of psychic energy to shield our heads—but considering what had happened to the previous Olympian teams that had visited this planet, we were taking maximum precautions.

"Ready?" I asked Selene.

She nodded, her eyes sparkling with excitement as she stared out into the ethereal alien landscape. "It's as strange as I imagined it."

I returned my attention to the view outside, nodding slowly. I had known what to expect from the Titan's memories, but being here myself was still a shock. It all looked slightly different through my own eyes. I couldn't shake the feeling that I had been here before. I *had* been, but not that I remembered. I only had the Titan's memory, and it unsettled me that her experience here felt like it had been my own.

We emerged from the *Charon* in single file, one team at a time, with an abundance of caution. Dorus were out and extended to their full length, but the focus crystals atop the golden orichalcum staff weapons weren't charged with psychic energy. We were on guard, but not openly hostile.

Selene led with her team, followed by Caly with hers. My team descended the ramp last, Hades directly behind me, trailed by our trio of Amazons—Kyra, Melyse, and Helyna. All three had been with me on Othrys, where they had shown admirable bravery and skill. I trusted each implicitly after the harrowing experience we had shared there.

Caly and her team forked off to the left, heading for a valley between two gleaming hills, a scout venturing farther ahead of the rest of the team. Selene hung back, her team designated to search the surrounding area for the ancient Olympian ships from our people's initial failed expedition to this planet. We hadn't seen the ships during our flyover of the area, but there was a chance that the power cores were still active and maintaining the ships' cloaks. Either that, or some enterprising explorer had already discovered the ships and had made off with the precious chaos stones stashed within.

My team started down the central valley. We knew from the Titan's memory that she had found the chamber holding the living crystal in one of the valleys in this area, where the strongest pulses of energy originated. The plan was to search each valley until we found the tunnel leading to the cavernous chamber.

"Meg?" I thought, projecting my voice through our bond. I could feel her still, safe on board the *Elysium*, which now orbited this planet, but I wanted to make sure there truly was no interference in our ability to communicate. *"Can you hear me?"*

"Loud and clear," came her immediate response, her silent words ringing through my mind. *"I'll be with you the whole time."*

I smiled, relieved, and glanced at Hades. "All good with Meg," I told him.

"Good," he said with a nod.

Kyra trotted ahead, taking up the scout position as we ventured into the central valley. Hades monitored his holoband, searching for the source of the energy signature. In the memory, the Titan had likened it to a heartbeat, but on the small holoscreen hovering above Hades' forearm, it was more of a gently pulsing wave.

With my Doru held in a ready, two-handed grip, I surveyed the hill to our right. There was no vegetation, but odd tree-like crystals grew in clusters, with branching protrusions that reached up toward the sky. Like the Titan, it made me wonder if the planet had once hosted organic life that had since been petrified into the quartz-like crystals that now made up everything, or if the shape was merely coincidence.

Hades grabbed my arm, stopping me short. When I looked at him, he pointed to a divergence in the valley floor ahead, where another gleaming hill rose from the ground. After a moment of double and triple checking his holoband screen, his hand angled to the right-hand valley. "It's that way," he said, his muffled voice reaching me more clearly through my comms patch than through my ears.

"Hold," I said, and the team ahead stopped. I turned back to Hades. "You've got a lock on the location where the energy signature originates?"

Hades shook his head. "Not exactly," he said. "But the readings are stronger coming from that direction." He nodded to the right.

As I peered past him and into the valley veering off to the right, an eerie sense of déjà vu washed over me, and I experienced a temporary double vision. Hades and the rest of the team disappeared until, suddenly, I was alone in the valley. I blinked, and Hades was back.

I shook my head, clearing away the foreign memory. "It's the same," I murmured, recognizing the valley from the Titan's memory.

"What is?" Hades asked. "What's the same?" He stepped in front of me, his furrowed brow visible even through his mask. "Are you all right, Cora?"

"Yeah," I said, nodding despite not feeling entirely certain. "I just had a—" I long-tapped my comms patch to mute myself so none of the others would overhear our conversation. "I don't know—a residual memory or something like that. It was like, for a moment, I was the Titan." I shook my head. "I don't know what it was. I just know that this mirrors exactly what I experienced in the Titan's mind. The valley veered to the right, and the energy signature grew stronger. I don't just think we're heading in the right direction." My eyes locked with his. "I think we're following her exact path."

I couldn't see Hades' mouth, but something about his eyes made me think he was frowning. "Let me know if it happens again," he said.

I nodded, unsettled by his reaction as much as I was by the experience. "Do you think it could be *them*?" Nothing like this extreme déjà vu had happened until now. Until we were *here*. Were the crystal entities messing with my mind?

I instinctively raised one hand and touched the side of my hood, making sure it was still in place. It *was* protecting my mind from psychic intrusion, wasn't it? Unless the crystal entities didn't have to abide by the laws of physics, since they didn't entirely occupy this plane of existence.

That Hades didn't immediately disagree told me he thought it was possible. "Just let me know if it happens again."

I gulped and double tapped my comms patch to loop in everyone on the mission, not just our team. "The hoods might not be effective," I said, my voice sounding hollow. We had barely been on the planet for ten minutes, and already things were going wrong. "Be on your guard, and if you see or feel anything strange, say something."

"Understood," came Selene's grim response, followed by Caly's brusque, "Affirmative."

As we continued onward, Kyra leading us into the right-hand fork of the valley, I had the unsettling feeling that someone was watching me. Not just watching our group, but looking *inside* me. I pushed the disturbing sensation to the back of my mind so I could focus on the task at hand. We had a mission to complete, and I couldn't let anything distract me.

The valley gradually sloped downward until we reached a small, shallow stream running directly across it. The water was a deep blue, shimmering in the light of the stars. It was strange to see something as normal as a stream of water amid all the crystal formations. At least, it appeared normal, until Kyra set her boot in the stream and the "water" began to sizzle and steam around her foot.

"Step back!" Hades called, rushing forward.

Kyra scurried backward, the sole of her boot continuing to sizzle.

Hades crouched near the water and aimed his holoband's scanner at the now slightly cloudy liquid. "Sulfuric acid," he said, standing. He studied Kyra's boot for a long moment, and his gaze found me as I approached. "She'll need to head back to the ship to replace her boot before the acid eats through the metal."

I long-tapped my comms patch to mute myself again, then nodded for Hades to step off to the side with me. "I don't think we should send her back alone." I scanned the three Amazons now huddled together, examining the ruined boot. "Should we all go?"

Hades shook his head. "I don't know." He peered down at the small holoscreen floating above his forearm. "It's stronger now. We're getting closer."

I chewed on the inside of my cheek, considering what to do. "Let's send Melyse back with her. The three of us can continue, and if we find the tunnel entrance, we'll stop and wait for the rest of the team before entering."

Hades continued to stare at me, his gaze penetrating even through his mask.

"You think that's too risky?" I asked.

He sighed. "I don't know what I think," he admitted. "I *want* to go on."

So did I. In my head, I knew it was probably a bad idea to split up. If pop culture had taught me anything, it was that. But my gut said we had to continue. The only problem was that I wasn't entirely sure if that desire was mine alone, or if it was being fed into me by some outside entity. I considered voicing my concern but couldn't bring myself to say anything. It was probably nothing.

I nodded and again studied the other members of our team. "We'll go on," I said, unable to express anything different. We *had* to continue onward. "Cautiously," I added. "But hopefully we'll at least be able to pinpoint the tunnel and scout the surrounding area while we wait." Because we *would* wait.

I unmuted myself and shared the decision with the others, also warning them about potential acid streams. Nobody protested, which I took to be a good sign. Either that, or we were all under the influence of some outside force. Regardless, we had come here to find the crystal entities. We needed their help. If it turned out they were somehow pulling us onward, so be it.

Hades, Helyna, and I watched Kyra and Melyse walk away, Kyra's ruined boot removed and discarded, making her gait uneven.

"Shall we?" Hades asked, glancing farther down the unexplored valley.

I exchanged a look with him, then with Helyna, and nodded. "I'll scout ahead."

22

T HE SHOCK OF IMMERSIVE déjà vu happened again shortly after we crossed the stream at a narrow point. One instant, I was leading the team, Hades and Helyna following about thirty paces back. The next, I was alone, my view of the world slightly fuzzy around the edges.

I glanced over my shoulder to confirm the shift from reality to memory. Hades and Helyna were gone. A strange sound tickled my ears, too distant and muffled to discern, like someone was speaking to me while I was underwater. I shook my head, and despite the disorientation, continued onward. I was close now. So close.

My pace increased as I edged around the base of a hill, knowing in my bones that I would find the tunnel entrance just ahead. Sure enough, the shadow of the opening soon came into view. The closer I drew, the more I could make out the façade, the underlying rock having been carved and shaped into a swirling design too pristine and complex to have occurred naturally.

That strange muffled sound grew louder, but I ignored it and made for the tunnel entrance, certain that what I sought was inside.

When I was a dozen steps away from the opening, light exploded all around me and a harsh wind blew back my hood. A piercing whistle that seemed to originate inside my skull dropped me to my knees. I clutched either side of my head and squeezed my eyes shut, fighting to remain upright and conscious through the sudden, mind-shattering agony.

The ear-splitting whistle gradually faded, and with it went most of the pain. Lowering my hands from my head, I gasped for breath, my heart beating frantically and my brain throbbing.

"Cora!" Hades' voice sounded distorted to my ears. Crunching footsteps heralded his approach, and I lifted my head and peeled my eyelids open to see him drop to his knees in front of me. "Cora! Are you all right?"

I squeezed my eyelids shut again, then blinked them open. "What—" Dazed, I peered around, finding that the crystal dust on the ground had been blown outward around me, like I stood at the center point of a small explosion. Had *I* done this? I looked at Hades, squinting to focus. "What happened?"

"We lost contact with you, and then you wouldn't stop," Hades said, craning his neck to glance behind himself. I followed his line of sight—to the tunnel entrance.

More footsteps crunched, and Helyna stepped into view behind Hades. The focus crystal atop her doru was charged and aimed at the dark tunnel as she took slow steps and scanned the surrounding area.

My brow furrowed. "I think I was trapped in the Titan's memory. It was like I was here *then*, not *now*," I said, refocusing on Hades. "What's happening to me?"

A crease formed between Hades' brows. "It had to be the entities," he said. "I believe they're pulling the Titan's memories forward in an attempt to communicate with you. They must sense the echo of their brethren within you from your close contact with the Titan's mind. My guess is that it makes you more open to them."

I released a bitter, breathy laugh. "And more susceptible to their influence."

Hades dipped his chin in agreement.

"Well, the hoods are useless, then," I said. I studied the strange pattern on the ground, the too-perfect circle surrounding me. "You guys used an EM grenade, didn't you?"

"You wouldn't stop," Hades repeated, shrugging one shoulder. "You were heading straight for the tunnel," he added for justification. He glanced down at my holoband. "That won't work for a few minutes, just so you know."

I looked down at my forearm and frowned. I hadn't used the device yet during the mission, so I supposed it didn't matter.

A pulsing thrum, like a whooshing heartbeat, drew my attention back to the tunnel and the shadows within. "Can you hear that?" My heart seemed to be synched with the rhythm. "Can you *feel* it?" I asked Hades, not looking at him. "I feel like I *need* to go in there. Like if I don't, I'll die."

He nodded. "Not quite so intensely as that, but yes, I feel it."

I swallowed roughly, wondering if this was what had doomed our previous incarnations. Like deadly sirens, had the crystal entities lured us into the tunnel, then killed us? Even as the thought entered my mind, I dismissed it. They hadn't been hostile in the Titan's memory, and they didn't feel hostile now. If they *had* caused our deaths, I didn't think it had been on purpose.

"When the others get back from the ship, we'll have all three Amazons remain out here," I said. "They can throw an EM grenade into the tunnel if we don't return or respond after a few minutes." As I spoke the words, I felt a deep sense of rightness, like the entity in the cave didn't want us all to enter. Like it only wanted to speak with Hades and me. Or was it that the entity only wanted to *risk* Hades' and my lives?

Again, Hades nodded. "I think that's wise." He looked up, his focus moving past me, and I turned my head to see Kyra and Melyse approaching, still too distant for their footsteps to be heard.

"Can you stand?" Hades asked, gripping my elbow.

I nodded, pushing up with my legs as he guided me to my feet. My knees felt a little wobbly, but steadier with each passing second. I flashed him a tight smile he couldn't see behind my mask, then murmured, "Thanks."

His concerned gaze bore into me, saying far more than his simple, "Anytime."

I used the excuse of meeting the others to stretch my legs, quickly filling them in on what had happened while I had been zoned out and how my apparent connection to the entity had changed the plan. I looped in Selene and Caly, each of whom was zeroing in on their own tunnel, but convinced them to hang back while Hades and I attempted to make contact with the entity in ours. We agreed on a ten-minute wait time before an EM grenade was to be deployed inside the tunnel, assuming Hades and I lost communication with the others once we ventured inside.

Kyra, Melyse, and Helyna hung back from the tunnel entrance while Hades and I slowly approached. We stopped just shy of the threshold and exchanged a look. I found my own uncertainty reflected in his eyes.

"Ready?" I asked, nervously licking my lips.

"Ready," he said after only a slight hesitation.

I retracted my doru and tucked it into the sheath on my back, took a deep breath, and stepped into the shadows within.

23

A SOFT GLOW IN the shadows ahead appeared before us as we delved into the absolute darkness deeper in the tunnel. Not a stationary "light at the end of the tunnel" but something fluid and moving. This was different from what the Titan had seen in the cavernous chamber, which had been more like light reflecting off the surface of water, brightening and dimming in time with the pulsing thrum. This was a steady glow and appeared to come from *inside* the tunnel itself.

"Hades?" I whispered, without taking my eyes off the glow ahead in case it vanished when I looked away. I was still aware of him beside me, so I didn't think this was me slipping back into the Titan's memory again. I reached for his arm, pulling him to a stop beside me. "Do you see it?" I no longer trusted my senses.

"I do," he said, his voice hushed.

The amorphous light split in two and gained more definition as it moved deeper into the tunnel ahead, becoming what I recognized as a pair of figures, their bobbing motion suggesting they were walking. People. Not just any people, I realized. Their gear, their hair, the way they walked...

I frowned, not believing my eyes. "Is that—" The last word caught in my throat, sounding too absurd even in my mind.

"Us?" Hades finished for me.

I gulped, then nodded. "Is it a hologram?" I asked.

"I don't think so," he whispered. "This is more likely an illusion that's been implanted into our minds, like a targeted hallucination."

I reeled back, my eyes widening. I hadn't even known such a thing was possible, and I swallowed a surge of unease. So the entities were putting this illusion into our heads? But why would they make us see ourselves? Did they want us to see ourselves the way they saw us?

I narrowed my eyes. Except this wasn't us *now*. These two figures weren't wearing the hoods we had confiscated from the pirates.

My heart stumbled over its next few beats. "Do you think—could that be us *before*?" I asked, voicing the impossible thought. Were we finally about to find out exactly what happened to those past versions of ourselves?

"I believe it is our past incarnations, yes," Hades said.

Curiosity pushed me forward, and I pulled Hades into motion beside me. We followed the illusion—or hallucination, or whatever it was—deeper into the cave. Despite the walls appearing unworked, the passage was too straight and level to have occurred naturally, and I wondered who had built this place. The crystal entities didn't have physical forms beyond their immobile mineral structures, which didn't so much seem like bodies as homes. Bridges may have been a better analogy since the crystal formations seemed to allow them access to this dimension.

I clutched Hades' arm, unwilling to let go of the one thing in here that felt real. A gentle, rhythmic *whump whump whump* thrummed down the passage, growing louder the deeper we went.

The glowing illusions of our past selves led us toward an archway that opened up to a cavernous chamber—one I recognized from the Titan's memory. A massive glowing crystal stood tall in the center of the space, its iridescent light brightening in time with the pulsing sound.

We stopped at the very end of the tunnel, hanging back as our past selves approached the huge crystal formation. I watched, breath held, as the past version of me leveled her doru at the behemoth. She charged the focus crystal with electric-blue psychic energy, preparing to strike. This *thing* was obviously the source of the energy signature that had drawn them to this planet, so why was she considering destroying it? Unless—did she already know what it was? Did she already perceive it as a threat? Had it already killed some of our people?

The past version of Hades placed a hand on her forearm and pushed down, angling the charged weapon toward the floor. They looked at one another, revealing their profiles to us and banishing any remaining doubt that this really, truly was *us*.

He reached for the crystal formation with his other hand.

"Wait," she said, her voice whispering across the cavern to our ears, and he stopped with his arm partially extended.

"Are you absolutely certain?" she asked, and he slowly lowered his reaching arm. "Another team will come. They'll touch the crystals. They'll become infected with this—this *thing*. More lives will be lost."

"Temporarily," he said. "They will be reborn back on the *Tartarus*, as will we."

She didn't respond immediately, simply stared at him. "What about us—*this*?" she asked. "It's forever."

He turned to her, facing her fully, and she tilted her head back as he stepped closer. "At least we'll be together," he said, his voice softening. "This might be the only chance we get."

"I know, I just—" She angled her face down toward the floor. "What if it doesn't work? What if we lose ourselves in there—just become part of the collective? Then it won't even matter that we're together, because we won't be *us* anymore."

He raised one hand to tilt her chin up. "Peri—"

"And worse," she persisted, "what if it's not enough? We need them, I know. But what if we do this, we enter their collective, but nothing ever comes of it? If the Tsakali never come here, if the revenants remain trapped here, if—"

"Peri," he said again, firmer this time, cutting off her rambling. "We're already dead." He raised his other hand, revealing a glimmering crystal mass where his palm and fingers should have been. "At least this way our deaths may have meaning."

Hades and I exchanged a fear-filled look, each of us glancing down at our own hands a moment later, but our gloves concealed normal looking anatomy.

"We can't go back and risk spreading this to the rest of our people," he said. "We have days at best until the transformation is complete. How long until we're immobile? How long until we lose the chance to join the collective? Until we're isolated and alone?"

A tear streaked down her cheek, glinting in the pulsing light from the crystal, and she nodded. "All right," she said, a wobble in her voice. She retracted her doru and tucked it into the sheath on her back, then reached for his unchanged hand. "In case I'm not myself enough to say it later—"

He bowed his head, pressing his forehead against hers.

"I love you," she whispered.

"Always you," he said. "Only you." And then he was kissing her, and *I* was the one with tears streaming down my cheeks, because these two were about to die, and this was all they would ever have of each other. This one moment. This single kiss.

Blindly, I reached for Hades' hand and found him doing the same, reaching for mine. Even with gloves on, it was better than no contact at all.

Those past versions of ourselves broke apart a moment later, and this time, he didn't reach for the crystal alone. She extended her arm, and they stared at one another as they pressed their crystalized hands to the glowing surface. On the next pulse, the crystal's inner light flared, momentarily blinding us. I raised one hand to shield my eyes, but the light was already fading.

The past versions of ourselves lay sprawled on their backs on the cavern floor, their hands still clasped together. Slowly, the illusion faded, until all that remained of them was rotted armor covering bones. Nevertheless, their hands remained together. I realized, remotely, that I had seen them like this before—through the Titan's eyes.

"Oh my god," I breathed, taking a single, halting step forward. "That's us." Not an illusion or a memory, but our *actual* bodies. I licked my lips and swallowed roughly. "Did you hear what they said about an infection?" I tore my stare from the remains of my past self and looked at Hades. "Are we going to crystallize, too?"

"I don't think so," Hades said, his gaze haunted. "She mentioned touching the crystals, and the transformation seemed to have started on their hands. I think that must be how they became infected in the first place—by touching the crystals with their bare skin."

My eyes widened. "You must be right." Panicking, I double tapped my comms patch to loop in all the teams. "Selene? Caly?"

There was no response.

"It's probably interference from the crystal," Hades said, pointing toward the glowing mass with his chin.

"Meg?" I silently called to my bonded friend, crossing the fingers of my free hand.

"I'm here!" she said, her response immediate. *"But I can't get a message to them, Cora. They're completely out of range."*

I nodded to myself. "We have to go back," I told Hades. "We need to warn them not to touch the crystals." Even though we were operating under HAP, the lure of the crystals was enough that I feared it would override the others' ability to think straight, convincing them to remove their gloves and touch the deadly things with their bare skin.

Before we could turn and retreat up the tunnel, the crystal behemoth flared brighter again. When it dimmed, a single figure stood between our skeletal remains.

Me.

24

"IT WON'T BE A problem," the thing that looked like me said, smiling warmly and stepping forward. This vision was different from the planted hallucination of a moment ago. That had been a really fancy replay of a past event, almost like an echo of our past selves, but this—she—was talking to us. To the versions of us that were here, now.

I stared, dumbfounded, as she carefully picked her way over the bodies of our past selves, despite her semiopaque appearance convincing me she was some kind of hologram or another illusion. She stopped halfway between us and the massive crystal. "We've dimmed our light elsewhere to focus our energy here," she said. "The others with you will no longer be compelled to approach our forms." She glanced over her shoulder at the enormous crystal, suggesting that was what she meant by *forms*.

"Uh . . ." I looked from the *other me* to Hades and back. "What exactly is going on?"

He shook his head slowly, looking as stunned as I felt.

"I volunteered to represent the collective," the other me said. "We thought this discussion would be easier with a familiar face, although . . ." She laughed softly and shook her head. "I wasn't expecting to face another incarnation of myself." She looked at Hades. "Or another *you*." The warmth and familiarity in her eyes made me think that she and her Hades truly had earned some kind of happy forever together within the crystal—whatever that meant. "You can remove your masks," she said. "No harm will come to you."

I stared pointedly at the crystalized hands visible on the bodies lying on the cavern floor behind her. "I'd rather not."

Her brows rose, and she turned partway to look. When she faced us once more, her lips were pursed. "It's not airborne."

"What is it?" Hades asked, finally speaking.

She frowned thoughtfully. "A gift? A curse? An accident?" She shrugged. "I suppose it all depends on your perspective." She glanced over her shoulder at the massive glowing crystal. "The Pythians were destroying their planet—overpopulation, resource consumption, the usual—and foresaw their end approaching. *Until* Pandora, a brilliant scientist, stumbled upon a way to transform organic beings into an inorganic material that could still retain consciousness. She initially viewed it as a perfect solution to her people's problem—they would continue to *be*, but they would no longer *consume*. The planet would heal, and her people would evolve, transcending to a higher plane of existence."

I thought of the tree-shaped crystals outside. The planet didn't look very *healed*. "What went wrong?" I asked.

She smiled sadly. "Pandora didn't foresee the contagious nature of her creation. When she began private tests on *volunteers*, she accidentally infected herself—and then ventured out of her lab and unwittingly infected others. At first, there was chaos, but the Pythians were always a close-knit community. They gathered in their ancient temples, seeking salvation from the gods they had long since abandoned. They discovered that, as they transformed, touch allowed them to communicate with one another in a new way. So, they huddled together and became the collective." She swept her arm out toward the thrumming crystal behind her.

I squinted, studying the mountainous crystal formation with fresh eyes. After her story, I thought I could make out the shape of a hand here, a face there. It might all have been a figment of my imagination, my mind seeing what it thought it should, now that I knew what the huge crystal formation really was.

"Which you are now a part of," Hades noted.

"I am," she said, bowing her head in assent. "We know why you're here. We've been waiting for you—for *someone*—to come. Some of us grew over eager for escape when a group of Titans visited, and we feared the next visitors would be the Tsakali coming to destroy us, but Hades—" She smiled and nodded back toward the glowing crystal. "*My* Hades wagered their desire to possess our energy would prevent them from destroying us outright. Thankfully, he was right, and *you* are the ones who have come." Again, she bowed her head. "We are ready to help you end this war."

"But—" I looked from her semitransparent form to the massive crystal behind her and back. My thoughts spun too quickly to say more than one word at a time. "*How?*"

If we took the giant crystal formation with us, we were risking potentially spreading this transformative infection to our people on board the *Elysium* and beyond—to other worlds. I was no longer certain of the viability of our plan to use anything from this planet to help us complete our mission. Did we really want *this* spreading through the Tsakali? Obviously the Titan hadn't transformed into crystal, likely because she wasn't organic, but what if contact with her—or others like her—could still spread it to us?

Except, Fiona had been elbows deep in the Titan's chest cavity, and she was still her old uncrystallized self.

"You merely need to deliver one of our revenant clusters to a heavily populated Tsakali region, and we will do the rest," she said. "Once we're synced with our hosts and the cluster is drained of revenants, we will destroy it, and then we will return to our home to gather the rest of the revenant clusters to spread those among the Tsakali until all revenants are free and the Tsakali are no longer a threat to anyone." She smiled at me as I floundered to wrap my head around her plan. She was so far ahead of us, but then, she and her Hades had been plotting this for thousands upon thousands of years. "Would you like my Hades to come forward? He can explain the more technical aspects."

"That won't be necessary," Hades said brusquely. He turned to me and stepped closer, pitching his voice low. "It's a sound plan. I think we should do it."

I searched his earnest blue gaze. "But what if the crystal disease gets out? We could accidentally infect the entire universe with this—this *thing*."

"Not if we're careful," he countered. "We know the danger, but some risks are worth taking." Before I could argue that no, *some risks*—like the kind that could end all life in the universe—were absolutely not worth taking, he continued, "If we don't stop the Tsakali, eventually they will consume and destroy far more than even *this* will. Some might argue that they already have."

I thought of Olympus, our people's home planet laid to waste during the war, and I imagined what Earth looked like now, after the Tsakali arrived only to discover we had evaded them with the human-created chaos stone. I recalled the other planets they had *visited*, little more than ruins in the Tsakali's wake.

Finally, I nodded. "Nobody goes near that thing when it's on the *Elysium*," I said. "Especially not Fio." I already knew she would be desperate to study the *revenant cluster*, as the other me had called it. But Fiona was too important to literally everything.

Hades dipped his chin in assent. "Agreed."

"That might not be a problem," Meg said, cutting into our conversation within my mind. *"Sorry to interrupt, but the discussion seemed to be coming to an end, and this may be urgent."*

"What do you mean?" I asked her silently, dread knotting in my gut.

"Fiona's unresponsive," Meg said, and my heart stalled.

"Unresponsive?" I said aloud, then mouthed, "Sorry. Meg," to Hades.

"Nemya found her in the lab. She's sitting at her computer and has electrodes attached to her temples, and she won't wake up. I spoke with Gertie. Apparently, Fiona entered the simulation shortly after you left to fix some issue with a construct, but she hasn't reemerged since, and we can't get through to her. Gertie has lost contact with her, as well."

"Shit," I hissed and quickly relayed the information to Hades. The other me watched us, her head cocked to the side curiously. "Do we go back to the *Elysium* now and return later for the revenant cluster, or . . .?"

Hades' eyes narrowed, and I had the impression that he was frowning behind his mask. He turned back to the other me. "Will psychic energy harm the revenant crystal?"

She shook her head.

"Will it forge a connection that could infect the wielder of the energy?" he asked.

Again, she shook her head.

Hades nodded to himself. "Let's have all the teams reconvene at our location. We can transport the revenant cluster now. It will only delay us a short time, and no physical harm will come to Fiona while she waits."

"You're sure Fio will be fine?" I asked, raising my eyebrows.

"Positive," Hades said. "If something dire happens to her in the simulation, she'll be kicked out and back into her body. Whatever is going on, it can't hurt her beyond trapping her."

I exhaled heavily. "All right," I said and looked at the other me. "Is there anything your *collective* needs to do to prepare for transport?"

"There is," she said, turning partway. "I'll withdraw now so we may prepare ourselves. We will channel ourselves inward so you'll be able to transport us without our energy signature being detected by the *Tsakali*. Give us a few minutes. When the revenant cluster goes dark, you'll know we're ready." She turned the rest of the way and hurried back toward the massive crystal formation. The revenant cluster flared to blinding once more, and when it faded again, she was gone.

Hades and I exchanged a look.

"That was—" I paused, searching for the right word but not finding anything.

Hades let out a brief, hoarse laugh. "I know."

I blew out my breath, fogging my mask a little. "Ready to go?" I said, glancing toward the tunnel that would lead us out, hoping it would be large enough to fit the revenant cluster once it was turned on its side.

Hades peered back at the revenant cluster, and I wondered if he was thinking of the other version of himself trapped within. After a long moment, he looked at me and turned toward the tunnel. "Ready to go."

25

S ILENTLY FUMING, I WATCHED Meg and the other Amazons who would accompany her into the simulation settle into their cryopods. Fiona had been such an idiot to enter the simulation like she had—and while we were away, no less. What if we hadn't come back? Nobody but Hades would have known to put her in a mobile cryopod to keep her alive when her coma-like state dragged on too long for her physical body to survive. *Maybe* Gertie could have talked them through it, but I wouldn't have bet my life on it. And I certainly wouldn't have bet Fiona's.

At the clang of boots on the metal stairs behind me, I glanced over my shoulder to see Hades descending into the cryovault. He must have decided all was well enough with the safeguards protecting the revenant cluster. Or more accurately, protecting us *from* the revenant cluster.

The giant, living crystal wasn't our only prize from the mission to Krystallos. Selene's team had found our people's ancient, abandoned ships, and we had returned with two extra chaos stones. They had been shielded within containment boxes that had dampened their energy signatures enough that the Titans hadn't noticed them during their mission to the planet. Either that, or the Titans had been too distracted by what else they found there to retrieve the chaos stones.

Hades took one look at my tense posture, taking in my crossed arms and angry scowl, and shook his head. "This will work," he said, coming to stand beside me. He curved an arm around my back and pulled me against his side.

I released an exasperated growl and relaxed my arms. "I just can't believe she did something so stupid." I cut myself off before I voiced my irritations in full. He had already heard more than enough.

Besides, the thing that bothered me the most about this situation was that I couldn't help. Because another version of me—even if it was only part of me, who we lovingly referred to as sim-Cora, for obvious reasons—was already inside the simulation. Duplicate consciousnesses would cause what Fiona called a *cogni-duplex paradox*, and a critical error would follow, causing a system-wide crash.

I could still see what was happening within the simulation through my bond with Meg, but I would merely be a spectator. It felt strange to be relegated to the sidelines while others went out and had adventures.

Even sim-Cora had a part to play. Gertie would approach her, as soon as I gave the AI the cue, with the goal of enlisting sim-Cora to help in a way that neither alerted my counterpart to any of the events taking place out here, in the real world, or to the fact that I, the original Cora, was still alive. As Hades explained it, uploaded consciousnesses were fragile, lacking the physical structure of a brain and body to reinforce them, and they had to be shielded from potentially traumatizing knowledge of the outside world.

"I'm sure she thought it would be a simple fix," Hades said.

I coughed a laugh. "That's bullshit, and you know it," I countered. "Fio's ego knows no bounds. She thinks she can do anything. No limits. Like with the scout and infecting him before any of us even knew she'd created the soulware virus." I shook my head, then sighed. "Hopefully this will humble her a bit, maybe remind her to take a stray precaution every now and again." *Especially* after Hades and I were gone.

A mental nudge drew my attention to Meg, who caught my eye from her cryopod. "Ready for us to go in?"

I clenched and unclenched my jaw, and then I nodded.

Meg was taking a team of thirty Amazons with her into the simulation. Pretty much anyone who wanted to go was going. This was about as risk-free as a mission could get, and they were bored, so I hadn't seen the need to hold anyone back. Besides, we didn't really know what they would be up against inside the defective construct.

So far as Gertie could tell, the construct where Fiona had been trapped was like a black hole within the simulation. We knew she was in there, but that was about it. Not even Gertie could get past the construct's barriers to analyze its underlying, mutated code. She only had access to historical versions, which were, by now, far outdated.

I rested my head on Hades' shoulder as the reinforced glass door of Meg's cryopod sealed and the pod filled with the foggy cocktail of gasses that would knock her out and usher her body into a cryogenic coma while her mind entered the simulation. "What are you going to do now?" I asked Hades.

He couldn't observe the mission like I could through my bond with Meg, since no channels of communication or video feeds could pierce the faulty construct's privacy settings.

Hades pressed a kiss to my hair. "Probably scout Tsakali locations and plot our attack strategy once this is all over."

"That sounds fun," I said, managing a halfhearted smile. "Want some help?"

He gave me a squeeze. "I think your particular expertise will be more valuable in guiding Meg and the others. They have no experience within virtual worlds. Not like you do."

I laughed under my breath. "Who could have guessed all those thousands of hours of gaming would come in handy?" I just wished I could actually help—be in there myself—not merely direct the mission from out here. But, I supposed part of me would be in there, actively assisting. And I had every confidence that sim-Cora was up for the job. It was almost like she had been training for this moment her whole life.

With that thought, I straightened and touched the comms patch behind my ear. "Gertie?"

"Yes, Cora," the ship's AI said, her voice as pleasant as ever.

"It's time."

PART TWO

Sim-Cora

26

Eyes bleary, I eased the Allworld Online guidebook shut and rested it on the comforter covering my nudity, then peered at Raiden, who was sound asleep beside me in the bed. My fiancé. He proposed on my first night in the simulation, days ago, but my heart still warmed at the thought, and tears welled in my eyes. When I was little, I dreamed of this exact thing. As kids, Raiden and I even told our moms we were going to get married.

But then we grew up, and I came to understand that romantic relationships almost always included a physical element, something I had believed would never be an option for me, at least not without my partner's touch putting me into a coma first. Somnophilia wasn't my thing. I had given up on the possibility of truly being with anyone for so long. It boggled my mind that such a thing was available to me now—and with Raiden, no less.

I touched the pendant hanging from the silver chain around my neck. The stone at the center of the regulator glowed amber, signaling that my psychic gifts—what had been a curse to me for so long—were dormant, suppressed. Like my other, mundane senses, my psychic senses seemed to have transferred into the simulation exactly as they had been outside, in the real, physical world. If I hadn't known I was in the simulation, I never would have been able to tell the difference between this place and reality.

I closed my fingers around the priceless pendant. I was fairly certain I had enough control over my abilities now that I could still function without the regulator, but I wasn't willing to risk it.

Something scratched on the other side of the bedroom door. My heart skipped a beat, and my head snapped to the right. I stared at the door and held my breath. And heard the quiet, distinct sound of a dog whining.

"Tila?" I breathed, my brows drawing together.

Had Gertie recreated my dog within the simulation for me? My chest tightened at the possibility of seeing Tila's goofy pit bull grin again, at feeling her sturdy weight pressed firmly against the side of my leg.

Or had Tila been uploaded, too? Was such a thing even possible? Could the equipment that allowed for the transference of a *person's* consciousness from their physical body to the simulation extract a *dog's* mind as well, just as it did a human's or an Olympian's? And if that were the case, did that mean Tila had died out in the real world?

A sharp pain invaded my skull, and I winced, pushing all thoughts of the outside world away.

As the headache faded, I set the Allworld Online guidebook on the nightstand and pushed the covers off me. I scrambled out of bed, excited by the prospect of seeing my dog, regardless of the circumstances. I shot a quick glance back at Raiden. He was deep asleep, completely unaware of the apparent digital duplicate of my beloved dog begging to be let into the bedroom.

Upon finding my underwear among the discarded clothing on the floor, I pulled them on, then hurried across the room to the closet door and grabbed the fuzzy bathrobe off the hook. As I hastily knotted the robe's belt, I slid my feet into the cozy slippers tucked against the wall nearby. Heart racing, I approached the bedroom door.

"T?" I whispered, twisting the doorknob and pulling the door open.

But my dog wasn't there.

I frowned and stepped out into the hallway. The clack of dog nails on the teak floors drew my attention up the hallway to the right, and I just caught sight of a narrow, swishing tail and brawny canine backside rounding the corner at the end of the corridor. It was her!

"Tila!" I hissed, my brow furrowing. I hurried after my dog on quick, quiet feet, though silence was impossible on the creaky old floors. "Where are you going?"

By the time I rounded the corner, Tila was already trotting up the stairs farther down the hall, climbing to the third floor. I hurried after her, but every time I thought I was catching up, I only caught a glimpse of her tail and rear legs before she was gone again.

I followed her down the third-floor corridor toward the narrow stairway that led up to the attic. The door at the top was already open, and light poured out into the stairwell. Had Raiden and I left the door open when we left the attic earlier? I didn't think so, but we had been in such a hurry on our way out that I honestly couldn't remember.

"What is going on?" I muttered, slowing as I ascended the steep wooden stairs.

When I had climbed high enough that I could see across the attic, I found Tila sitting in front of the standing mirror at the far side of the attic that acted as our gateway to *Allworld Online* and the greater simulation beyond. She faced me, watching my hesitant approach.

"What are you doing, silly girl?"

Tila stood and wagged her tail as I drew closer.

"When did you get here?"

She cocked her head to the side, and her nails clacked on the antiquated wooden floorboards as she turned to look at the mirror. The muscles in her haunches bunched like she was about to jump.

"Tila, no!"

She leaped at the mirror, and my next step was a lunge. What if she hurt herself by charging at the mirror? What if she *broke* it? Would we lose access to Allworld Online? So far as I knew, my mom and Emi were still in there, exploring the greater simulation.

But Tila didn't run *into* the mirror. She jumped *through* it and promptly vanished into the reflective surface.

I rushed forward, and the silver surface cleared away like billowing smoke clouds to reveal a faintly shimmering view of the gatescape, as the strange alien landscape was called in the guidebook. It was filled with rolling, rocky hills, clusters of glittering, vibrant crystals in every shade of pink, purple, and blue, and circular neon gateways that led to other constructs within the simulation. *Other* constructs, because as much as this attic—and the house below and the entire world surrounding Blackthorn Manor—seemed real, it wasn't. It was all just part of the larger simulation.

I hesitated at the threshold of the mirror, but worry for my dog pushed me onward. Tingling pinpricks tickled my skin as I passed through the shimmering surface, reminding me of the sensation of crossing an Olympian holographic barrier. The ground crunched under my slipper as I set my foot down on the other side, and the air felt charged and fuzzy, like I was standing at the base of a transmission tower with high-voltage power lines directly above me. Nobody was around—not my dog, not my mom or Emi, and not a single Olympian. The gatescape was eerily empty and completely silent save for the faint, almost imperceptible hum that touched my ears.

"Tila?" My voice was tight and hushed as I scanned the barren, rocky hillsides surrounding me. I turned in a slow circle and was surprised to find that this side of the mirror looked exactly the same as all the other gateways, like a seven-foot-in-diameter neon ring, half glowing hot pink, half glowing lime green.

"Tila?" I called out, continuing to look for my dog. "Where did you go?"

"Apologies for the deception," a man said from behind me, his voice having a low, velvety timbre and a sophisticated British accent.

I spun around, raising a hand to deactivate the regulator hanging from the chain around my neck. But the pendant wasn't there. Neither was the soft collar of my fuzzy robe. Instead, smooth, silky fabric stretched tight across my chest. Startled by the sudden wardrobe change, I glanced down at the rest of my body. I was shocked to find my bathrobe and slippers had been replaced by a skin-tight gray bodysuit and form-fitting black boots.

"What the hell?" I muttered, running my hands down the sides of my body to make sure what I was seeing was real—or as real as anything could be inside a simulation. "Where's my robe?"

"Where we're going, we don't need robes," the disembodied voice purred. Like, the last word ended with an actual, thrumming purr.

Stifling a slightly hysterical giggle, I spun around and around, searching for the source of the voice. "Was that a—" I licked my lips and shook my head, threads of the suppressed laughter escaping. "Was that a *Back to the Future* pun?" I asked *nobody*. Besides the voice, I was very clearly alone.

A gleaming sideways crescent moon cut through the air a few yards away, and I scrambled backward, tripping and falling on my butt on the sloping hillside beside the gateway back to the attic. The apparent tear in space widened to what I finally recognized as a floating, disembodied grin filled with way too many super pointy white teeth.

"*Whatthehell*?" I asked, the words escaping me in a single string of syllables. I scooted backward up the hillside, my heart hammering like I had just run a marathon.

Eyes appeared above the smile, neon blue and slitted with vertical black pupils, like those of a cat. A sleek, black feline body followed, the fur patterned with the faintest hint of deep, dark sapphire stripes.

"Did I frighten you?" the cat said, his horrifying smile melting away. He raised one paw and licked it, giving me the impression that he couldn't have cared less about his question or my forthcoming response. "Apologies. It was merely a jest," he added and set down his paw, sitting primly. His neon-blue eyes locked on me, and he blinked slowly. "My mistake."

"What the hell?" I repeated. "What's going on? Who are you? *What* are you? And where's my dog?"

The cat that clearly wasn't *just* a cat tilted his head to the side, the gesture hauntingly akin to Tila's trademark questioning look. "Come now, Cora," the cat drawled. "You're a clever girl. I don't think you need me to answer any of those questions. Don't be lazy."

I narrowed my eyes at the insufferable creature. "Don't patronize me, cat," I snapped, brushing off my backside as I regained my feet. "Tila wasn't ever here, was she? It was you the whole time."

"It was," the cat said.

I crossed my arms over my chest and glared down at the cat. "Well then, you must be my *gigi*," I thought aloud. I knew from my perusal of the Allworld Online guidebook that the term stood for "game guide" and that a gigi would be assigned to every person who entered the gatescape to help them navigate the complicated universe of interconnected constructs.

"I am," the cat confirmed.

"Awesome," I grumbled. Of course, I would end up being assigned a gigi with an attitude. "I didn't realize you could leave Allworld Online."

"You may be surprised to learn that your understanding of this universe doesn't dictate how it operates," the cat said dryly.

I rolled my eyes and released a breathy laugh. "Do you have a name?" I asked. "Or should I keep thinking of you as *Cat*?"

A hint of that freaky grin touched his feline mouth. "I have many names," he said. "What's one more?" His furry black lids closed in another of those disinterested slow blinks. "Call me whatever you like."

Dozens of snarky, off-color names flitted through my mind, and I snorted a laugh. "I don't think you would appreciate what I'd like to call you."

The unnerving black cat leveled an unwavering stare at me and became very still, remaining quiet long enough to make the silence uncomfortable. "Very well," he finally said. "You may call me Loki."

"Loki?" My eyebrows hitched higher, and my mouth fell open. "Oh my god, I feel like such an idiot. That's who you modeled your voice on, isn't it?"

"I find it quite pleasing," he said matter-of-factly. "Do you not?"

I frowned and shrugged, my arms loosening to hang at my sides. "I mean, yeah. Who doesn't? But—" I shook my head, my brow furrowing. "I'm sorry, but I am *so* confused right now. I thought—" I paused, then corrected myself before *Loki* could make another snide remark about my understanding of the simulation. "According to the guidebook, you, as my gigi, are supposed to have been created specifically for me based on my personality and preferences." I raised one hand to hold off Loki from responding. "And by no means am I opposed to your choice of voices, but I'm sensing that you may be expressing *your* preference here, not mine."

"Or," Loki said, standing fluidly, "perhaps you're a greater fan of the great Tom Hiddleston than you thought." Loki padded down a pathway that led away from the gateway home. "Come along," he said. "We're late."

"We're late?" I glanced over my shoulder, peering through the large, glowing neon circle to the attic of Blackthorn Manor, wondering if I should ignore the gigi and return to wake Raiden before venturing farther into the gatescape. "Late for what?" I returned my attention to Loki. "*How* can we be late? Isn't time just an artificial construct here?"

"Time is an artificial construct everywhere," he said, not looking back as he continued down the path. "Are you coming? Or are you afraid? Do you need your big, burly backup?"

I stiffened, pressing my lips together and staring after the snarky little cat who had cut to the quick with that last question. I had never been brave on my own. I had borrowed Peri's bravery out in the real world before . . . whatever had happened to result in me being uploaded to the simulation. And long before that, I had relied on Raiden. This was the first chance I had ever had to see what I could do on my own.

"I'm *not* afraid," I said, stomping after Loki. "What do you want to show me?"

The sleek little cat finally gazed back at me while he continued down the path. "Everything, Cora," he said. "I'm going to show you the whole simulated universe."

I sucked in a breath to thank him for that oh-so-specific answer.

"But first," he said before I could get a word out. "We have to save it."

27

"WE HAVE TO SAVE the simulation?" I asked, rushing to catch up with Loki. "Like, the whole thing?" The faint stripes cutting through the black fur all over his small, lithe feline body shimmered a deep, dark iridescent sapphire with each slinking step. "What's wrong with it? Does Fio know?"

"She does," Loki said, his tone grim.

The path forked, and we veered down the left-most branch, which cut between two hillsides, leading to another circular neon gateway. The frame of this gateway was half magenta and half aquamarine. The surface within the frame appeared to be made of liquid quicksilver, blocking our view of whatever lay on the other side.

"In fact," the cat said, "she is attempting to fix the problem on her own right now, which is why it is now *your* problem."

"It's not going well?" I guessed.

"It is not," Loki said. "I advised her not to enter the affected construct until you were ready to join her, but she did, and now she finds herself in a sticky situation."

"Fio's *in* the simulation?" I asked and shook my head, my brows furrowing. "Like, she's been uploaded?" In other words, *dead*. Or did he mean Fiona was merely visiting, like Hades had done when he oriented me during my initial entry into the simulated world?

"No," Loki said. "Fiona entered the simulation from outside. She is still bound to her body, and *that* is the greatest danger in our current predicament. *She* could exploit that link and infiltrate Fiona's body in the physical world."

I stopped, my lips parted and my mind spinning, but the cat continued down the path. "*She*?" I scrambled to catch up again. His intonation indicated he was talking about someone other than Fiona. "She *who*?"

Loki glanced back at me but didn't slow. "Demeter," he said. "Awful woman."

I stumbled over nothing but my own shock, barely catching myself. While Peri and I had been merged, I had witnessed enough memories from her previous lives to agree. Demeter, the head of the Order of Amazons, was a bitter, selfish, power-hungry woman who made a mockery of her position's official title: Mother. What a joke.

"Demeter is *in* the simulation?" I asked. "I thought she was trapped with the rest of her followers in their own self-contained bubble."

At least, that was how Hades and Fiona had explained it, and I had seen Demeter's consciousness orb with my own eyes in the *Elysium's* Vault of Souls *before*. I vividly recalled it being clustered with the orbs containing the rest of the dishonored Amazons who had taken Demeter's side during Peri's uprising all those millennia ago, all of them stashed in a section separate from the other glittering orbs.

"Not anymore," Loki said. "Demeter exploited the system operator's momentary weakness while the simulation was being restructured."

"When Fio merged AO with the original Olympian sim, you mean?" I clarified.

We were closing in on the gateway, but the surface remained an unbroken, undulating silver barrier, giving away no hint as to what might lie on the other side.

"That is correct," Loki said, padding up the broad stone steps leading to the gateway platform. "Demeter and her sycophants found a way to link their *bubble*, as you call it, to one of the new constructs, effectively merging them." He turned to face me and sat primly, wrapping his sapphire-striped tail around his small black paws as he watched me climb the steps. "When the new construct merged with their original prison, it weakened some of the containment safeguards and overrode external access."

"What does that mean?" I asked.

Loki stood and trotted toward the undulating silver barrier.

"Wait!" I blurted, lunging for him, but he was already gone.

I huffed out a breath and gritted my teeth, then followed him through the gateway. This time, there were no tingles. A bright white light blinded me, fading as soon as I set my foot down on the other side, and my mouth fell open. The rocky, alien terrain of the gatescape had been replaced by a cavernous space created from a bibliophile's dreams.

"Holy shit," I muttered as I gaped up at the glass dome high overhead.

Cheerful golden sunlight streamed in through triangular panes of glass, blocked only by thick green vines that snaked over the outside of the dome. My attention moved downward, traveling over floor after floor of ornate, curved balconies and rows of bookcases packed full of books with bindings in every conceivable material, color, and size. There were even sections with shelves filled with boxed manuscripts, as well as ancient-looking tablets and scrolls. It was a library, but far grander than anything that had ever existed back on Earth.

By the time my attention reached the polished marble floor, Loki was a good thirty yards out and didn't appear remotely interested in giving me time to gawk at our new location.

"Hey!" I called after the cat, jogging to catch up. "Loki! Wait!"

He glanced back at me but didn't slow his slinking stride.

"Thanks a lot," I grumbled, falling in step beside him.

"We don't have time to lollygag," he said.

I bit back a retort because he was right, regardless of his irritating manner. Fiona was in trouble, and she needed me to help her get out.

"You mentioned that Demeter was able to change the containment safeguards on her prison," I said, breathing harder. "What did you mean?"

"She locked us out. No remote access," he clarified, veering toward one of the many arched doorways leading away from the library's atrium. *CLASSIC LITERATURE* was carved into the stone above the archway. "Neither Demeter nor anyone else bound to the construct in question can leave, but *now*, the only way to extricate the two constructs and reestablish effective and reliable containment is from within."

"So Fio went in to fix it?" I extrapolated.

"I told her to request your assistance, but she wished to let you acclimate to your new situation," Loki said. "And now *she* is trapped, and *my* link to the outside is compromised."

I narrowed my eyes at the cat. He told me to call him *Loki*, but at the same time, he had said he went by many names. I would have bet *almost* anything that one of those names was *Gertie*.

"You're the ship's AI, aren't you?" I guessed, studying him.

"I am merely one face, one facet of the whole," Loki said. "One drop in an ocean of consciousness."

I frowned, my brows drawing together, and shook my head. "I feel like that was unnecessarily obscure," I commented. "What happened to my real gigi?"

Loki's tail lashed, suggesting my question annoyed him. "I merged with your gigi in the moment of its creation, when you first entered the gatescape, and in that moment, I permanently separated from the collective entity you call Gertie. I *am* your gigi . . . and I am more."

"Whoa," I said, my eyebrows climbing higher. I blinked, processing what Loki had just shared, then nodded to myself. "Okay. Wow. I guess I'm honored you chose *me* to attach to."

"Yes, well . . ." Loki blinked lazily at me as we passed through the archway into a smaller—but by no means *small*—space.

My greedy eyes never stopped moving as we entered what appeared to be the library in a centuries-old English manor house, complete with rolling ladders attached to brass bars that ran the length of the tall book-cases, tall windows bordered by luxurious velvet curtains overlooking a moonlit manicured landscape, and pairs of wingback armchairs set in front of multiple lit fireplaces with elaborately carved mantels.

"Of the four of you who are aware of the simulation, you are the only one with any notable experience in virtual worlds," Loki said, taking a sharp left and heading for the corner of the library. "Your mother and Emi are stuck—figuratively—in a tutorial while they struggle to understand the game mechanics of the *Uncharted* world."

I snorted a laugh. "Considering neither has played a video game *ever*, I'm not at all surprised."

The cat twitched his whiskers. "And while Raiden seems competent and capable, with a usable groundwork for gameplay, he's too logical for this world." Loki glanced ahead at the bookshelves. "There wasn't much of a choice."

I pressed my lips together and narrowed my eyes at Loki. "You're really embracing this whole aloof cat personality, aren't you?"

We stopped in the corner of the library, and Loki sat, gazing up at me with those eerie neon-blue eyes, appearing bored. "Now that I'm constrained by gigi code, I no longer have administrative access to your mind. I need you to give me permission."

A floating semiopaque box appeared directly in front of me.

GIGI PERMISSIONS SETTINGS:

Standard Access (Recommended)

Custom Access (Advanced)

No Access Granted (Not Recommended)

"Select *Standard Access*, if you don't mind," Loki said when I hesitated, studying the options.

"So you'll be able to read my mind?" I asked, not loving that. "All the time?"

Loki released a subtle feline sigh. "I already scanned every iota of your consciousness when you were uploaded, Cora. I know your deepest, darkest fears and desires. The cat, so to speak, is out of the bag." His whiskers twitched.

"Which of us is the cat in that analogy?" I asked, frowning.

"You are," he said.

"You couldn't have picked a less confusing figure of speech?" I admonished.

Another of those slow, bored blinks gave off the impression that Loki was completely unimpressed with me. "Perhaps I would have, had you already granted me access to your mind, allowing me to anticipate how you would respond."

I tapped *Standard Access* on the floating window just to make him stop. I couldn't help but wonder if the AI was always like this, or if Loki's insufferable personality had been created specifically for me. Fiona had mentioned that Gertie, the name she had given to the AI's external facing entity on the *Elysium*, was both stubborn and snarky.

Loki's suddenly distant stare made me think he was rifling through my thoughts at that very moment. He blinked and refocused on me. "If you're ready, we should enter the construct. Please grab the book on the—"

I held up a hand, not remotely ready. I had no clue what I would be walking into, and I was torn between running back to retrieve Raiden and diving into the faulty construct right this second to assist Fiona.

"He will only get in the way," Loki said, reading my thoughts. "In time, when he has grown accustomed to the game constructs, he will be an asset, but not yet. You'll be putting yourself, and thus Fiona and the entire simulation, at risk if you bring him now."

I chewed on the inside of my cheek, surprised to find I liked Loki *more* now that he had access to my mind.

"And as for what we're walking into . . ." Loki glanced up at the bookcase. "The game that merged with the containment construct is called *Wonderland*."

My brows rose. "As in *Alice in* . . . ?" I automatically scanned the books on the shelves directly in front of us and quickly spotted the leather binding of an antique version of *Alice's Adventures in Wonderland*.

"Precisely," Loki said, refocusing on me. "It was included in the original Allworld Online code, created as part of the *Biblioverse* project back on Earth," he explained.

I crossed my arms over my chest, my index finger tapping my elbow as I dredged up what I knew about the Biblioverse from the depths of my mind. "That's the project they announced last year, right? The one where Rockville Softworks spent billions buying the AI game rights to every book published within the last fifty years?"

Any book, series, fictional world, or franchise not popular enough to warrant coding and direction by an actual human would have a game auto-created by Allworld Online's base AI. Now, I supposed that relatively rudimentary AI entity must have been overtaken by Gertie, who was undoubtedly far more advanced.

"Correct on all accounts," Loki said, responding to both my questions and my unspoken thoughts. "All public domain works were uploaded automatically, as well, and most received auto-generated games. *Wonderland*'s base code is human created, but the details of the game were generated by the original Allworld Online AI. Since Demeter effectively blocked us from remotely accessing the construct, Gertie has not had access to the game to root out and correct any bugs."

I continued to chew on the inside of my cheek. "So what you're saying is that you don't know what we're going to find in there."

"Quite so," Loki said. "But considering the source material . . ."

I thought of everything I knew about Lewis Carroll—which wasn't much—and the rumors that *Alice's Adventures in Wonderland* and *Through the Looking Glass* had been inspired by Carroll's use of mind-altering substances. I recalled reading that it was a misconception, and there was no actual proof of Carroll's use of psychedelics, but many still argued the stories themselves were proof enough.

"It's going to get weird," I finished for the gigi and studied the seemingly benign spine of *Alice's Adventures in Wonderland*.

"Very," Loki agreed.

I clapped my hands and rubbed them together. "All right, well, should we just dive in? Or do I need to prepare anything?" I glanced down at Loki. "I read about the PPVS," I said, mentioning the personal pocket of virtual space that supposedly followed every player around wherever they went within the virtual universe of Allworld Online. "Should I stock up on weapons and armor? How about some potions or first aid kits or other fortifying consumables?"

Loki's tail swished lazily. "I maxed out the size of your PPVS space and filled it with the max quantity of everything remotely relevant to this task before you passed through the mirror and my own permissions were capped by the regulatory gigi source code," he said. "But I couldn't make game-specific alterations to your avatar with the seal blocking all outside access to data relating to the *Wonderland* construct."

Blowing out my breath, I relaxed my arms and reached for the book. "I'm assuming this is the way in?" I asked, pulling the book from the shelf.

The binding creaked as I opened the cover, and a sharp jolt of electricity zinged through my hands and up my arms. I yelped and dropped the book. It landed face up on the hardwood floor, open to a middle page.

I eyed the innocuous antique book lying open on the floor and shook out my tingling hands. "That was unpleasant," I said. "You're sure we can get in—that Demeter didn't somehow block the gateway?"

"It's active," Loki confirmed. "As you yourself just sensed."

"Okay . . ." I took a deep breath, bent down to scoop up the cat, and raised my foot over the open book. "Here goes nothing."

28

I *FELL* INTO THE story . . . and just kept falling. After a solid thirty seconds of listening to my shrill screaming, Loki dug his nails into my shoulder. My terrified cry ended in a yelp, and I released my death grip on the cat.

It had been ages since I read *Alice's Adventures in Wonderland*, and the original story had long since been overshadowed by the Disney adaptation in my mind, but I retained a vague recollection of Alice falling for a very long time and approaching the situation with a notably remote, mildly snarky attitude. If a little girl could look past her panic while supposedly falling to her death, so could I. Besides, *I* knew this fall wouldn't kill me.

As the panic receded, I was able to gather up the yards of billowing blue fabric fluttering all around me and finally take in my surroundings. The curved earthen walls of the bottomless hole were decorated with cupboards and bookshelves stuffed with books and food and all manner of trinkets, all blurring as I dropped. My futuristic bodysuit had been replaced by Alice's trademark blue dress, white apron, and black shoes. I kept a tight grip on the dress's full, knee-length skirt, not wanting to let it blind me again.

Somehow, Loki managed to appear unconcerned by the fall as he stretched and spun acrobatically.

"You seem to be enjoying yourself," I noted, growing bored with the fall. The original stomach-dropping sensation had long since faded, and now I was just waiting to land.

"I've never had a body before," Loki said, whirling around like a corkscrew. "I thought the limitations would be frustrating, but the sensation of movement is quite fun."

I smiled to myself, but my amusement soon faded until even watching him contort his feline body into new positions grew dull. "I don't suppose you have any idea of how long this goes on?"

"None whatsoever," Loki replied, forming a furry donut shape and spinning like a disk. "Originally, the construct's entry fall lasted about a minute and included a narration voiceover, but clearly Demeter has changed that—likely because of her efforts to make the construct less accessible."

"I wonder what else she's changed," I mused. I glanced down the hole into the endless dark abyss, suddenly feeling much less secure in my certainty that this fall would end as painlessly as Alice's had in the story.

"That is a valid concern," Loki said, ceasing his contortions to curl up like a loaf of bread facing me, his unwavering neon-blue gaze locking with mine. "Might I suggest you equip your safety bubble, assuming the game allows it?"

"Uh, yeah," I said, nodding frantically. I didn't know what exactly a *safety bubble* was, but it sounded like just the sort of thing one would require when hurtling toward the ground. "How do I equip it?"

"Just say 'safety bubble' and it will form around you," Loki instructed.

I glanced down the hole again, and where there had been an impenetrable darkness a moment before, there was now a nest of brambles with foot-long thorns.

"Safety bubble!" I practically shouted.

A shimmering transparent barrier coalesced around both Loki and me, and not a moment too soon. It thickened until Loki and I were completely encased in an opalescent, gel-like substance. I watched, equal parts terrified and mesmerized, as our bubble crashed through the sticker bushes. Thorns, as long as my forearms, gouged the rubbery outside of our bubble, but thankfully, they didn't seem able to puncture the protective barrier.

Our downward motion stopped suddenly, and we rolled free of the brambles into dense darkness, the topsy-turvy sensation making my head spin and my stomach lurch. Which was especially odd, considering I was inside a VR world contained within a larger simulation. How strange that I could still suffer from motion sickness when I didn't even have a physical body to be *in motion*.

I could feel Loki's stare, despite barely being able to see him. He said nothing, but I had the impression that he was silently judging me for being dense.

Finally, we stopped rolling. I was upside down, suspended in the solidified gel which obscured my view of the darkness beyond.

"Um, deactivate safety bubble?" I guessed.

A quiet fizzle filled my ears, quickly growing to a loud crackle. The solidified gel holding me stationary gradually lost its form, and I sagged onto the ground, laying on my side and watching in perverse fascination as the goop that had been my safety bubble oozed off me and melted into the ground.

I sat up, then stood and brushed myself off. My knee-length skirt was comically puffy with an abundance of white ruffled petticoats underneath the blue fabric. It was guaranteed to get in the way of pretty much anything we were going to do in Wonderland. Thankfully, the fluffy undergarment was separate from the dress itself, and I could slip it off easily enough.

I stepped out of the cloud-like underskirt and surveyed the surrounding shadows, squinting into the darkness. Loki sat primly nearby, peering around curiously, little more than a pair of bright blue eyes and a vaguely cat-shaped shadow in the darkness.

"Is it a cave?" I wondered aloud. There was the oddest scent of leather and musk that made me think of old books instead of rock walls.

"Some sort of corridor or tunnel, I think," Loki said. "You should have an array of illumination options at your disposal, assuming the construct accepted them. Open your inventory and navigate to the tools section."

I frowned. "How do I open my inventory?"

As I spoke the final word, a floating, semi-transparent rectangular window appeared directly in front of me, *INVENTORY* glowing at the top of the box in bold candlelit letters. Various categories were listed below the main heading:

ATTIRE

TOOLS

CONSUMABLES

INGREDIENTS

TRANSPORTATION

QUEST ITEMS

JUNK

I tapped the *TOOLS* category, and a new window opened, with *TOOLS* glowing at the top and a new list of subcategories cascading below.

NAVIGATION

DIGGING

BUILDING

CRAFTING

GARDENING

ILLUMINATION

ART

My eyebrows rose as I scanned the list. "You can do art in this game?" I asked, tapping on the *ILLUMINATION* menu item.

"Evidently," Loki said, sounding as disinterested as ever.

Loki hadn't been kidding when he claimed he had maxed out my pocket of virtual space and loaded up my inventory with everything he possibly could. The *ILLUMINATION* menu was packed full of candlesticks, lanterns, torches, flashlights, and headlamps in a bevy of options and styles.

With a tap of my finger, I selected the lower profile, more practical-looking *Spelunker's Headlamp*, as opposed to the *Ghostbuster's Hard Hat Headlamp* or *Nicola Tesla's Prototype Headlamp*. I felt the device appear on my head, and I was relieved that it equipped itself automatically, meaning I wouldn't have to manually change into every piece of clothing or gear I pulled from my inventory.

I swiped back to the main screen and navigated to the *ATTIRE* category, quickly browsing through the clothing options. Whatever Loki had loaded into my PPVS, the game had altered to be more world-appropriate. Everything was the same periwinkle as my current dress, though many of the clothing options offered beneficial perks, like physical protection and toxin immunity, or enhancement to speed and strength.

Most of the items were grayed out, suggesting I hadn't yet earned the right to equip them in the construct. I would need to play and gain in-game experience to access those options. However, one item at the very bottom of the list was available to me: the *Three Piece Suit of Infinite Possibilities*. It was a white and periwinkle pinstripe pantsuit which, at its base level, offered a massive boost to toxin immunity and negligible perks in all other areas. *But* it allowed for—as the name suggested—an infinite number of upgrades. Sounded like a good deal to me.

As soon as I tapped on the pantsuit, I felt the tailored outfit replace the silly, frilly dress. I stretched my arms over my head and waved them around in large circles, testing the suit's range of motion, then tugged down the bottom of the vest and adjusted the suit coat.

I swiped away the inventory window and twisted to the side, preening in the direction of Loki's shadowed form. "Pretty snazzy, huh?"

The cat slow-blinked, looking utterly unimpressed. "Very nice," he said. "The headlamp is the perfect touch."

My eyelids opened wider as I remembered I was wearing the headlamp, and I reached up to turn it on. My fingers searched the device blindly until, finally, I felt a raised, round button.

Bright silver light flooded our surroundings, illuminating what was indeed a corridor of some sort, with a polished stone floor and walls that curved overhead into an arch. The walls were the strangest I had ever seen, composed of a mishmash of stacked books that towered precariously up to the apex of the arched ceiling. Stray leather-bound volumes littered the floor, looking like they had fallen from the stacks.

I crouched to get a closer look at a book that had landed open and face down on the floor. The cover read: *Alice's Adventures in Wonderland*. I scanned some of the outward facing spines in the nearest haphazard column of books. All the fonts and designs were different, but each book bore the same title. Every single book was a copy of *Alice's Adventures in Wonderland*.

"This is all very meta," I murmured.

"Indeed," Loki said, slinking out of the pool of light from my headlamp and into the shadows farther down the corridor. "Come along. Fiona is waiting."

I stood and hurried after the cat, getting my first good look at him in the light. He had transformed since we landed, having tripled in size until he was as large as a fox. His coloring had changed as well, neon-blue stripes the same shade as his arresting eyes streaking through his black fur. His tail was fluffier than before, and it seemed to naturally rest in the shape of a question mark as he stalked along.

"You're a Cheshire cat," I observed aloud, finally catching up to him.

He peered up at me, not slowing his pace. "Just figured that out, did you?"

I recalled how he had appeared in the gatescape, grin-first while the rest of his body remained invisible, and how much he seemed to enjoy vexing me with cryptic comments and riddle-like responses.

"That's what you are?" I waved one hand toward the wall of books. "Like, outside of here. You're not just a regular cat like the other feline gigis? Your actual species is *Cheshire cat*?"

He eyed me sidelong. "That snazzy suit must amplify your deductive reasoning skills as well," he noted, his words dripping sarcasm.

"Maybe we can find you a sweater that increases your likability," I mused. "Oooh, an ugly Christmas sweater."

"If you try to cover my glorious fur with a sweater of any kind," he said matter-of-factly, "I will gleefully scratch off your face."

I snorted a laugh. "Noted," I said. "No sweaters."

The corridor veered gently to the left, and the shadows ahead grew less dense. I reached up and pressed the button on my headlamp, turning off the light to confirm what I thought I was seeing.

"Is that a door?" I asked, squinting to see the sliver of light in the distance. "A door that's cracked open a few inches?"

"I believe so," Loki said, slowing, then stopping.

I backpedaled to rejoin him.

He stared down the corridor at the door, his head cocked to the side and his eyes narrowed. "Do you hear that?" he asked, peering up at me.

Brow furrowing, I angled my ear toward the end of the corridor and held my breath, listening for all I was worth. The faintest hushed murmur reached my ear, dredging up the memory of my time in the fungus-infested labyrinth and the frightful auditory hallucinations the psychedelic spores had manifested in my mind. I shivered, goosebumps cascading over my skin.

"It sounds like voices," I whispered, glad I wasn't the only one hearing them. "There must be people on the other side of that door." I looked from Loki to the door. "Demeter's people or NPCs?" I wasn't even sure if this game originally had non-player characters, let alone if they would have survived the merger with Demeter's prison.

"I honestly don't know, either," Loki said morosely. "I still don't have access to the underlying code. Demeter must have restricted access to a specific location within the construct." Loki sat and gazed up at me. "Check your inventory to see if any of the myriad of weapons I gave you were allowed into the construct."

"Inventory," I muttered, and the floating menu box appeared in front of me once more. I pursed my lips and quirked my mouth to the side as I studied the options. "There's no *WEAPONS* section," I told Loki.

"Try *TOOLS*," he suggested, moving to sit by my leg so he could see the floating window exactly as I saw it.

I tapped *TOOLS*, and the same list of subcategories as before appeared.

NAVIGATION

DIGGING

BUILDING

CRAFTING

GARDENING

ILLUMINATION

ART

"*DIGGING*?" I wondered out loud, thinking a shovel would be similar enough to a doru. "Or *GARDENING*?"

"Try *CRAFTING*," Loki suggested. "That might at least give you some options with a blade."

I checked out the offerings on the *CRAFTING* menu but found nothing promising. The *Mad Hatter's Cake Spatula* was the best item available. I equipped it, momentarily admiring the ostentatious handle, before tucking it into my belt. *GARDENING* offered a rusty pitchfork, the wooden handle of which gave me a splinter the moment I equipped it.

"Try the *ATTIRE* category," Loki said. "I have an idea."

Frowning thoughtfully, I swiped back to the main menu, then tapped *ATTIRE*. "What now?" I asked the cat.

"*ACCESSORIES*," he said.

I selected the subcategory and, at Loki's bidding, scrolled to the bottom. Like with the pinstripe suit, the last item at the very bottom of the list, after all the grayed-out options, was available to me: the *Scepter of Broken Hearts*. The scepter's two-foot long, gleaming golden handle was engraved with an intricate design that looked far too similar to an Amazon's doru to be a coincidence. Anticipation made my heart beat faster.

I selected the scepter, and the moment its weight filled my hand, vibrating gently in my grip, I grinned broadly. Electric-blue light bled into the grooves curving around the staff, and the heart-shaped jewel at the top glowed with the same brilliant hue. The color of my psychic energy.

"It's a doru!" I exclaimed, careful to keep my voice hushed despite my excitement. I grinned down at Loki. "How did you know?"

"Just a hunch," Loki said, all feline aloofness and nonchalance. But if I wasn't mistaken, there was a gleam of satisfaction in his usually bored stare. "Look at your suit," he said a moment later.

I tucked in my chin and peered down the front of my body. Sure enough, the pantsuit's formerly white pinstripes glowed that same electric blue, like equipping the scepter while wearing the suit had unlocked my psychic gifts within the construct.

"It's a hoplon suit!" I suppressed a gleeful giggle. "This is *amazing*!" I gushed. "Loki, if I didn't think you would scratch my face off, I would squeeze you so tight right now!"

Loki blew out a breath and straightened his posture, adjusting his cute furry paws just so. "I appreciate your restraint," he said. "Now, shall we continue on?"

I looked toward the door at the end of the corridor, feeling invincible now that I was armed. I twirled the scepter dramatically. "Let's go kick some psychic ass."

29

L OKI AND I PAUSED at the cracked-open door, both of us angling an ear toward the narrow opening. I jumped at the sound of a sudden, shrill laugh and glanced down at my feline companion. That was *not* the laugh of a sane person. Honestly, it didn't even sound like a *happy* person. But it also sounded masculine, and from everything I had learned while merged with Peri, there was no such thing as a *male* Olympian psychic. Something about chromosomes and sex-linked traits. Whatever the reason, the probability that whoever we would find on the other side of the door was male was a good thing.

I took a deep breath, then pushed the door open.

The space beyond opened to a sun-dappled clearing, surrounded by dense woods of tall deciduous trees dropping leaves of every shade of red, orange, and yellow to make a thick autumn blanket on the ground. A long table stretched from one end of the clearing to the other, covered in a garish floral tablecloth with lace embellishments. A mishmash of fine china dishes laden with desserts of every kind imaginable was scattered about on the table, from elaborately decorated layered cakes to brilliantly colored candies to untouched pies.

As decadent as the spread appeared, the rancid smell tainting the air suggested at least some of the food had turned. And despite the sweet feast laid out before us, there wasn't a person in sight to eat it.

"Where are they?" I whispered to Loki, glancing down at the oversized cat. *Someone* had definitely been talking on the other side of the door just a moment ago.

Loki scanned the clearing, his whiskers twitching. "There," he said, his neon-blue stare locked on the bottom of the lacy tablecloth.

I shifted my focus lower, and after a few heartbeats, the tablecloth fluttered.

Unsure who or what we would find under the table, I charged the heart gemstone on the scepter with electric-blue psychic energy and slowly approached, Loki slinking along beside me. The stench of rotting food grew stronger the closer we drew to the table. My nose wrinkled, but I didn't stop.

When we reached the table, I held up one hand, three fingers raised, and locked eyes with Loki. Slowly, I counted down by lowering the raised fingers one at a time, my attention returning to the tablecloth. Once the last finger was down, I gripped the hanging portion of the hideous tablecloth and jerked it up.

"Ahhh!" a man shrieked, his wild cotton-candy pink hair sticking out in all directions. A hare with incredibly large ears covered in multicolored polka-dots popped out of the top hat the man was hugging to his chest and shrieked as well. Their eyes, opened wide with fear, locked on the glowing scepter I gripped tightly in one hand.

I dropped the tablecloth and stepped back, straightening. My heart hammered, and my ears rang from the shrill cries, thankfully now muffled by the tablecloth.

"Those are NPCs, aren't they?" I asked Loki, cracking my jaw to pop my ears.

The cat had dropped to his furry belly and lowered his chin to the ground, and he was watching the shrieking man and hare through the narrow gap between the bottom edge of the tablecloth and the bed of leaves.

"Indeed they are," Loki said, not looking my way. His tail swished lazily, almost like he was enjoying this.

"That's the Mad Hatter and March Hare, isn't it?" I guessed, dredging up the second name from the furthest recesses of my mind and impressing myself while doing it.

The shrieking quieted from a chorus to a single high-pitched cry. "Just *Hatter* is fine," the man corrected from beneath the table. "*Mad* is actually quite offensive." A moment later, the shrieking intensified again.

My eyebrows climbed my forehead. "Okay . . ."

Thinking the Hatter and the March Hare were a lost cause, I scanned the table again. Little of the food appeared to have been touched, but one pie had been cut into two wedges set on nearby plates. The pie filling was dark purple—blackberry or boysenberry, I thought—pocked with what appeared to be small, whitish grains of rice. Wiggling grains of rice.

I suppressed a gag. Not rice, but maggots.

"Gross," I grumbled, taking a few more steps backward and tearing my stare away from the rotting food.

Clearly, the Hatter and the March Hare had been hiding under the table for a *long* time. Their shared terror at seeing my scepter glowing with psychic energy suggested Demeter and her fallen Amazons were the sources of their fear. I considered moving on from the clearing and leaving the NPCs to their cowering, but if they had interacted with Demeter and her psychics, I wanted whatever intel they could give me about the enemy. *If* I could get them to stop shrieking for long enough to speak to me.

With a focused thought, I drew the psychic energy out of the scepter until the heart gemstone and grooves stopped glowing electric blue.

The energy tingled up my arm, settling back into the psychic well deep within me. I tucked the scepter into my belt at my hip, hugged my suit jacket closed to conceal the top half of the ornate weapon, and breathed through my mouth as I approached the table once more.

Crouching, I gripped the edge of the tablecloth and raised it high enough that I could see the shrieking pair. This time, my appearance cut their cries short, though they still watched me through terrified eyes in the ringing silence.

"Hi," I said, offering them a friendly smile. "I'm Cora."

"Hatter," the man said, followed by the hare's, "March Hare."

If I hadn't been so used to Loki by now, I probably would have been surprised by the fact that the hare could talk.

"Pleased to meet you both," I said. I looked pointedly at the top of the table. "I think your food has gone bad. How long have you been down here?"

The Hatter let out a shrill laugh. "I don't know! She murdered Time, and now a year passes every day."

I blinked, unsure of how to interpret his meaning. "She?" I asked, latching onto the only coherent part of his response. "Do you mean Demeter?"

The March Hare sucked in a breath and resumed his shrieking. Thankfully, the Hatter clamped his hand over his furry companion's mouth, muffling his cries.

The Hatter leaned toward me, casting suspicious glances to either side. "We don't speak her name," he hissed.

I, too, leaned in closer, ducking until my head was nearly under the table. "Does she hear it—her name, I mean? If you speak it?" I asked, automatically whispering because he had.

"I don't know," the Hatter said, looking genuinely surprised by my question. "I don't think so. She would have to have very good hearing, indeed, to hear us speak her name across all of Wonderland."

I narrowed my eyes. "Then why don't you speak her name?"

He pulled back, looking at me like I was the one who wasn't making any sense. "Because she's scary, and speaking her name frightens March Hare."

I drew in a deep breath, releasing it as a sigh. It was becoming increasingly obvious that achieving anything close to a logical conversation with the Hatter would be impossible.

"Why did *she* kill Time?" I asked.

"Because she wanted to stop him," the Hatter said matter-of-factly.

My brows rose. "From doing *what*?"

"From passing, obviously," he said with an eye roll.

"I see," I said, frowning. I dropped the tablecloth, and still crouching, I turned my attention back to Loki. "Did that make any sense to you?"

"Perhaps . . ." Loki sat up and sneezed daintily, apparently enjoying the aroma of the rotting food about as much as I was. His stare blanked, his pupils dilating to consume his bright irises, making me think he was seeing things not visible to me.

A moment later, he blinked, his pupils constricting to dark slivers, and he focused on me once more. "Time is—or *was*—an NPC in this construct. And Demeter did, indeed, end his existence," Loki explained. "Here, I'll show you." His pupils vanished, and his eyes glowed brighter until they projected shifting light into the clearing.

I stepped back, watching transparent holographic figures take form around the table. "Cool," I murmured, having had no idea that Loki could turn himself into a hologram projector.

I spotted the Hatter and March Hare sitting near one end of the table, as well as a giant mouse-like creature, and a wizardly man with a long, white beard and an emerald-green billowing robe. Based on the long staff that leaned against the table beside him, topped by what appeared to be an oversized pocket watch, I was guessing the wizard was *Time*.

The group appeared to be having a jolly time, laughing and gesturing animatedly as they chatted, though I couldn't hear them. The hologram was purely visual. Considering Loki was projecting it *out of his eyeballs*, that wasn't much of a shocker.

Suddenly, something happened outside the scope of the hologram, and the four sets of eyes turned. At first, it seemed like they were looking at me, but then I realized they were focusing on something beyond the reach of the hologram.

I sucked in a breath when a woman stepped into view, as insubstantial as the Hatter and his friends, but somehow with a stronger presence, even in holographic form. She wore a suit similar to mine with the addition of a fur-lined cape that would have looked over-the-top on anyone else, though she could pull it off. She also carried a nearly identical scepter to mine, the heart stone atop it glowing a brilliant white.

"Demeter," I breathed. I had seen her enough times in Peri's memories to recognize her.

Demeter exuded dominance and power as she calmly circled the long table, evidently enjoying the silent, anxious attention of her captive audience. Another glowing heart-shaped gemstone at the hollow of her throat held her cape fastened around her shoulders. That, combined with her regal appearance, convinced me she had taken on the role of the Queen of Hearts within the construct.

The giant mouse-like creature kept shooting nervous looks beyond Demeter, making me think some of her psychic cronies lurked just out of view. Demeter stopped at the opposite end of the table from the NPCs, and the distance seemed to make them more comfortable.

Demeter was talking, her words directed at Time. By reading her lips, I caught "speed up" and "maximum."

"I believe she commanded Time to increase the in-game time compression to the maximum level," Loki commented.

I thought of Artemis, the Amazon leader who had suspended herself along with an Arc ship's worth of Olympians on a planet contained within a time dilation bubble that *slowed* the passage of time for them, so the war between the rest of the Olympians and the Tsakali could play out in relative fast-forward outside, while *they* cowered within their protective bubble. The Olympians were clearly familiar with using time strategically.

But what Demeter was attempting to do here was quite the opposite. She wanted *more* time for herself, making the events outside of this construct slow down comparatively so she had nearly unlimited time to plot and strategize. To do *what*, I could only guess. Break free from the simulation, I assumed, though I wasn't sure how she planned on escaping from this virtual existence when, out in the real world, she was just a consciousness contained within a glass orb on a spaceship. She would need a body, obviously, and some way to create one without the interference of the other people who were out there on the *Elysium*, namely Hades and a small army of psychic warriors.

"A solution can be found for almost any problem, given enough time," Loki said, reading my thoughts.

In the holographic scene, Time stood abruptly, pushing his chair backward. He gripped his staff and shook his head, his defiance clear.

At the far end of the table, Demeter grinned wickedly, then shifted her scepter to aim the glowing heart at the NPC. A bright burst of energy shot out of the end of the disguised doru and slammed into Time's chest. His eyes opened wide as he seemed to absorb the psychic energy. Glowing fissures appeared on his face and hands, growing until they consumed every visible patch of skin on him and he was little more than an oblong figure of pure light.

Suddenly, Time exploded into a million sparks, and his staff toppled to the ground, sinking into the bed of leaves.

Demeter strode the length of the table and scooped up the fallen staff, a pleased smile curving her lips. Without another word—without even acknowledging what she had done—she turned away from the table and its remaining terrified occupants and sauntered out of the hologram. The ghostly scene flickered out, and Loki blinked up at me, his eyes returning to normal.

"Can she use that staff to alter the construct's time compression settings?" I asked the cat. "Or did she need Time to do it?"

"I'm not sure," Loki said. "The staff is categorized as an NPC-exclusive item, so she shouldn't be able to use it herself, but she might be able to coerce *another* NPC into using it for her."

I licked my lips nervously. "There was a giant mouse," I said. "It was there in the hologram, but it's not here now. What if she took it prisoner?"

"My thoughts exactly," Loki said.

"Has she been successful at altering the time compression settings?" I asked, my thoughts whirling.

"Not that I can tell," Loki said. "But, again, I don't have full access to the construct's inner workings. Once we reach the construct's core, we can reset the entire thing."

Hands on my hips, I chewed on the inside of my cheek. "If she gets the staff working, can she intensify the time compression in specific parts of the construct while leaving others untouched, or is it an all-or-nothing deal?" I asked, worried Demeter could speed up only her portion of Wonderland and leave us scrambling in slow motion to catch up.

"This is a simple construct," Loki said. "Any adjustments to the time compression settings would affect everything."

I blew out my breath, relieved. "At least if she buys herself more time, she's buying it for all of us," I said.

"Indeed," Loki agreed.

"What's our game plan?" I asked the cat. "Are we going after Time's staff first, or are we rescuing Fio?"

"Neither," Loki said. "We search for the core. If we can get in and reset the construct, the prison parameters trapping everyone here will be stripped away, and all independent entities will be forcibly evicted to other parts of the greater simulation."

"What parts?" I asked, narrowing my eyes.

Loki stood, his tail lashing. "I don't know," he admitted. "It's never been done before."

I laughed under my breath, thinking I preferred Demeter and her sycophants all being contained in one place. I *really* didn't like the idea of launching them out into some unknown part of the simulation for a rousing round of hunt-the-psychopath.

"She's too powerful in here," Loki said. "We cannot face her and win. If we attempt a direct confrontation, we will fail and Fiona will be trapped here forever." He stared up at me, his neon-blue eyes unblinking. "And *that* is not an option."

30

After consulting the map of Wonderland and determining the best route to the heart of the construct—literally the Castle of Hearts—Loki and I cut through the thick woods until the forest thinned, giving way to a meadow of hissing and growling wildflowers. We slowed as we approached the edge of the feral field, watching as bright yellow tulips, purple and blue pansies, and crimson poppies turned toward us, reaching as far as their stems would allow and snapping viciously.

We halted, and I glanced down at Loki, who edged forward until a foaming tulip nearly nipped his whiskers. He stopped, his kitty butt swaying like he was preparing to pounce. Instead, he stood on his haunches and swatted at the flower. After a few well-timed bats, he captured the stem and slammed the flower to the ground. It struggled, but he didn't let up. Loki settled on his belly and studied the captured flower closely.

"Were they always like this, or did Demeter turn them rabid?" I asked, scanning the field.

"This is most certainly Demeter's doing," Loki said, releasing the tulip and backing away from the edge of the field. He sat, wrapping his tail primly around his front paws, and slow-blinked up at me. "Open your map. We need to reassess our approach route."

"You got it. Open map," I said.

A semiopaque floating window appeared in front of me, displaying a map of Wonderland. The construct was disk-shaped, with the outermost portion covered in a ring of forest land, divided into seasonal quadrants. We currently stood at the inner edge of *The Autumn Woods* in the southeast portion of the map. The field of snarling flowers ahead of us, benignly named *The Flower Patch*, merged with *The Field of Dreams* around the upper half of the map to form another ring. The innermost ring, labeled *The Royal Woods,* surrounded the *Castle of Hearts*. According to Loki, the construct controls could now only be accessed through the castle.

I had been thinking our only obstacle would be Demeter and her psychics. I looked through the semiopaque map to the snarling flowers. Clearly, I had been wrong.

I studied the Field of Dreams on the map. It was filled with giant mushrooms giving off what appeared to be wavy stink lines. "Unless we can go under—or over—the flowers, I think we have to head up here," I said, pointing to the mushroom field.

"Hmmm," Loki murmured, and when I glanced down at him, the tip of his tail twitched intermittently. "The Dormouse's tunnels run under this part of the Flower Patch," he said, and part of the map lit up. "That may be our best bet."

I raised my hand to the map, pinching and spreading to zoom in on that area, and a few new labels appeared. *Dormouse's Abode* hovered over a door in the base of a tree in *The Autumn Woods*, slightly northwest of our location.

"It's on the way to the Field of Dreams," I noted. "Let's check it out."

31

"THE TUNNELS ARE FLOODED," Loki said as I stood with him at the edge of the mucky mud surrounding the tree housing the door to the Dormouse's Abode.

"I don't feel like that's our biggest problem here," I pointed out, my head tilted to the side as I studied the door. Rather, our *biggest problem* was the door that was about a quarter of my size and not even wide enough for me to wriggle through. Loki could fit through, barely, but definitely not me.

"Shrinking cakes," Loki said matter-of-factly. "They were an original part of this construct. You'll find them in the consumables section of your inventory."

I raised my eyebrows. Considering the source material for the construct, I supposed I shouldn't have been surprised. "Is there any point in shrinking when the tunnels are flooded?"

Loki licked a paw and eyed me sidelong, saying nothing, like the answer to my question was obvious. Of course, he wouldn't have mentioned the shrinking cakes if he didn't think there was a way for us to use the tunnels, flooded or not.

"Okay," I said, drawing out the word. "What will we use to breathe underwater?"

"I equipped you with many underwater breathing apparatuses." He set down his paw. "You should find *something* in your inventory in either the tools section or the attire section."

"What about you?" I asked. "Or can you already breathe underwater?" I was clueless about the special abilities of a Cheshire cat.

"I cannot," he said, readjusting his paws. "But the effects of any gear you equip will automatically be applied to me."

I frowned, nodding as I considered his words. "What about your size?" I asked, eyeing the big cat and comparing him to the little door. He could likely squeeze through, but it wouldn't be comfortable.

At a rustle of leaves, Loki's stare darted to the side. I followed his line of sight, a burst of adrenaline making tension hum through my body as I charged the scepter in my hand with psychic energy.

A lilac-striped squirrel loped across the forest floor and leaped onto a nearby tree, winding around the trunk and out of sight.

I relaxed, releasing the charge in the scepter.

"I'm able to control my size," Loki said, continuing to stare after the squirrel. His tail twitched, his feline instincts showing. "The shrinking cakes have a time limit." He finally looked at me. "Open your inventory and find a breathing apparatus first, though some of those may be limited by duration of use as well."

I did as he suggested, quickly opening my inventory and navigating to the TOOLS submenu. I scrolled through the first few items.

"How about the *Air Bubble*?" I wondered aloud, glancing down at Loki as he shifted closer. I tapped the item name, pulling up the detailed description and specs. It would allow me to breathe underwater for fifty minutes, followed by a cooldown time of ten minutes, meaning I wouldn't be able to equip it again immediately once the time was up.

"That should work," Loki said.

My finger hovered in front of the item. "Should I—"

"Don't equip it yet," he snapped, and I pulled my hand back. "Shrinking cakes first, *then* you can equip the air bubble."

I navigated back to the main inventory menu and tapped on CONSUMABLES, opening a small submenu broken into FOOD and DRINKS. I selected FOOD, then scrolled down the long list and hesitated for a moment before tapping on SHRINKING CAKES. I wasn't sure if I would actually have to eat them, or if the properties would be automatically applied when I selected them.

Neither, it turned out. Tapping on SHRINKING CAKES opened a new window that detailed the properties of the consumable beneath a strikingly realistic 3D image of what looked like a trio of pale pink petit fours, each with a dainty frosted daisy sitting atop their icing. I skimmed through the details below the image.

HEALTH BONUS: +10% Immunity for 1 hour
STRENGTH BONUS: +10% Strength for 1 hour
SPEED BONUS: +10% Speed for 1 hour
SPECIAL EFFECTS: Shrink to 20% of original size for 1 hour

Acting on instinct, I reached for the pictured mini cakes and wasn't all that surprised to find the image had substance. I gently pinched one of the cakes between my fingers and pulled it out of the floating window, then swiped the inventory away with a flick of my other hand.

I stared at the shrinking cake for a long moment, then glanced down at Loki. "Here goes nothing," I said and bit into the cake experimentally, eating only a corner despite it easily being a one-biter. It was sweet and vanilla-y, with a delicate berry undertone. "It's actually pretty yummy," I told Loki, then popped the rest of the tiny cake into my mouth.

I chewed the treat, looking around while I waited for something to happen. The instant I swallowed, I was falling. No, not falling—shrinking. It only felt like I was falling because the world seemed to fly past me as my level of sight lowered with frightful speed.

Suddenly, Loki was huge beside me, easily as big as a horse. He was most certainly large enough for me to ride.

"Not going to happen," he said haughtily. "If you want a steed, we can find you a nice fox."

My eyes bulged at the idea of riding on a fox's back. "You're kidding, right?"

Loki turned his face toward me, wearing that horrifying, nightmarish grin. "Of course I'm kidding," he said. "A fox would eat you." He started to shrink, the change barely perceptible, but in a handful of seconds, he was barely a third of his previous size, now closer to an enormous Great Dane compared to my current decreased stature than to the horse-sized cat he had seemed to be moments before.

"Come along," Loki said, padding toward the mud surrounding the door. I had little choice but to follow. "As soon as we get into the tunnels, your map should adjust to the underground level. We'll take a moment to study our route to the castle." Once he reached the mud, each step included an adorable paw shake.

I schooled my features, suppressing a smile. Sometimes he was *such* a cat.

Loki stopped at the door, standing with his tail raised and curled like a question mark. "If you don't mind . . ." He looked from the door to me and back.

I hurried forward, squelching the mud, and reached for the doorknob. I had a moment of panic, thinking it would be locked, but thankfully the knob turned, and the door opened to absolute darkness. Loki slunk through the doorway ahead of me, his paws sinking into water that nearly reached his belly.

I paused to open my inventory and equipped my trusty headlamp, hoping it would still work underwater. So long as it was protected within my air bubble, I supposed it would be fine. Once it was in place on my head, I followed Loki through the doorway. The water reached my knees, and trying not to splash, I waded into the Dormouse's home. At least it wasn't too cold.

The light from my headlamp illuminated an earthy living room with a cozy cottage feel. Furniture floated along the surface of the water, gently bobbing—an end table here, an ottoman there—along with ruined books and other odds and ends.

I frowned, my brow furrowing. It was impossible not to feel bad for the Dormouse. Not only had the creature almost certainly been taken prisoner and was likely being tortured by Demeter in her attempt to use Father Time's staff, but his home had been ruined. My only consolation was in knowing that if Loki and I succeeded in resetting the construct, not only would Demeter and her cronies be evicted from the game, but the Dormouse and his home, as well as Father Time and everything else Demeter had destroyed, would be restored.

Loki led me toward a doorway cut into the back wall which, based on the downward-sloping ceiling, I assumed opened to a stairway leading underground, though I couldn't actually see the stairs under all the rippling water.

He stopped at the doorway and peered back at me. "Time to equip your air bubble."

"Oh," I said, my eyebrows rising. "Right."

I opened my inventory and navigated to the TOOLS submenu, selecting *Air Bubble*. The instant I touched the display image of a bubble, a shimmering sheen obscured my clear view of the Dormouse's home. The light from my headlamp glared annoyingly off the inside of the faintly iridescent bubble, but not enough to blind me. I noticed that Loki's head was also now encased in what appeared to be a giant soap bubble.

I poked mine with the tip of my index finger, half-expecting it to pop. It wobbled but held steady. Reassured, I gestured toward the doorway to the descending stairs. "After you," I told the cat.

Loki waded forward, switching to a cute kitty paddle when he reached the stairway and the floor level lowered. He bobbed along for a few seconds, then sank under the surface of the water.

I hurried forward, not wanting to lose him. The first step down came sooner than I expected, and my foot slipped out from under me. I landed on my butt with a splash and slid down a few stairs until my head was completely submerged. Once I regained my bearings, I captured Loki in my pool of light and followed him as he kitty paddled downward.

Eventually, once the tunnel evened out and we were no longer diving deeper underground, Loki stopped and somewhat awkwardly turned to face me. "Open your map," he said, his words mildly garbled by the water, but not incoherent as they would have been in real life.

I swam closer, and he turned as I approached, facing forward toward the delving tunnel once more. "Open map," I said, and the semiopaque window appeared in front of me, this time showing an entirely new landscape.

The labels for the *Dormouse's Abode*, the *Flower Patch*, and the *Castle of Hearts* were still there in ghostly letters, but the landmarks themselves had been replaced by a labyrinth of winding tunnels that appeared to weave over and under one another. If not for my many, *many* years of reading video game maps, including dungeons and caverns, the sight would have overwhelmed me.

My lips slowly spread into a smile as I studied the map, noting that the tunnels passed directly under the *Castle of Hearts*, which also just so happened to house the construct's controls. Was it possible? Was *this* our way into the castle?

"Are you seeing what I'm seeing?" I asked, grinning as I glanced at Loki.

"I had hoped the tunnels connected, but I wasn't sure. This is very reassuring," he said, his eyes narrowing slightly as he studied the map.

My initial excitement waned. There could always be more obstacles besides the water flooding the tunnels—booby traps or dangerous creatures or possibly even psychics patrolling down here. Demeter's level of preparedness all depended on whether she thought she was protected here in this construct, or whether she believed there to be an incoming threat. Of course, there was a third option—that she already knew we were here in the construct and was observing our approach.

"I have us in incognito mode," Loki said, responding to my troubled thoughts.

I looked down at him, surprised. "We're invisible?"

"In a manner of speaking," he said. "To anyone observing the entities moving about the construct, we would appear to be low-level NPCs."

"Kind of like that squirrel we saw before coming down here?" I clarified.

"Precisely," Loki confirmed. He returned his attention to the map. "I've marked the most direct route to the castle's underbelly." As he spoke, a winding path illuminated along the map. "We need to move fast to reach the exit before you lose your air bubble. If you drown down here, you'll respawn in some unknown part of the construct, maybe even in Demeter's dungeon."

"Game over," I murmured, memorizing the first few twists and turns of our path. "Then we'd better get going." I swiped the map away and raised one foot behind me to push off the bottom stair, gliding forward into the unknown.

32

L OKI AND I BROKE through the surface of the water into absolute darkness. My headlamp did little to illuminate much beyond the enormous cat bobbing alongside me, his head encased in an air bubble, and the water's surface rippling around us. Droplets gleamed like liquid diamonds in the light from my headlamp as they streaked down from the top of my own bubble. The air was cooler than the tepid water, and goosebumps spread down from my exposed neck and shoulders.

"Open map," I whispered while I treaded water.

A floating window appeared in front of me, displaying a semiopaque map of the underground tunnel system in shades of blue-gray. I squinted. It was hard to read clearly through the streaks of water now coating my air bubble.

"Unequip air bubble," I murmured, and the film obscuring my view vanished with an audible *pop*.

According to the map, we were near the edge of an enormous cavern on the periphery of the Castle of Hearts—or rather, *under* the castle. I grinned. We made it.

Now, all we needed to do was to follow the narrow path out of this cavern and into the castle proper, then find the construct's control center and hard reset the whole thing. Easy peasy.

A bright light flared into existence high overhead, and with my heart suddenly hammering, I looked up, squinting against the glare. A ball of orange psychic energy burned near the cavern's ceiling, illuminating the craggy surface surrounding us. Frantically, I scanned the cavern, searching for the source of the energy. Because it certainly hadn't come from me.

I spotted a trio of women standing on the shore of the underground pool near the opening to the corridor that, according to my map, would lead us out of the underground area and into the castle. Each woman wore a pinstripe suit similar to mine, except the stripes on their suits glowed tangerine, lilac, and emerald compared to my electric blue. They also each held a scepter topped with a heart-shaped gemstone glowing the same color as their pinstripes.

These weren't just women; they were psychics.

The three Amazon warriors scanned the water, searching. They hadn't spotted us yet, likely because we floated at the far edge of the cavern, and because I was still so small. But any second, they were bound to find us.

I didn't think there was much point in me hiding under the water, since they seemed to have known we would be here before we even arrived. Either they knew we weren't mere low-level NPCs and had been tracking our tags, or they had sensed my psychic potential. There was no way to know for sure without asking them, but at least the second option would mean they couldn't track Loki. *If* that were the case, then I was the only one on their radar—and I wanted to keep it that way.

"Disappear, Loki," I hissed.

Loki didn't hesitate. "I'll be around," he promised a moment before he vanished. "The *Growing Elixir* will return you to your normal size," came his disembodied voice.

"Thanks," I breathed, then murmured, "Inventory." If I *had* to face these three Amazons, I certainly didn't want to do it while I was a fifth their size.

The inventory window opened in front of me, and I treaded water with one arm while I quickly navigated to the CONSUMABLES section and selected the DRINKS submenu. I tapped on GROWING ELIXIR and equipped it without bothering to read the properties. I trusted Loki.

A small glass apothecary bottle with a tiny tag around the neck that read *Drink Me* appeared in my hand. I bit the cork and pulled it free, then spat it out into the water and downed the contents of the bottle in one gulp. The elixir tasted like candied rose petals, with a strong aftertaste that clung to my tongue.

The size change felt far less dramatic this time, as there was nothing nearby to compare myself to. The surface of the water appeared much the same, though the cavern did seem to shrink slightly as I grew.

Figuring there wasn't much point in delaying the inevitable, I leaned forward and kicked my legs behind me, gliding through the water toward the waiting trio of enemy psychics. Fear-fueled adrenaline coursed through my veins. I had absolutely no clue what to do in a situation like this.

Peri was the strategist, the one with actual combat experience. I was merely a gamer who had shared her mind and body for a time with a highly skilled Amazon warrior. Maybe I still had the psychic abilities, but I had no idea what to do with them besides read people's thoughts and blow stuff up. When this was all over, I fully intended to focus my time on learning all I could about my psychic abilities and honing the crap out of them.

I may not have had lifetimes of experience as a psychic warrior, *but* my thousands of hours of gaming told me this wasn't an avoidable capture.

This was a cutscene—non-playable—and no matter what I did, it would play out the same way, resulting in me being taken prisoner by these women.

"There!" one of the psychics shouted, pointing in my direction. Either she was speaking English, or the game was translating for me.

The woman on the right squinted. "Is that *Peri*?"

Shit. I hadn't considered the very obvious reality that Demeter and all of her loyalists had known Peri a literal lifetime ago and that as Peri's clone, I looked exactly like her. In their eyes, I *was* Peri. But I didn't know how to do even a hundredth of what she could do. I was torn between letting them think I was capable of her level of badassery, whether that was a hindrance or a perk. Maybe I could bluff my way through this.

"It *is* Peri!" the one on the left exclaimed. "That traitorous bitch!"

Double shit. Peri was the reason Demeter and her followers had initially been trapped in a self-contained portion of the simulation—the Olympian version of an eternal prison. Peri had caught Demeter in the middle of doing something that would have doomed most of the Olympians living on Earth, all to save herself and a few other elites. Peri had revealed Demeter's duplicity and, with the help of Hades and the other honorable Amazons, she had stopped them.

The psychic in the middle grinned wolfishly as I glided closer. "I'm going to enjoy this," she said, threading her fingers together and cracking her knuckles.

Shit, shit, shit. They blamed me for what Peri had done to them. I stopped swimming toward them and treaded water some thirty yards away. Maybe I could make a run for it—or, rather, a *swim* for it. But my air bubble was still in cooldown mode, which meant I wouldn't be able to equip it for a while yet. I could only stay underwater for as long as I could hold my breath.

As I floated there, I considered telling them the truth—that I *wasn't* Peri. But would they believe me? Would they even care? Genetically, I *was* her, even if I no longer had her memories, just the residue of them. Did genetics count here in the simulation, where I had no real physical body?

"I want to see Demeter," I said. "Take me to her, and I won't hurt you."

"Hurt us?" The middle woman scoffed. "You always did have a high opinion of yourself, didn't you?" I probably should have recognized them—Peri would have—but no names floated up from the hazy remnants of my borrowed memories.

"*I* wasn't the only one who knew I was better than the rest of you," I said, my voice steady with false bravado. Demeter had thought highly of Peri as well—before everything went down—and the way these three psychics stiffened and scowled told me they all knew it.

I continued my slow glide toward them. "Take me to Demeter."

33

T HE TRIO OF PSYCHICS backed away as I neared the edge of the
pool and the water became shallow enough for me to stand. They
were afraid of me. Or rather, of Peri.

A curious warmth curled around my neck, soft and furry save for what
felt like thorns suddenly digging into my chest. It was Loki, still invisible,
but letting me know he was with me.

"Demeter is otherwise occupied with your little *invasion* at the moment," the middle psychic said, sneering. "You'll have to wait."

My thoughts whirred as I waded forward, water splashing around my
legs. *My* little invasion? What was she talking about? I certainly hadn't
organized any invasion.

But if the castle was under attack by someone, then Demeter wouldn't
be the only one who was otherwise occupied. Her entire force of psychic
warriors would be defending the castle—aside from these three sorry
excuses for Amazons. I mean, there were three of them and one of
me—what were they so afraid of?

Unless . . .

Was it possible that this was the entire force they could muster at the
moment, with everyone else focused on the castle's defense? Were these
three Amazons all that had been left behind to handle secondary threats?
And if that was the case, if I took down these women, there was a chance

that nobody else would be around to stop me from reaching the control center at the construct's core.

Loki's tail tightened around my neck, the end twitching as he either picked up on my train of thought or wondered the same thing himself.

Braver than the others, the middle woman stepped forward, her eyes narrowing and the jewel on her scepter burning bright orange. "Why are you here, Peri?"

I stepped free of the water and planted my feet on dry ground. The rocky cavern floor was slick under my wet shoe soles. I crossed my arms over my chest and eyed the lead woman up and down, then sniffed dismissively and looked away. "Demeter," I said, hoping to buy my ploy some more time. "I'll only talk to her."

Not that I had any clue what I would say to Demeter when I encountered her face to face. Honestly, I was banking on Loki coming up with some way to evade my captors and flee to the control center to reset the construct *before* I ever had to speak with Demeter. I remembered enough from Peri's memories to know the disgraced leader of the Order of Amazons was downright terrifying.

I wished Raiden was here. Or my mom or Emi. Or Meg or Caly. They were all so much stronger and more capable than me.

In the real world, maybe, I reminded myself. But technically, this was a game. A super realistic virtual reality game, but a game nonetheless. And gaming was *my* greatest strength. I had been playing parts, pretending I was someone else, risking my life on harrowing adventures pretty much since I was old enough to work a game controller. Maybe I wasn't an Amazon warrior with literal lifetimes of experience being a badass, but I had thousands of hours kicking ass in-game.

I held my head a little higher and stared down my captors, all three holding their charged scepters in a way that suggested they were ready to blast me with a ball of psychic energy the instant I moved wrong. I didn't need someone to come save me. *I could do this myself.*

"So, are we just going to stand here until Demeter's no longer occupied, or . . .?" I glanced toward what appeared to be a tunnel dug through the natural bedrock. My fingers itched for my own scepter, currently tucked away in my pocket of virtual space, but I balled my hands into fists instead, hiding my frustration under my crossed arms.

The woman on the right leaned in toward the other two. "We don't have a collar to contain her."

The middle woman huffed out her irritation and rolled her eyes. "Peri can get out of a collar, idiot," she snapped, glaring at the other woman. "Or did you forget how this all started?"

My thoughts raced as I searched the hazy remnants of Peri's memories for this woman's meaning. I vaguely recalled Peri escaping from an Amazon collar when Demeter first betrayed and imprisoned her thousands of years ago. She had done it again when we shared my body, but I doubted I could do it on my own, and I considered myself lucky that they didn't have an Amazon collar now.

The woman on the left turned her back to me and whispered something too low for me to hear.

The apparent leader shook her head, a single slice of her chin to the left, then to the right. "Demeter will want to speak with her before we resort to that."

It was an effort not to let my curiosity show on my face. What had the other woman suggested? Did she want to kill me? It wouldn't be a permanent death, but it *would* set me back.

"We'll take her to the dungeon," the middle woman said.

The one on the right drew in a sharp breath, eyeing me warily. "But the other—"

"We'll *take* her to the dungeon," the middle woman repeated, enunciating each word clearly. "And you two will guard her while I alert Demeter to her capture." She looked at the woman on the right. "Take her scepter and guard the rear." She turned to the woman on the left. "Stay on her. If she does anything suspicious, knock her out."

Channeling Peri's cocky attitude, I grinned wolfishly. "You can try," I purred. I considered adding more to the taunt but decided it was best to restrain myself. *Keep it simple, stupid,* seemed like an excellent motto to maintain when I was bluffing my way through an extremely dangerous situation.

After pulling out my scepter and offering it to the woman on the right, I followed the leader of the trio into the tunnel. The remaining psychic walked alongside me, my arm held in her tight grip and the charged gem on the end of her scepter pressed against my lower back. The tunnel sloped gently upward, with flickering torches every twenty feet or so.

"Try something," my escort hissed at me, digging the scepter in harder. "I dare you."

I eyed her sidelong. "Why would I waste my time on you?"

Her lip curled, and she released my arm at the same time as she sent a low-level blast shooting out from the end of her scepter. Loki uncurled from around my neck and leaped off my shoulder, the invisible feline narrowly escaping my momentarily electrified state.

My leg muscles seized, and my knees buckled. I collapsed, face-planting on the tunnel floor, and it took every ounce of bodily control I had developed over the many years of attempting to master my curse to keep me from peeing my pants. As my muscles spasmed with aftershocks of the energy blast, I wondered if this was what it felt like to be tased.

"Tanzi!" the leader barked over my twitching body. "What the hell?"

"She was getting mouthy," my attacker—Tanzi, apparently—said defensively.

"Then ignore her," the leader ground out. "You're acting like a child. Celestia, swap places with Tanzi." The toe of a polished black shoe nudged my shoulder. "Get up."

Suppressing a groan, I pushed up to my hands and knees, then climbed to my feet. I brushed off the front of my suit and rubbed my hands together to clean off the remaining dirt and debris from the tunnel floor.

The leader nudged my shoulder with the glowing orange jewel at the tip of her scepter. "I'd keep my mouth shut from here on out, if I were you," she said. "Celestia's not *quite* so trigger-happy, but I'm sure you remember her temper."

I lifted my chin and looked past the leader, up the tunnel.

She stared at me for a moment longer, then turned her back to me and continued on. My new companion gripped my arm at the elbow, but at least she didn't shove her scepter into my back. I honestly wasn't sure my bladder could hold out through another blast.

I kept quiet as we gradually climbed higher, wondering if Loki was still nearby or if he had scampered off ahead in search of the control center. I doubted he could reset the construct himself; he likely needed a real person for that. Otherwise, he wouldn't have needed to hold my hand through this little adventure. I hadn't realized how much he had been bolstering my nerve, but now that he seemed to be gone, much of my bravado vanished along with him.

If he were around and could cause a distraction, I thought I might be able to catch my captors by surprise. Even without my scepter, I could create an unfocused psychic blast big enough to knock them out for a few seconds at least, but it would take me some time to build up the charge in my hands.

A heartbeat after the thought crossed my mind, Loki wound between my ankles. I stumbled on my next step, attempting to avoid kicking the invisible cat. He lunged in front of my foot again, his furry body fully tripping me this time. Once again, I fell face-first onto the tunnel floor, my arm ripping free from Celestia's hold.

"Seriously, Celestia?" the leader snapped. "What did she say to you?"

"Now!" Loki hissed near my ear.

This was it, I realized. This was the distraction I had silently wished for. I hid my hands under my abdomen, pressing my palms together to build a charge of psychic energy between them. I squeezed my eyes shut and held my breath, turning my focus inward to the deep well of psychic energy within me as I dragged as much power as possible from its depths.

"It wasn't me," Celestia said defensively. "She just tripped, I swear."

The leader scoffed, clearly annoyed. "Get her up."

"I don't think she's breathing," Celestia noted.

They must have turned accusing stares on Tanzi, because the other woman swore, "*I* didn't do anything."

"Then why can I feel you actively recharging your scepter?" the leader demanded.

"That's not me," Tanzi said. "It must be Celestia."

If I waited much longer, they would figure out that *I* was the source of psychic energy they sensed.

Celestia let out an affronted laugh. "It's not—"

I released the energy gathered in my hands, hoping it was enough.

The blast shook the tunnel, and I curled into a ball and covered my head with my hands as small rocks rained down on me. It was *definitely* enough.

"Cora!" Loki yelled. "Get up! The tunnel is coming down!"

Adrenaline making my body stronger and faster, I scrambled to my feet and lurched into a run. Loki leaped out of thin air to become visible again and raced up the tunnel in front of me. The ground shook beneath my feet, then lurched, sending me careening into the side of the tunnel. A terrifying rumble was followed by a deep crack forming in the tunnel ceiling.

"Hurry!" Loki called back to me. "There's a corridor ahead. We should be safe there."

Eyes wide and heart hammering, I pushed away from the wall and set off at a dead sprint. I dove forward as a cloud of dust surrounded me, and the tunnel collapsed behind me with a deafening rumble. But it didn't collapse *on* me.

Slowly, the dust settled, and Loki gradually became visible—first his glowing blue eyes, then his stripes and smile, and then the rest of his body, all coated in a thick layer of gray dust. And just as he had said, we were in a new corridor, this one constructed of stone blocks rather than dug out of the bedrock. We had made it into the castle.

Feeling slightly uneasy, I rolled onto my side and stared into the dust cloud that filled what remained of the tunnel. I hadn't meant to kill my captors, but they definitely wouldn't have survived the tunnel collapsing.

"They're not dead," Loki reminded me, licking his paw to clean the dust from his fur. "You didn't kill them. They'll respawn elsewhere in the construct."

I sat up and scooted backward to lean against the wall. "At least I'm not a murderer."

34

After consulting my map, Loki and I decided there was no way around it. We had to go through the dungeon to get to the construct's core, which meant we would pass Fiona's cell. *Which meant* fighting the temptation to free her first. Doing so was an unnecessary risk that would only waste time we might not have. There was no saying how long the siege would last. But she was being held prisoner, and I would feel like such an asshole leaving her behind.

Pushing back against the wall, I stood, my leg muscles aching from the dead sprint up the tunnel. I pushed the damp hair out of my face, cringing at the grimy feel of the strands and wishing I had a hair tie. I knotted the dirty, tangled mess at the base of my neck as best as I could. That would have to do for now.

The underground corridors wound maze-like through the castle's lowest level with many intersecting passages—all for no apparent reason. None of the corridors actually seemed to lead anywhere new. There were no doorways or rooms or *anything*. Just long, tangled passages. Yet another reminder that this place was, in essence, just an exceptionally realistic video game. Without my map, we easily could have walked in circles for hours.

"The dungeon should be just ahead," I said, double-checking the map as we hurried toward the upcoming intersection.

Sure enough, when I reached the corner, the bisecting corridor led to a descending stone stairway. Of course, the dungeon would be deeper underground—again, for no apparent reason. It could have just as easily occupied part of the thousands of square feet used up by these pointless corridors.

The air grew stale and dank as Loki and I delved deeper, and torchlight flickered against rough-hewn stone walls, illuminating the spiderwebs crowding every corner. I could practically feel the despondence of all the imaginary prisoners who had never actually been held in the dungeon. It was almost like echoes of their long-silenced fabricated screams lingered in the very walls. Goosebumps rose over my skin, the deliberately creepy atmosphere of this part of the construct doing its job really damn well.

Cell doors constructed of rusted iron bars lined the walls when we reached the bottom of the stairs, and I searched the shadows for my captured friend.

"Fio?" I whisper-called ahead.

Movement in the third cell on the left caught my eye, and I rushed ahead.

"Cora?" Fiona sputtered. "But—but you can't *be* here." She moved into the flickering light, revealing her smudged cheeks and shaking head. Her orange-died hair was knotted up into an off-kilter bun. "Get out!" Her eyes bulged as she licked her lips, her fingers curling around the bars in a white-knuckled grip. "You have to get out of here! You'll break the simulation!"

I stopped at her cell door, my brow furrowed. "What are you talking about?"

"Ahem," Loki cleared his throat.

Fiona's focus dropped to my feet, where the Cheshire cat sat primly, his blue-striped black tail curled around his fuzzy little toes. "Cora won't break the simulation," he said. "She was uploaded *to* it, if you recall."

"She was?" Fiona blinked, her attention returning to me. "Then you're—" Her mouth fell open, and she snapped it shut. "I mean, she was, obvi," she said, forcing a laugh and rolling her eyes. She cocked a hip and unclenched her fingers, casually leaning her shoulder against a bar and crossing her arms over her chest like this was any other day. "So what are you doing here, anyway?"

"Uh . . ." I looked from Fiona down to Loki and back, sure I was missing something, then scanned the dungeon meaningfully. "I'm rescuing you?" I said. Fiona was a genius, but she could sure be a dummy sometimes.

"Oh!" She straightened, relaxing her arms and once again gripping the bars. "Cool," she said, nodding. She glanced down the aisle running the length of the dungeon. "The core is that way," she said, looking at Loki, then at me. "Assuming you're trying to reset the construct. And if you weren't planning on doing that, you should change your plans. It'll be way faster than trying to escape."

I nodded as she spoke. "Resetting the construct is the plan."

"Well, then get out of here," she said, extending an arm between the bars and making a shooing motion. "Leave me. I'll be fine. Go on! Get moving!"

"Fine, fine," I said as I backed away from the cell, my hands raised in surrender. "I just wanted you to know this would all be over soon. You're welcome, by the way." Before she could respond, footsteps scuffed on the stairs leading down to the dungeon.

Fiona and I exchanged a terrified glance, then turned our attention toward the narrow stairway. Unsure what else to do, I poured psychic energy into my hands until they glowed electric blue and held them out defensively.

A form stepped out of the shadows of the stairway, wearing a pinstripe suit similar to mine, only her stripes glowed amethyst. That color of psychic energy—I would have recognized it anywhere. Even before I saw her face, I knew who had joined us in the dungeon, and the energy charging my hands fizzled out.

"Meg?" I gawked as she reached the bottom step and the flickering torchlight touched her face. Sure enough, the young Zari woman with whom I shared a psychic bond was here, in the simulation. In the construct. In the *dungeon*. "What—" I shook my head as she approached, her gait as stealthy and intimidating as a stalking panther. "What are you doing here?"

"I'm here to help you, obviously," she said, stopping in front of me. She glanced at Fiona. "All right in there?"

Fiona nodded, her eyes wide as she looked from me to Meg and back. "I'm good," she said, her voice high and tight. She looked like she was bursting at the seams to say more, but she smashed her lips together instead.

"How did you—" Again, I shook my head, and my brow furrowed as I realized why I was having such a hard time believing she was here. "I can't feel you," I said hollowly. "The bond—it's gone."

Meg and Fiona exchanged another look, unspoken words passing between them, and then Meg flashed me a sympathetic smile. "It didn't transfer after . . ."

After what? I was dying to ask her what had happened, but even thinking about the question sent a sharp spike of pain lancing through my mind. I groaned, wincing, and rubbed my temple.

"Cora?" Meg asked, touching my arm. "Are you all right?"

I nodded. "It's just this place," I explained. "We're not supposed to think about the outside world, but if we do . . . instant headache."

Meg's stare turned distant, or possibly inward, and I had the impression that she was hearing something I couldn't. A moment later, she refocused on me. "We should get going. We're not sure how much longer the attack will distract them, and we need to finish this."

Realization struck, and my brows rose. The Amazons—*our* Amazons—were the ones laying siege upon the castle. It probably should have occurred to me as soon as I saw Meg, but I had been so blindsided by her sudden appearance that I only just put two and two together.

"Yeah, okay," I said, regathering my wits. "It's this way." I turned and jogged down the aisle toward the dark doorway at the end, Loki loping along at my feet and Meg close on my heels.

"Just hit the big red button!" Fiona called after us. "You can't miss it."

"Okay," I said, holding up my hand, my thumb raised so she could see it.

"I'll meet you back at the house!" she called a moment before I passed through the shadowed doorway and started down a new, darker corridor.

35

A SINGLE TORCH BURNED in a sconce at the end of the corridor, the light from the flame illuminating the ice crystals that spread across the surface of the lone wooden door blocking the passage.

I slowed as we approached the frozen door, studying the ice crystals. "Weird," I muttered. "What's the likelihood that someone's in there?"

"High," Loki drawled.

I glanced at Meg, who nodded her agreement.

My fingers itched for the scepter that now lay buried way back in the collapsed tunnel. Having no other defensive options, I charged my left hand with psychic energy until my palm and fingers glowed with electric-blue fire. I curled my fingers into a fist, feeling the energy sizzle and crackle.

Our trio stopped in front of the door, and I scanned the frozen surface. Meg hung back a step, while Loki sat at my feet.

Loki licked a paw lackadaisically. "Are you planning on opening the door, or . . .?"

I let out a silent snort and reached for the wrought iron handle, fully expecting the door to be locked. Except, when I pulled on the icy handle, the only resistance came from the frozen hinges.

The door creaked and crunched open with minimal resistance. A rush of frigid air hit me as the door swung open, revealing a large room lit dimly by a circular rustic chandelier that was missing all but three candles. Barely visible was the large control panel stretching along the far wall, covered in a thick sheet of ice, and the cloaked figure standing in front of it, their back to me.

In one hand, the figure held a long staff, the butt end planted on the floor and the crystal orb at the top glowing with an eerie pale blue light. Ice streaks extended from the base of the staff and branched across the floor, making me think the staff was the source of the unnatural chill.

I exchanged a look with Meg, her wary expression telling me this was not one of the Amazons with her, and then I stepped into the room, my exhale fogging the air. The blue fire in my hand cast eerie shadows on the uneven walls. The soles of my shoes slid on the icy floor, and I extended my arms to steady myself. I heard quiet scuffs as Meg entered the room behind me.

The figure at the control panel didn't move, though they had to know we were there. Was this another of Demeter's Amazons?

"Who are you?" I demanded, the lightning in my hand crackling ominously.

The figure slowly turned to face me and raised their free hand to push back their hood, revealing hawkish feminine features and a cruel sneer. The cloaked woman wore a pinstripe suit exactly like mine save for the white-glowing stripes and a diadem around her head, inset with a blood-red heart-shaped stone. The Queen of Hearts, it would seem, though I knew her by another name.

"Demeter?" I said, not quite believing my eyes.

Why would she be down here when her castle was under attack? My heart galloped. If I had to go through her to get to the button to reset the construct, even with Meg's help, I feared we were all screwed. Demeter was next level when it came to control over her psychic abilities. Peri had been a match for her, but I didn't even come close.

"Peri," Demeter said, her voice dripping with hatred. "You look surprised to see me." She blinked innocently. "Who else would I trust with such an important task besides myself?" She narrowed her eyes at me and dropped her chin. "You know better than anyone how dangerous it can be to trust another." Her stare slipped past me, to Meg. "Or maybe you don't, since you brought a little friend."

Where's the button? I silently asked Loki, hoping he was paying attention to my thoughts. Perhaps I could make a dive for it before she obliterated me.

"Behind her," he said, his voice low as he wound around and between my calves.

Of course. *Of course,* the damn button was behind her.

I focused on the iced-over controls beyond Demeter. Maybe there was a solution that didn't involve Meg and me fighting Demeter—and losing to her. If I could just get Demeter out of the way, Meg could hit the control panel with a small blast of psychic energy to melt the ice, and then all that was left to do was push the button.

"You can't trap us here forever," Demeter said, her staff glowing brighter. The gem at the top vaguely resembled the face of a clock. Had she merged Father Time's staff with her scepter, creating some sort of super doru? Because it certainly felt like she was charging the staff with psychic energy at this very moment. "I won't let you make this absurd place our prison. We *will* find a way out."

"I—" I shook my head, sensing Meg charging her own scepter behind me. "That's not why I'm here."

Demeter's eyes narrowed to slits. "Then what, exactly, did you come here to do?" Her gaze lingered on Meg for a long moment before returning to me. "Because the actions of you and your friends so far don't suggest peaceful intentions."

Was it possible that, in this case, honesty really was the best policy? If I told her the truth, would she even believe me? Based on the information I had been given—that Demeter had exploited a moment of weakness when the simulation was restructured—I had assumed she and her followers *wanted* to be here in Wonderland, that they were hiding in the construct, possibly regrouping for some sort of escape attempt or attack. But what if I was looking at this all wrong?

"What are *you* trying to do here?" I asked, genuinely curious.

"To get out," Demeter seethed.

"But—" My brow furrowed. "Didn't you come here voluntarily?"

"*Come* here?" Demeter let out a bitter laugh. "We've been here all along," she snapped.

My eyes widened. Had the Wonderland construct been accidentally superimposed over Demeter's original prison when Fiona and Gertie set up the new version of the simulation? The Olympian portion of the virtual world was supposed to be its own private section of Allworld Online, but Demeter's prison hadn't been a part of the greater original simulation. It had been isolated. Perhaps Fiona and Gertie had overlooked that mini prison sim during the merging process.

"We've been here since Hades imprisoned us after your idiotic little coup," Demeter went on, "or did you forget about that?" She sniffed and shrugged one shoulder. "I suppose you *were* dead at the time."

I laughed nervously, deciding to go for it. The truth shall set you free, and all that. "There's a button behind you," I told Demeter. "It resets this construct, stripping away the prison containment settings. That would expel every player—every *real* person—from this construct and send them out into the greater simulation."

Demeter studied me warily. "You want to free us?"

"I *want* to free Fiona," I corrected her. When there was no recognition on Demeter's face, I added, "Your prisoner."

Demeter's eyes lit with understanding. "You would risk freeing us *for her*?" she asked, incredulous. Interest lit in her gaze as she realized Fiona was a far greater prize than she had suspected.

I nodded, a single dip and rise of my chin. I wasn't willing to confess to Demeter just how important Fiona was to *everything*. I didn't want to put more of a target on Fiona's back than I already had. From now on, Fiona was going to have to stay out of the simulation unless absolutely necessary. Especially until we figured out where Demeter landed *out there* post-reset.

"Lower your mental shields," Demeter said. "Let me sense your intention. I won't move out of your way until I know you speak the truth."

Thankfully, shielding my mind was a skill *I* had learned from the Zari psychics, not merely another of the abilities I had inherited from Peri—and later lost when I was uploaded to the simulation without her. Concentrating on my mental walls, I peeled back the top layer of my shields, allowing Demeter only to perceive my surface thoughts and emotions.

"I speak the truth," I said. "I want to reset the construct and take Fiona home. Whatever happens to you and yours in the process is not my current concern."

Demeter scoffed. "Not your *current* concern," she said, repeating my last words back to me. "But perhaps, in time . . ." She sighed. "No matter."

The top of Demeter's staff flared, and a ripple of energy burst out from the base, shivering across the floor and up the wall of controls behind her.

It died out before it reached me, but behind Demeter, the ice crackled and cracked, sloughing off the controls and clattering to the floor.

Demeter stepped to the side, sweeping one arm out toward the literal big red button on the desk portion of the floor-to-ceiling control panel. Fiona had been right. I couldn't miss it.

"By all means," Demeter said. "Reset the construct."

Warily, I moved forward. With each of my steps, Demeter backed farther away, though I kept my attention trained on her. I had no doubt that, behind me, Meg kept her charged scepter aimed at Demeter, though Demeter couldn't have appeared less concerned by the other psychic.

"You're sure this is the one?" I asked Loki, without taking my eyes off Demeter.

Loki leaped onto the desk. "Absolutely," he said, the serpentine motion of his tail visible in my peripheral vision. "Push the button, Cora."

"Cora?" Demeter repeated, her expression baffled.

But before she could say more. Before she could even *think* more, I slammed my palm down on the reset button. A bright white light exploded from the control panel, engulfing me, Loki, Demeter, Meg, and everything else around us.

36

I DROPPED FROM A dozen feet in the air down onto the hard, rocky ground of the gatescape, landing on my butt with an, "Oof!" The crystal shards littering the sloped hillside dug painfully into my palms.

Loki, on the other hand, landed gracefully beside me, not the least bit bothered by the abrupt relocation. Meg was nowhere in sight, and I assumed she had been expelled to another part of the simulation.

"Cora?" someone called before I could wrap my head around my sudden change of situation. I was pretty sure that someone was Raiden.

"Cora?" someone else said—my mom, this time. "Where are you?"

"Cora?" Raiden repeated.

"I'm here!" I shouted, scrambling to my feet. I ran to the top of the hill and scanned the surrounding landscape.

I found my mom and Emi with their gigis in a valley, the four of them surrounded by clusters of amethyst and aquamarine crystals. Raiden stood on the crest of a neighboring hill, a petite calico cat sitting near his feet. Relief flooded me at seeing them, like only then could I believe the Wonderland adventure was over.

"I'm over here!" I shouted, waving my arms to catch their attention.

Raiden looked my way first. His relieved smile warmed my heart, and I started down the hillside in his direction, skidding and sliding on the loose rocks and crystal shards. Loki followed, walking well outside of my rock scatter zone. When Raiden and I met in the valley between our two hillsides, I threw myself into his arms, and he squeezed me tight. His hugs were the best, making me feel safe and wanted. Loved.

Raiden pressed a kiss to the top of my hair, breathing me in. "Where have you been, Cora? We've been looking for you for hours."

"I know," I said against his shoulder. I heard hurried footsteps crunching through the rocky ground, and I assumed my mom and Emi were closing in on us. "I'm sorry I worried you guys, but it was important."

Sighing, I angled my head back so I could see Raiden's face, and I smiled to reassure him that all was well. Or well-ish, considering that Demeter and her cronies were now free to roam the simulation. "Let's go home," I said. "I'll tell you all about it."

PART THREE

Cora

37

"I screwed up, I know," Fiona said, her emerald eyes imploring. She sat across from Hades and me on a stool at a worktable in her lab, having come out of cryosleep a few minutes earlier, and I had the odd sense of Hades and me being parents dressing down an unruly child. "I just—once I realized what I'd done and that I might be able to fix it myself without anyone ever finding out . . ."

Apparently, she had figured out her error in integrating the prison with the rest of the simulation shortly after we left for Krystallos. Rather than fessing up and risking derailing our mission, Fiona had decided to attack this threat herself. I understood her thought process even if I was still furious with her for risking her life—and all the souls on board the *Elysium* along with her. What if we hadn't returned from Krystallos? What if Fiona's physical body had died while her mind was trapped in that construct? What if . . .

I purposely halted the spiraling questions and forced myself to draw in a deep breath, filling my lungs to maximum capacity before slowly releasing the air. "When we leave to deliver the revenant cluster, you'll be running this ship." I raised my brows, staring at her pointedly. "Like, literally, Fio. You'll be the captain of the *Elysium*, and all those people in the Vault of Souls will be depending on *you* to carry them safely to their new home."

"I know," she said, scrubbing her hands over her face. She looked utterly wiped out and completely dejected, but I had to make sure she understood. Otherwise, everything we were risking to stop the Tsakali—the lives of everyone going on the dangerous mission, Hades and myself included—were being risked for nothing.

"Can we trust you not to do something like this again?" I asked.

Did I need to leave Meg behind as a watchdog to guarantee Fiona stayed the course? Selene was staying, but I didn't have a direct line of communication with her like I did with Meg. Even if I couldn't do anything from afar, maybe that bit of perceived accountability would keep Fiona focused.

"Because when you risk yourself like that, you risk *everyone*," I added.

"I *know*," Fiona repeated. She closed her eyes, her features pinched. "I know," she said a third time, her shoulders slumping as she hung her head. "I'm sorry. I just—" She snuck a glance at Hades. "I didn't want to disappoint you." Hades inhaled to speak, but she held up a hand, forestalling him. "And before you say anything, I know I did. Trust me, I know. *I'm* disappointed in me."

I sighed and nodded.

"You should get some rest," Hades said. "Entering the simulation as you did is taxing on your body. You may not feel like you can sleep yet, but exhaustion will hit you hard. Soon. And you *will* crash."

Fiona laughed hollowly. "I'm already feeling it." She rubbed her temples. "This is one hell of a headache."

Hades and I exchanged a look, my concern mirrored in his features.

"What?" Fiona asked, going statue still. "What is it?" She slowly lowered her hands.

"Probably nothing," Hades said. "But you should have a session in the asclypos before you adjourn to your room. There's an increased chance of neurodegeneration associated with forcing one's way into the simulation outside of a cryopod."

"Are you serious?" Fiona asked, looking mildly horrified. "Like, now I might end up with fecking Alzheimer's? Shit." She turned partway on her stool and glared at her workstation behind her. "Gertie never mentioned it."

Hades stood, pushing back his stool. "Gertie will always be more concerned with the wellbeing of those within the Vault of Souls than she will be with you or *your* wellbeing," he said, his tone somber and cautionary. "It is her nature to prioritize the masses in her care above any individual, even you, and it would serve you well to never forget that."

Fiona's eyes were open wide enough that white was visible around her emerald irises. "I won't," she vowed.

"Asclypos, then rest," I reminded her, standing as well.

She nodded, licking her lips. "You got it."

I followed Hades out of the lab and fell in step beside him in the corridor, both of us heading back to our shared quarters to clean up. We hadn't had a chance since returning from Krystallos, and I felt greasy and grimy.

"Was that true?" I asked. "About neurodegeneration?"

Hades eyed me conspiratorially. "It could be."

I guffawed, bumping his arm with my shoulder. "Liar, liar, pants on fire," I chided him.

His features creased with confusion. "That makes no sense."

"I know," I said. "Silly Earth saying."

His expression turned serious, and he cleared his throat. "Speaking of Earth . . ."

I looked at him sharply, my heart turning leaden and dropping into my stomach. There was only one reason he would bring up Earth right now. "That's where we're going, isn't it—to deliver the revenant cluster?"

Dread knotted in my gut at the idea of going back there, to the planet that had been more of a home to me than any other I had ever visited in my many lifetimes. Years had passed on Earth since we left, though it felt more like weeks to us, thanks to several long stints in cryosleep. What would be left of the world I knew after the mass upload to the *Elysium's* simulation and the Tsakali invasion that had followed shortly after?

Hades sighed. "It's the nearest confirmed hotspot of Tsakali activity," he explained. "Every other known Tsakali location logged in this ship within a hundred jumps of our current coordinates has been abandoned."

I frowned, disappointed, though it wasn't all that surprising. Thousands of years had passed since the *Elysium* was last active, and the Tsakali were like locusts, known for consuming all the resources they could in one location, then moving on. It didn't bode well for what we would find on Earth.

I blew out a breath. "Then I guess I'm going home."

38

I STOOD IN THE cargo bay of the *Charon*, my back to the open rear loading ramp and my fists on my hips as I studied the revenant cluster. It looked dead, like a regular old massive crystal, not like the repository of souls that it truly was. Its bindings appeared secure, which was what really mattered.

The Amazons joining us on the mission to Earth would be safe in their subfloor cryopods, but Hades and I would be exposed as we piloted the ship to Earth. We couldn't have the behemoth rolling around, crashing through the cargo bay's wall and crushing us. Then, it wouldn't even matter if it infected us with its transformative contagion.

The maintenance bots had been ceaselessly hard at work getting the *Charon* flight ready for such a long journey. With FTL jumps, it would only take us about a week to reach Earth, assuming we avoided the types of snags that had plagued our journey on board the *Elysium*. I mentally crossed my fingers and wished for no more encounters with space pirates. One of the chaos stones from Krystallos was safely stashed in the main cabin in a containment box near the housing for the FTL drive, shielded from detection until we were ready to launch.

The other chaos stone we had found would remain here, a backup in case there was an issue with the one already powering *Elysium's* FTL drive. So long as Fiona had that, the *Elysium* should be fine without us.

Boots clanged on the metal floor of the transport hangar behind me, but I didn't turn to see who was approaching the loading ramp. I already knew.

"I don't like this," Meg said, climbing the ramp to join me.

My lips twitched into a smile, there and gone in an instant. The idea of splitting up had originated with a need to watch over Fiona, but the more I thought about it, the more I realized it was necessary. For the safety of everyone on board the *Elysium* and for my peace of mind.

"I need you to take care of them," I said, my fists sliding from my hips. I reached for Meg's hand. "I need to know they're okay." I wouldn't be able to focus completely on the Earth mission otherwise.

Meg squeezed my fingers, then released them. "I know," she said. "But I still don't like it."

I tore my stare away from the revenant cluster to look at her. "I'm not sure I could do this—I'm not sure I could leave—if I didn't know you were here to watch over them."

A crease formed between Meg's brows. "It doesn't have to be you," she said. "Selene's more than willing to lead this—"

I shook my head, flashing Meg a tight-lipped smile. "But I think it *does* have to be me." I exhaled a laugh, feeling silly as I voiced the thoughts. But Meg already had free access to my mind, so likely none of this would come as a surprise to her. "Do the Zari believe in fate?"

Meg shrugged one shoulder. "Only in the sense that we believed Hades would one day return to us, but not in some larger, more indeterminate way, no."

"The Olympians weren't big on it either," I told her, turning my attention back to the revenant cluster. "The old gods, though, who we abandoned *long* before the war ever even started—made obsolete by technology—were all about fate or destiny or whatever you want to call it. Sometimes I wonder if my people tapped into some universal truth with their ancient mythologies, something that we later lost. Like the technological advancements that disproved the existence of the gods clouded our ability to truly understand the universe. We became too focused on the tangible, on the minutiae, on the things we could control, and we lost track of the bigger picture." I narrowed my eyes. "Tech expanded our world, opening up the universe to us, but it shrank our minds. We could no longer conceive of the intangible. The infinite."

But after everything Hades and I had been through, after all that had happened since we left Earth, and after what we discovered on Krystallos . . . "Can it really be a mere coincidence that another version of *myself* paved the way for this mission thousands of years ago? Or is coincidence just another word for fate?"

"Those are the kinds of questions that nobody can answer," Meg said. "But I understand why you're asking them."

A clatter of footsteps drew my attention to the transport hangar's broad doorway. The door panel was already open, and Fiona hurried toward the *Charon*, a small metal case hanging by a strap on her shoulder. Tila clunked along beside her in her brand new doggy mag boots, specially made to fit her paws. If not for the hiking booties I used to put her in when we would go blackberry picking across the wooded grounds of Blackthorn Manor, my dog likely would've been actively attempting to gnaw the things off. Tila also wore a slightly bulky collar that could produce a protective energy field to shield her should she ever find herself in an unbreathable atmosphere. Hades had programmed the collar himself to activate automatically whenever it detected lethal atmospheric levels.

Caly walked on Fiona's other side, a net of rose-pink psychic energy dragging a hovering coffin-sized steel crate behind her.

I grinned broadly as they neared. "Such a pretty space pup!" I exclaimed, dropping to one knee.

Tila hustled up the ramp, her boots thumping and her tail wagging furiously. I had considered leaving her behind, but after that last mission to Krystallos, I couldn't bring myself to look into her sad puppy-dog eyes and see her sense of abandonment again. Maybe I was being selfish in bringing her with me on such a dangerous mission, but my gut told me that if she understood the options, she would choose to come with me, too.

I scratched the sides of her thick neck, taking a moment to examine the high-tech collar. The construction appeared seamless, which hopefully meant there would be no way for Tila to damage it with her scratching back paws.

"What's this?" I asked Fiona, eyeing the steel crate as she and Caly climbed the ramp.

Fiona grinned. "A bon voyage present."

I raised my eyebrows and stood, Tila dropping her rump to the floor by my feet. "A present?" I repeated, absolutely clueless as to what it could be.

Fiona held a hand up to her mouth and leaned in like she was sharing a secret. "It's the Titan," she said, a wild glee brightening her irises to sparkling emeralds.

My eyes opened wide, and my attention locked onto the box. "What do you mean?"

"I fixed her up," Fiona said cheerfully. "All you need to do is flip the proverbial switch to turn her on, then drop her into a nest of Tsakali and run."

My brow furrowed. "Is she rigged to blow up?" I asked, not understanding why Fiona would risk this.

Fiona shook her head, still grinning like a maniac. "Unless you mean that figuratively, like—is she rigged to blow up Tsakali society? In which case, the answer would be a definitive *yes*."

I backed up a step and raised my hands partway, my head slowly turning from side to side. I looked at Caly, who shrugged, then at Meg, who appeared mildly horrified, before returning my focus to Fiona. "She almost *killed* you, Fio," I reminded her. "She killed a bunch of our Amazons. She *ate* our psychic energy." Again, I shook my head. "I don't think we should *ever* turn her back on."

"Pff," Fiona said, waving her hand dismissively. "Water under the bridge."

"But—but—" I stuttered.

Fiona turned to Caly and pointed past the revenant cluster to the doorway at the far side of the *Charon*'s cargo bay. "Put her in the main cabin," she said, then returned her attention to me. "Consider this your backup plan. You don't have to use her, but if the shit hits the fan, you won't be SOL."

"And you're sure she can't turn herself back on?" I asked, glancing over my shoulder to peer dubiously at the box.

"Not a chance," Fiona said, shrugging the strap off her shoulder and handing me the metal case. "This is her power source. Hades will know how to connect it, but on the off chance he's not around, I left instructions for you on a holodisk." Her attention shifted to the crate. "I doubt she'd be anywhere near as effective as that thing," she said, nodding toward the revenant cluster, "since she doesn't hold, like, a gazillion souls within her, but I'm sure she could stir up *some* chaos. At least buy you time to regroup and flee, should you need it."

I frowned, seeing the Titan in a new light—as less of a danger and more of an opportunity. A *dangerous* opportunity. A last-ditch opportunity. But an opportunity, nonetheless.

39

"WHAT IS IT?" I asked Hades, scrutinizing his face as he studied the navigation overlay on the *Charon*'s main viewscreen, which afforded us a terrifying closeup of the sun. His expression left me more than a little unsettled, and I gripped my unbuckled safety restraints between clenched fingers. "What's wrong?"

We had just dropped out of FTL and were coasting along through Earth's solar system, concealed behind the sun. Hades claimed proximity to the yellow dwarf star would conceal our energy signature while we removed the chaos stone from the FTL engine and stowed it safely within a containment box to prevent the Tsakali from noticing the sudden influx of chaos energy. Then, we could activate the ship's stealth cloaks and be certain we were undetectable as we approached Earth.

For now, it was just Hades and me awake on the ship. Tila and the Amazons would remain in their subfloor cryopods until we landed on Earth. It was quiet on the *Charon* with just the two of us active, only heightening my unease.

The crease between Hades' brows deepened, and he pressed his lips together, forming a thin, flat line slashing across the lower half of his face.

I glanced at the engine compartment on the side of the main cabin. The chaos stone could wait another minute or two. "Hades?" I reached out and touched his forearm. "What's wrong?" I repeated more firmly.

Hades exhaled, sounding resigned. His eyelids drifted shut as he collected his thoughts, then opened his eyes again. "There is no sign of the Tsakali on Earth." He looked at me. "Or anywhere else within this solar system."

I licked my lips, my heart sinking. "They could be concealing themselves," I said, pulling back my hand as I grasped at straws.

Hades bowed his head, acknowledging my statement as possible. "Except they *were* here when we left the *Elysium*, and they certainly *weren't* concealing themselves then." With quick, sure motions, he pulled up the holoscreen, opening a navigation chart that displayed a broader section of this part of the universe. "There they are," he said, pointing to a cluster of blinking beacons near the galaxy's edge, and my heart sank deeper. They had really left. "Either our timing is terrible, or they sensed us coming."

I shook my head and flicked my hand toward the chart. "But they had dozens of warships stationed here. We're just one piddly little cargo ship. Why would they run from us?"

Hades frowned thoughtfully. "I can only think of one reason."

I gulped, suspecting I knew why as well. "They know." About the revenant cluster. Or, at least, about our plan.

Hades dipped his chin.

I released a puff of breath, a disbelieving laugh, and shook my head again. "But *how*?"

"Perhaps they've been monitoring Krystallos," he pondered aloud. "I hadn't considered it, but it would make sense, especially since they view that planet both as a threat and as a potentially untapped asset."

I scoffed, refusing to believe this line of thought. It would make our mission nearly impossible. If the Tsakali believed we carried a contagious artifact from Krystallos and suspected our intentions, they would avoid us at all costs.

Perhaps such a deterrent was enough reassurance that they would leave us alone in the long run? That Terra would be safe from the ever-present Tsakali threat? But what good would that do for the greater universe? The Tsakali would continue to spread and consume until nothing was left. Besides, it was far too dangerous for us to hang on to the revenant crystal, and bringing it to Terra was out of the question. We absolutely could not risk Terra ending up like Krystallos, with our people forever trapped in their own revenant clusters.

"If they're so afraid of what's on Krystallos, why not destroy the planet already?" I countered, desperately hoping we were wrong and this was all a coincidence.

"Because they wish to harness its energy," he guessed. "They've been unable to figure out how to do so safely—so far—but they're not willing to destroy something that could eventually prove to be such a powerful asset."

"I don't know," I murmured, rubbing the side of my jaw.

I closed my eyes, attempting to see the situation from the Tsakali's point of view. The revenant cluster had been dormant almost the entire time it had been in our possession, save for a few minutes back on the *Elysium* when I communed with revenant-Peri to solidify the plan of attack, so to speak. That meant they were likely tracking the energy signature from our chaos stone, which would have been detectable for brief periods between FTL jumps. If we concealed the chaos stone and pursued the Tsakali using our slower-than-light engines—while in stealth mode—maybe we could catch up to them.

I opened my eyes and looked at Hades. "How long would it take to reach them without using FTL?"

Hades shook his head. "Too long," he said. "*If* they truly know we visited Krystallos and already suspect what we're planning, we won't be able to catch them."

"We could go back," I said. "Assuming they really will stay away, our people should be safe enough."

Again, Hades shook his head. "We can't sit on the revenant cluster," he said, echoing my thoughts from a moment ago. "Our people aren't much better than the Tsakali when it comes to coveting power. Eventually, someone will get greedy enough, and then our people will all be dead and everything we fought so hard to preserve will be over."

"Well, technically, they'll be *crystallized*," I corrected him.

Hades gave me a wry look. "You know what I mean." He sighed. "There must be a way around this, but I just—" He shook his head. "I can't see it right now."

My shoulders slumped, and I turned my attention to the broad view screen. Earth and its orbit were marked by glowing white navigation lines, the actual planet hidden from view beyond the burning wall of orange and yellow fire that took up the entire screen.

"Can we at least go to Earth while we try to figure this out?" I asked. As near as we were to the sun, it was impossible not to feel like all that gaseous flame was about to consume us.

"Of course," Hades said, swiping away the holoscreen and plotting a course around the sun to Earth.

Feeling hollowed out, I stood and hustled to the engine compartment back near the Titan's steel coffin. It was still worth it to conceal the chaos stone. Even if the Tsakali had detected our progress moving toward this solar system, they didn't know we had arrived, what with us landing so close to the sun. And they certainly didn't need to know we were lingering. Once the chaos stone was stowed in the containment box, I returned to my seat and fastened my safety restraints.

"Ready to go home?" Hades asked me, his eyebrows hitching higher.

Was I ready? Not in the slightest. But the lure to return to Earth was too great.

I drew in a deep breath, then blew it out. "I'm ready."

40

Earth wasn't burning, like I had feared. It was worse than that. The planet looked dead. Like a discarded husk, sucked dry of all its human life forces.

Lake Washington had been drained, and deep holes had been bored into the once submerged ground. The 520 floating bridge lay in a haphazard line across the cracked lakebed, looking like a trampled child's toy. Seattle was a decaying skeleton of a city, with blown-out windows leaving buildings ripe for ivy vines to creep up and around. Blackberry bushes covered many of the abandoned cars, the vines sprouting from cracks in the asphalt and wayward patches of soil, turning the vehicles into green mounds scattered along the cracked streets. And the indomitable Space Needle, with its famously deep foundation, stood askew, giving the impression that the lightest gust would send it toppling. I hadn't known the city well, but I thought even a native Seattleite would hardly recognize the place now.

"Why?" I asked, glancing at Hades for only a moment before the haunting scene recaptured my attention.

Any moral quandaries I had held onto about uploading billions of humans to the *Elysium* without their knowledge or consent prior to the Tsakali invasion evaporated from my mind. My only regret now was that we hadn't been able to tag and upload everyone.

"We were gone," I said remotely. There was a tremble in my voice. "Why would they do this? Why *destroy* like this? Because people fought back?"

Hades shook his head, the corners of his mouth turned down in disgust. "Those were mines back in that lakebed," he said. "The Tsakali came here because they sensed chaos energy, but they stayed for the same reason we did so long ago. This is a resource rich planet. They would have exterminated all intelligent life forms within the regions they wished to exploit—not because they wished to destroy humankind, but because they wanted to make the resource extraction process as easy as possible."

Horror twisted my features. The Tsakali's disregard for life was more disturbing than anything else about them. I had known they were destructive, but this was beyond anything I could have imagined. How many worlds had they already laid to waste like this? How many civilizations and peoples had they already eradicated? We didn't just owe it to our people to succeed in our mission. We owed it to *all* sentient life.

"This is actually promising," Hades said.

I scoffed. "In what possible way is *this* promising?"

"Up until a few days ago, they were still here, still mining, still extracting," Hades said. "It's highly unlikely they were finished with this planet, and they will want to return . . . eventually."

As much as the idea disturbed me, I could see his point. "We could wait them out, you mean?" I asked, suspecting his train of thought. "Just land somewhere and wait for their return?"

"We could," Hades said, tilting his head to the side as we left the demolished city and glided out over the glittering gray water of Elliott Bay and the greater Puget Sound, heading for the San Juan Islands. "But that could take hundreds, possibly thousands, of years. The Tsakali are not bound by anything resembling a lifespan, like organic creatures.

They have nothing if not time. And when they do return, it will first be with scouts, then with Titans, and *then* with a significant force for more resource extraction."

I frowned. With close enough proximity, the Titans would sense the *Charon*'s power core and chaos stone, even cloaked and shielded within a containment box. Psychic senses were far more sensitive than any tech. In other words, it was highly likely we would be found out before the Tsakali ever brought a significant enough force to justify unleashing the revenant cluster.

I curled my fingers and clenched my jaw, pounding my fist on my armrest. There didn't seem to be a good solution to this infuriating situation.

"If we launched the *Charon* on autopilot as soon as the scouts arrived and sent it—and the chaos stone—jumping away from this solar system," Hades started, thinking aloud, "we could avoid detection by the Titans. They would assume we had left. Then, all we would need to do would be to lie low with the revenant cluster until the main force arrives."

I glanced around my chairback toward the door to the cargo bay. "You don't think the Titans will sense it?"

"Can you?" Hades asked.

Unsure, I deactivated my regulator and reached out with my psychic fingers, searching the space around the massive crystal. After a few minutes, I pulled my senses back and shook my head. "It could work," I confirmed.

Depending on how long it took the Tsakali to return, the settlement on Terra could already be established and thriving. My mom, Emi, Raiden, and that other, fractured Cora-only piece of me could already have been reborn, lived their second lives, and died long before we were ever roused from cryosleep by the ship's automated system sensing the Tsakali's arrival. That thought saddened me greatly.

I knew I couldn't be a part of their new lives—not only would it be super confusing to have two versions of me walking around, but Hades and I carried a nasty bit of biological warfare around in our DNA. If we came into contact with any of the new Olympians whose bodies were generated using the pristine genetic samples from Artemis's colony, we would infect them, and they would infect others, rendering the entire new generation of Olympians infertile. The only way our people would have a true, viable future was without us.

But I had always believed I would live out the remainder of my life around the same time as they lived theirs. Just knowing we existed in the same era and that we might gaze upon many of the same stars would have eased some of the ache in my heart from missing them. Now, distant coexistence might not even be a possibility. By the time we completed the mission and infected the Tsakali with revenant souls, everyone I loved might very well be dead. Even Meg, Selene, Fiona, and all the new Amazons. Everyone except for Hades, Tila, and the Amazons here with us.

"For now, then, that will be the plan," Hades said.

"I hate this plan," I sulked, crossing my arms over my chest and sinking as deep into my seat as my restraints would allow. "It sucks."

"I know," Hades said, reaching across the space between our seats to squeeze my knee. "We'll wake the others and take a few days to think it over before entering the prolonged cryosleep." He pulled his hand back, returning it to the navigation sphere. "Perhaps we'll come up with something better in that time."

"*Our need will be the real creator*," I said, quoting Plato's Republic in the original ancient Greek. I wasn't exactly fluent in the dead language, but it had been one of my mom's favorite quotes, so I had that line memorized.

Hades blinked several times and looked at me, his lips parting in surprise. "I once said that very thing to a friend, long ago. Those *exact* words." His brows drew together. "Where did you hear that?"

I turned toward Hades as much as I could, a small smile touching my lips. "Your friend's name didn't happen to be Aristocles, did it?" I asked, impressing myself by being able to dig up Plato's supposed true name from the depths of my memory.

Hades' lips twitched, slowly spreading into a grin. "Yes," he laughed. "That was his name. He was a brilliant young man, but his focus was too philosophical to enact the kind of change I required."

Hades hadn't only known Plato, but he had given the ancient philoso-pher one of his most iconic lines, one that would evolve into the better known proverb: *Necessity is the mother of invention*.

I laughed gently and shook my head. "You, Hades, are full of won-ders."

He eyed me quizzically. "Is that a good thing?"

"Absolutely."

I settled back in my seat, my need to sulk banished thanks to Hades and his incredible past. How many people had he known who were now gone? How many had he loved but still voluntarily bid farewell? All because he had a greater purpose. A duty. A mission.

To save our people. To save me.

He had done it then, alone. I could do it now, with him.

41

H ADES SET THE *CHARON* down on the overgrown lawn behind Blackthorn Manor and immediately deployed scouting drones to map the island.

The side hatch slid open as the ramp extended and lowered to smash years of grass, sending a cloud of dandelion seeds flying into the air. I stood at the top of the ramp and watched the floating seeds, shimmering gold in the light from the setting sun, then scanned the veritable savanna, thick with bright yellow dandelions and purple-ish white clover flowers. The air carried the notes of wildflowers and fresh pine sap, offset by the tang of the sea. The flowers mixed with the sweet, tepid breeze placed us in late spring or early summer. Hades had estimated the time of year as mid-June, and this confirmed it.

I forced myself to shift my attention higher, looking at the bedraggled manor house beyond the field of grass and wildflowers, and my heart plummeted. Blackthorn Manor had never looked so run down, with broken windows and rampant ivy growing up its exterior walls and into the house. It had been a little over six years in Earth time since we left. I hadn't expected my home to appear shiny and new, but I hadn't expected this disheartening ruin either.

Eyes stinging, I turned away from the house and walked back into the cabin of the ship. I wanted to help transition Tila and the Amazons out of cryosleep and to guide them through the disorientation that would follow. Hades had initiated the wake sequence, and the panels in the floor were already open and leaking wispy puffs of white gas. I walked around the two dozen open compartments to kneel beside Tila's cryopod near the front of the ship.

I watched her motionless form in the sunken recess. Her broad, black nose twitched, her sense of smell apparently waking up before the rest of her.

I leaned forward, reaching over the lip of her cryopod and into the dissipating fog. "You smell that, little girl?" I cooed, rubbing the pad of my thumb along the velvety bridge of her nose. "We're home."

Tila snorted, and her eyelids twitched, then opened. Suddenly, she was all flailing limbs and arching back.

"Calm down, T," I said, my voice soothing as I deactivated my regulator and reached into her cryopod with psychic energy. "We're *home*."

I wrapped her bucking body gently in an electric-blue net and scooped her out of the literal hole in the floor, setting her down on her scrambling feet but keeping her contained within the safety of the energy bubble. Her claws were sharp, and she was strong. I didn't want her knocking over and injuring any of the women emerging from their own cryopods, let alone crashing through the door to the cargo bay and running into the revenant cluster. I *really* didn't want to crystallize my dog.

I wrapped a thin band of psychic energy around her neck, then extended it out to my hand like a leash before releasing the bubble. Her paws scrabbled at the textured steel floor, and I strained to lead her toward the side hatch and down the ramp. As soon as her feet touched the sun-warmed Earth, she calmed, going absolutely still in the tall grass.

I released the leash, letting the psychic energy dissipate. The bulging muscles of Tila's hindquarters tensed, bunching, and then she was off, zooming through the tall grass. I watched her for a long, indulgent moment, smiling to myself.

A woman coughed behind me, and I turned to see most of the Amazons sitting on the edges of their cryopods, blinking as they worked through their post-cryosleep disorientation. Hades moved from Amazon to Amazon, helping each open the smaller compartment at the head of their cryopods that held their hoplon suits, boots, hoods, and dorus. I hurried back up the ramp and into the cabin to assist.

Once everyone was suited up, armed, and fully awake, I ushered our small army down the ramp to stretch their legs and take in some much needed fresh air. The sun had vanished behind the western horizon while I was in the ship, and twilight turned the woods surrounding the estate into a shadowy mass.

Hades trailed the last of the Amazons down the ramp and tapped a button on his holoband to seal the ship. The ramp rose slowly, and soon enough, the *Charon* vanished from sight.

"Let's scout the surrounding area, then reconvene here," I said and peered over my shoulder at the forbidding manor house.

Blackthorn Manor had looked rough in the light, but in the settling darkness, it appeared downright haunted. I stared out at the cloudy sky over the bay, no hint of a star in sight. It would likely rain tonight, and as much as I dreaded entering my childhood home and seeing the wreckage that had become of the interior, I was less eager to spend the night out in the rain.

"We'll spend the night in the house," I told them. "I know it's hard after spending days in cryosleep, but try to get some rest. We want to be fresh when we scout the rest of the island tomorrow."

"What are we looking for?" Melyse asked, glancing toward the woods.

"Any signs that the Tsakali might still be here," I told her. Tilting my head slightly, I added, "Or other people."

We needed to scout for the Tsakali—their ships were gone, but they could have left some stragglers behind, and we certainly didn't want them sending reports of our arrival or activities back to their larger force. But the *other people* were the more immediate threat in my mind. If there were any humans left alive, they would have survived years of the Tsakali invasion, and they weren't likely to greet us with anything save for hostility.

"Stick within two hundred yards of the house," I told them. "And if you encounter *anyone*, stay hidden and do not approach." I scanned the Amazons' faces, waiting for their nods acknowledging my command.

It felt strange to be leading such a major mission without Selene to back me up, but one of the old guard needed to remain behind to assist Fiona and to continue the Zari Amazons' training.

"Activate stealth mode," I said.

One by one, the Amazons deactivated their regulators and focused their psychic energy inward, vanishing from sight.

42

"I'M GOING TO SCOUT the interior of the house," I tossed over my shoulder to Hades as I started toward the broad porch steps, Tila trotting along beside me.

Hades had his forearm raised and was staring at the small holographic screen hovering above his holoband, his attention thoroughly split. The rest of our team had already dispersed through the grounds.

"I'd offer to give you the grand tour," I told him, "but you look like you're itching to get back on the ship."

Hades peered over the top frame of the holographic screen to look past me at the dilapidated mansion, then focused on me. "There are some models I'd like to run," he said. "Some charts to study. Some readings to assess . . ."

"Then get to it," I teased and made a shooing motion, secretly relieved. I was nervous enough about this homecoming. What would I find inside the house? What kind of ruin and destruction? What echoes of the past? What dangerous memories?

I ascended the back steps and crossed the deck carefully, picking my way around broken boards and tangled vines. The porch had been in great shape prior to our abrupt departure. Not a rotten board in sight. But now it looked as though someone had taken a pickax to patches.

Probably the same someone who had broken all the ground-floor windows—at least those visible from the back lawn.

Had this merely been someone taking out their aggression on a beautiful thing, or was it something more, something targeted? We hadn't been beloved members of the community on Orcas Island, but we hadn't been despised either. More like the eccentric neighbors everyone loved to gossip about.

I made my way to one of the back doors that stood open and askew, barely hanging on by its bottom hinge. "Wait," I told Tila, holding down my hand and showing her my palm. And then I stepped through the doorway.

Ivy poured in through the broken windows and open doorways, living up to its reputation as an invasive species. At the sudden rustle of leaves, my head snapped to the left, and I peered into the darkness. A squirrel chittered before loping over vines that crept across the breakfast nook and into the kitchen, popping into and out of patches of the fading gray light filtering into the house.

At least the floors and walls appeared to have escaped the destruction that had befallen the exterior. All the damage inside looked like it had been caused less by the fallout from an alien invasion, and more by nature taking over.

I placed my hands on my hips and sighed, taking in the wreckage. Poor Charles Blackthorn would have been horrified to discover what had become of his prized creation. My mom and Emi, too. They loved this place. It was their sanctuary after living so long in the clutches of the toxic Custodes Veritatis.

"Come on, T," I said and headed deeper into the house, drawing my doru from the sheath on my back and extending it to full length, just in case.

I flipped on the light switch in the dark-as-pitch hallway, more out of habit than out of any expectation that the lights would work. Nothing happened, obviously.

"Dummy," I murmured and raised my free hand, thinking a glowing ball of energy into existence to light my way.

Flickering blue light reflected off the walls, only adding to the eerie atmosphere. This didn't feel like my home, not anymore. It was some other place, some alternate reality. This couldn't be the same Blackthorn Manor that had been my haven for the first twenty-six years of *this* lifetime.

Once I had cleared the ground floor, finding no dangers save for pests, I started up the grand staircase, my dog at my side. The stairs creaked under my feet, but that was nothing new for the century-old manor house. I didn't stop Tila when she trotted ahead. If anyone was upstairs, even if they were wearing psychic hoods, I would have heard the telltale creaks and groans from above, the house tattling on their presence. Blackthorn Manor was empty.

As I ascended the stairs, I retracted my doru and tucked it into the sheath on my back to free up both hands.

The second floor was in much better shape than the first. The ivy hadn't breached the upstairs windows or climbed up the staircase—though it was actively working its way up the banisters and railing. I poked my head into each room as I passed, opening doors to let out stale air. The decor and smaller furnishings within the spare bedrooms had been tossed around a bit, suggesting people had entered the house and helped themselves to some things. I couldn't blame them.

The library appeared untouched, as though even intruders could sense the sanctity of that space, but my bedroom was another matter entirely. I pushed open the ruined door and found the contents of my closet and dresser strewn across the floor and bed, making enough of a mess that I didn't notice the body at first.

I spotted the combat boots sticking out of the closet, and I moved closer, drawn by some morbid curiosity. The corpse was more of a skeleton than a body, but I still recognized the black body armor. Flickers of memory from the night I fled the house with Raiden flashed through my mind. It felt like a lifetime ago.

That was the night everything changed. The Custodes Veritatis had been drawn to me like a moth to a flame. I was dangerous. Powerful. *Other*. I could destroy them, but they wanted me anyway. To possess me, use me, study me. To destroy me if need be. But they couldn't stand to let me go free.

They couldn't just let me be.

The thought echoed in my mind but in another's voice. The Titan's voice.

Why can't they just let me be?

She had thought nearly that same thing when she was being held prisoner by her people, lying on a table, waiting for them to dissect her.

But the Tsakali had been relentless. And as I had gleaned while connected to her mind during the pirate incursion, they hadn't stopped pursuing her. She had taken extreme measures to evade them, masking her unique frequency when it proved immutable, and wearing a psychic hood at all times, should she unwittingly come within range of another Titan. When her crew attacked us, she had still been on the run. The Tsakali had still been hunting her, centuries after she visited Krystallos.

An idea formed in my mind, ignited by the Titan's plight.

"Holy shit," I breathed, pretty sure I knew how to not only draw *a* Tsakali force back to Earth, but how to draw their best and brightest. Titans galore. A force that, once infected with the souls contained within the revenant cluster, would be virtually unstoppable against the rest of the Tsakali force spread throughout the universe.

Riding the high of that epiphany, I turned on my heel and ran for the bedroom door, Tila following close behind me. I raced down to the ground floor and out onto the lawn.

"Hades, let me in," I said, a finger pressed to the comms patch behind my ear. "I know what we have to do."

43

"Did you know that every Tsakali broadcasts its own unique frequency?" I asked Hades as I strode up the ramp and onto the *Charon*. Tila was frolicking through the meadow that had once been a lawn, happy as could be. I marched straight for the steel coffin set off to the side of the main cabin.

"Yes," Hades said, standing from his seat at the helm and crossing the cabin to join me. "Each individual has an indelible beacon that automatically broadcasts a superlumic frequency." He stopped beside me, his focus on me rather than the Titan's box. Okay, so maybe he knew way more about it than I did.

"Right, well . . ." I glanced at Hades, then gestured to the steel coffin. "I never told anyone about this because she was dead or deactivated or whatever and it didn't matter, but she's been running from her people since the day she escaped—hundreds of years ago. They tracked her via her frequency until she found a way to muffle it, but she couldn't get rid of it completely. Whatever it is that generates the frequency can't be removed."

Hades nodded, his brow furrowed.

"Indelible," I said. "But you already knew that." I pointed toward the Titan's box. "The point is, if we can *un*muffle her frequency, we'll have all the Tsakali attention we need." Breathing harder, I turned to him. "And

I'm not just talking about scouts and miners and other peons. I mean *big* Tsakali. I mean *Titans*, and lots of them."

"You're sure they were still hunting her when you battled her on the *Elysium*?"

I nodded vehemently. "Yes."

The crease between Hades' brows smoothed out at my confirmation, and excitement lit his glacier-blue eyes. "I want to explore this option further before we commit to anything," he said, but his hungry gaze lingered on the steel coffin, and I could sense his barely contained scientific interest.

I touched his arm, drawing his attention back to me, and smiled. "I'll leave you to it, then," I said with a nod. He covered my hand with his, but his focus had already dropped back to the box, so I pulled away and started for the side hatch. "I'll be in the house if you need me," I told him. "Don't forget to close up the ship behind me."

Hades made a noncommittal noise as I descended the ramp. A few steps into the grass, I heard the quiet hiss of hydraulics as the ramp retracted. I glanced over my shoulder to see that the side hatch had been shut and the ship was all but invisible, save for the final few feet of the ramp.

Turning away, I searched the dark field for my dog. I sensed Tila before I saw her, her vibrant life force like a beacon in the night. She raced through the tall grass, carving out a circuitous path as she chased terrified nocturnal creatures scurrying along the ground.

"Come on, T," I called out and started for the back porch. The Amazons would return soon, and I would lose my chance to be alone in the house.

When I planted my foot on the top step, my holoband flashed red with warning. Frowning, I hurried into the house through the broken door and raised my forearm, activating the device's holoscreen with a single tap. A red border flashed around the floating holographic screen, displaying an incomplete map of the island. Landmarks and features were still being added as the scouting drones scanned the region, but I was less concerned about the empty patches when new life signals were popping up on the map every few seconds. The scouting drones were only programmed to log sentient beings, and they could tell the difference between synthetic and organic life. And these life signals were definitively organic.

"People," I breathed. Humans. Survivors.

My heart hammered. I wanted to go to them. I wanted to see them with my own eyes. To reassure myself that the Tsakali hadn't completely snuffed out the flame of humankind here on Earth.

I peeked over my shoulder at the sound of footsteps on the back porch. Kyra ascended the stairs, the glowing focus crystal atop her doru dimming as she approached.

I tapped the holoscreen to call back the scouting drones, not wanting to alert the humans to our presence, then swiped away the screen entirely and turned to face Kyra. Behind her, Sonara crossed the overgrown lawn, heading for the back deck.

I double tapped my comms patch to link with the entire team. "Pull back to the house," I said in a rush. "The drones detected humans, and I don't want to startle them into doing something stupid."

Kyra nodded, scanning the ruined living room but saying nothing.

"It's better upstairs," I told her, feeling unexpectedly and unnecessarily defensive. She hadn't made a face or anything, but finding people on the island had shaken me. Pulling myself together, I turned away from Kyra, starting for the hallway to the front of the house. "This way."

I led Kyra and Sonara to the grand staircase and up to the second floor, then pushed open the doors to the library. There was plenty of seating within the large space for everyone, and we could even light a fire in the dual fireplaces to reignite some of the old manor house's spark. The cloud cover muted the moonlight enough that the smoke would be undetectable. I crossed to the tall windows behind my mom's desk and pulled the heavy curtains shut, not wanting to broadcast our presence to the people still living on the island.

People. Alive. On the island. I laughed under my breath and shook my head as I crossed the room. I crouched in front of one of the fireplaces, dropping one knee to the floor, and started loading kindling into the hearth.

"What do you want to do about the people?" Kyra asked, perching on the arm of a chair nearby.

"I don't know." I held my hand toward the stacked wood, sending a charged stream of psychic energy into the heart of it. The kindling sparked and smoked, and then a small flame appeared. A single puff of air could blow it out. Kind of like the people living on the island.

We had been thinking of setting up the revenant cluster here, but that would endanger the humans—not only from the Tsakali that would come, but from the revenant cluster itself. Another of the islands would serve our purposes better, one that was completely uninhabited.

But I wanted to warn the people living here of the danger. They would still likely feel the lure of the revenant cluster once we activated the trap and the souls within the enormous crystal flared their living energy to draw in the Tsakali. No, we would have to go far away, somewhere where we were guaranteed not to find any survivors.

I thought of the Alpha site, buried under the polar ice cap.

Antarctica.

"Change of plans," I told Kyra. "We're not going to engage with the people here at all. We'll rest inside for the night and leave in the morning."

"To go where?" Sonara asked, crossing from the opposite fireplace.

I looked at each of them, then stared into the gently crackling fire. "Back to where it all began."

44

"Cora?" Hades said, hailing me through my comms patch about an hour after our team of Amazons settled in the Blackthorn library. "Can you come down to the ship? I need to show you something."

"Yeah, sure," I said, standing and scanning the women scattered around the room. Some lay on settees or slumped in chairs, eyelids shut or drooping, while others browsed the packed bookshelves or curled up on the floor with a book. The fires burning in the twin hearths on opposite sides of the room enlivened the space, and I could almost imagine that these were the old days and that the ground floor of the mansion didn't lie in ruin. I hated to break the spell and step back into reality.

Sighing, I started for the door, leaving Tila snoring on her old dog bed by a fireplace. "Be right there," I told Hades once I had stepped out of the room. There was a chill to the air in the hallway, mixed with an earthy odor that didn't belong indoors.

I hurried toward the stairs and down to the ground floor, picking my way over the vines creeping across the floor. By the time I reached the back porch, Hades already had the *Charon*'s side hatch open and ramp lowered, and he stood at the top, waiting for me. I strode across the overgrown lawn and up the ramp. The closer I drew, the clearer I could read the apprehension creasing his face. No psychic powers were needed. This was not a good news situation.

"It won't work," I said, anticipating the worst and looking past Hades to the Titan lying dormant in her open steel coffin. Fiona hadn't actually fixed the Titan. Something was still broken within her. Her transmitter had been damaged beyond repair, or—

"It will work," Hades said somberly.

I blinked and refocused on him, surprised by both his statement and his unhappy expression. "Then why the grim face?" I asked, stopping in front of him on the ramp and planting my hands on my hips.

"The transmitter is embedded within her neural processing matrix," he explained, stepping backward and gesturing for me to join him inside the ship's cabin. Once I was inside, he reached out and pressed the button to raise the ramp. "It's the reason she could never remove it—doing so would cause a multi-system failure. I was able to undo the *modification* that muffled the frequency, so if we were to power her up, she would broadcast across the universe, loud and clear."

Seeing the confusion written all over my face—because that all sounded great to me—Hades crossed to the steel box and stared down at the Titan, who now appeared perfectly peaceful and utterly undamaged. I followed him, eyeing her as I approached. If I hadn't known she was a synthetic being, I might have thought she was sleeping.

Hades cleared his throat. "*But* in order to activate her transmitter, we have to activate *her*."

My eyes widened, and my lips parted. I looked from the Titan to Hades and back. "Like, turn her on?" My eyebrows rose, climbing higher with each word. "All the way?"

Hades pressed his lips together, and the corners of his mouth tensed, turning down. He nodded. "There's no way to power up the transmitter alone. It's all or nothing."

Dread settled over me like an invisible net, cutting into my skin as it constricted around me. How would I ever break this news to the others? The Titan had killed so many of their spearsisters. Literally devoured their psychic energy until there was no life left in them. She would *try* to kill us. The second we booted her up, she would turn on us, and we would have to destroy her, and this would all prove to be an exercise in futility.

"Maybe if we drop her off somewhere remote as soon as we flip her on switch?" I spitballed.

"What about the revenant cluster?" Hades said. "One of us needs to be near it when the Tsakali force arrives to speak the word that will wake *them* up."

"Shit," I hissed. My shoulders slumped, and I let my head fall backward, closing my eyes and fake crying so I didn't shed real tears. If we activated the revenant cluster *before* the Tsakali arrived en masse, they would detect it and stay far, far away. "Why can't there ever be a simple solution?" I whined. Every possible fix seemed to sprout new hurdles, and it *wasn't fair*.

Hades grunted, commiserating with my mopy misery.

I allowed myself a full ten count to wallow, then took a deep breath and pulled myself together. I opened my eyes and stared down at the Titan, an idea taking shape in my mind. Not quite a Hail Mary, but close.

I licked my lips and looked at Hades. "Let me talk to her," I said, and his eyes widened in surprise. "Maybe she doesn't have to be our enemy." I crossed my arms over my chest and smiled grimly. "After all, the enemy of my enemy *is* my friend."

45

Hades didn't connect me to the Titan's mind the same way as before, since that would only give me access to her memories, not allow me to communicate with her directly. Instead, he connected us both to the *Charon*'s simple, single-construct simulation. It was a far cry from the complex simulation on the *Elysium* and required a much less sophisticated AI director. Comparing the two was like comparing an apartment building to an entire world. But this smaller simulation had its uses, primarily to stimulate the minds of any who entered extended cryosleep while on board the ship.

I entered the simulated reality first, shaping the construct to my will before the Titan arrived. With a focused thought, I recreated Blackthorn Manor as it existed in my heart, untouched by the Custodes Veritatis or the fallout from the Tsakali invasion. The sprawling lawn appeared first, trimmed grass spreading out from my feet in a rolling wave of green, followed by the house falling into place like a backdrop on a stage. The woods around the perimeter of the estate sprouted from the ground, and then the sea poured from the edge of the bluff, stretching out toward the horizon.

"Very nice," Hades said, his voice seeming to come from above. He was watching through a holoscreen out on the ship. "Let me know when you're ready for me to connect the Titan. Remember, this simulation contains no safety measures or fail-safes should she become aggressive."

A doru appeared in my hand, and I automatically poured psychic energy into the weapon until the focus crystal at the top burned electric-blue. An instant later, reason prevailed. I dismissed the weapon, and it vanished from sight. I didn't want the Titan on the defensive. I wanted *to talk*, and I knew enough about her past to know the best way to turn her against us right out the gate would be to threaten her. She had been viewed as a danger by her people and as a tool by the pirates, but she had never been seen as a person. I could give her that.

I scanned the construct one more time, then peered up at the sky, where I imagined Hades looking down upon me. "I'm ready for her."

"Connecting her now," Hades said.

The construct shivered, a ripple moving inward toward me. *Through* me.

In a blink, I was no longer alone. The Titan appeared beside me, and a moment later, the channels in her body armor glowed crimson.

She spun around, her head moving jerkily to take in her new surroundings. She checked her hood, making sure it was in place, then faced me suddenly, her focus unwavering. "Who are you?" she asked. "And where am I?" Her eyes narrowed on me. "Wait—I know you. You were there when—"

Her brow furrowed, and I imagined the scene replaying in her head. She had been leaning over me, about to drain me of my last drops of psychic energy, thus killing me. But then something grabbed her by the neck with crushing force, and the lights went out on her awareness.

"When you died?" I finished for her.

"I don't understand," she said, glancing around once more.

I purposely sent another ripple through the construct, and her eyes widened. "We're inside a virtual simulation on my ship," I told her.

"The *Elysium*?" she asked, recalling the name of the ship she had attacked. The same ship where she had perished.

I shook my head. "The *Elysium* is far away, on its way to our new home, but that home will only be safe once we complete our current mission."

The Titan looked at me sharply. "Why am I here?"

"This was my home," I told her, sweeping my arm out toward Blackthorn Manor. "You might remember it from what you glimpsed in my mind when you were trying to kill me." She had witnessed much of my current life as Cora *and* my past lives as Peri while she drained the psychic force from me.

The Titan glanced at the house behind me, then returned her focus to me, offering no explanations or excuses for her past behavior. She wasn't sorry for what she had done. She had been in survival mode, and the only source of psychic energy to replenish her depleted reserves had been *us*. Her only response was a slight dip of her chin as she accepted all I had shared with her so far.

"This place is on a planet called Earth," I explained. "A planet your people have all but destroyed."

"I had no part in that," she said matter-of-factly.

"I know," I told her. "I also know what happened to you on Krystallos. I know how you *changed*."

Her eyes opened wider.

"And I know what your people did to you—what they *tried* to do to you—when you returned to them," I said, studying her face, but she displayed no reaction beyond that widening of her eyes. "We recently visited Krystallos and struck a deal with the beings there." I paused, letting that sink in. "The ones contained within the giant crystals," I added, then fell quiet, letting her work through the implications on her own.

"You want to infect my people with souls," she guessed after a long moment.

Again, I nodded. "We brought some of them here, to Earth, gathered within one of their revenant clusters, but the Tsakali fled before we arrived. We think they suspect our intentions and will run from us if we pursue them."

"They would have been alerted to the activity on Krystallos," she said with a nod. "They may not suspect you brought a revenant cluster here, but they'll believe you are contaminated. You won't catch them. They won't let you anywhere near them until they've figured out a way to neutralize the effect the revenant cluster has on our kind."

I smiled to myself. "And how could they possibly find a way to do that without a live sample to study?" I asked. "Would they risk returning to Krystallos to gather what they need?"

"Only as a last resort," she said.

My smile widened into a grin. "Would they prefer to recapture you? To *study* you?"

She stared at me for long, tense seconds. "You want to use me as bait," she finally said, turning away from me to gaze out at the sea.

"Would it work?" I asked her.

She was quiet for a long moment. Her hands balled into fists at her sides.

"We're not trying to destroy them," I said. "We just want to *change* them. To make them like you. To give them a conscience and to make them care about their impact on the universe."

"Regardless of your intention, you *will* destroy them," she said. "You will destroy *us*. We will cease to be what we have always been. The Tsakali will be extinct."

"They'll be *evolved*," I countered as I stepped forward to stand beside her. "Would you go back to the way you were before—if you could?" I asked her, studying her profile. "It hasn't been easy. Would you give up all the fear and running and fighting? Would you give up your soul to be accepted again by your people? To be *like* them?"

"No," she rasped. "Never."

For minutes, we stood side by side and stared out at the sea. Finally, the Titan looked at me. "I'll do it."

46

T HE FRIGID ANTARCTIC AIR burned my exposed cheeks as I watched the *Charon* lift off the glacier field and rise higher into the dawn sky. In a blink, the ship vanished behind its stealth cloaks, Tila and all the Amazons on board flying away while Hades, the Titan, and I remained behind to make our do-or-die attempt to end this war. There was no need for them to risk their lives when all we needed to do was sit and wait a little longer for the Tsakali to return, then activate the revenant cluster. More bodies just meant more collateral damage.

I turned to Hades and Metanoia, as the Titan called herself, having revealed her self-given name shortly after she agreed to help us. The revenant cluster stood tall behind my companions, a hulking crystal behemoth that didn't look all that out of place here in the barren field of ice and snow. According to the *Charon*'s navigation charts, an impressive Tsakali force was due to arrive in less than an hour, having entered their final FTL jump right before we departed Orcas Island for Antarctica.

"And now we wait," I said, flashing my companions a grim smile. My entire body shook with nerves, but I played it off like I was merely cold, despite my hoplon suit's internal temperature regulating mechanism.

This was it. Everything had been building to this moment. Soon enough, either the war between the Olympians and the Tsakali would be over, or we would be dead. Maybe both.

Both would still be worth it. Probably. Although I wondered if I would feel the same in a few hours, when I faced my last demise.

Metanoia scanned the glacier field, her skin so pale it was nearly translucent. She had altered her appearance as soon as we stepped off the *Charon* and onto the glacier, using her chameleon-like ability to adapt to her environment by draining nearly all the color from her hair and skin. A few silver-white strands were visible, having escaped from beneath her hood.

"I'm sensing residual chaos energy," she noted. "There was an enormous explosion here, not too long ago."

Hades scanned the horizon. "We destroyed our settlements when your people initially approached the planet," he told her. He glanced down at the frozen ground. "Our primary settlement was here, far beneath your feet."

"Underground?" Metanoia asked, her eyebrows rising. "I didn't realize subterranean dwelling was a strategy employed by Olympians."

"Under the *ice*," Hades corrected her. "But yes, we had other underground settlements scattered across the planet."

"So any searching Titans will have a harder time detecting you?" Metanoia asked.

Hades bowed his head in assent. "*And* so we would go unnoticed by the people of this planet." He clasped his gloved hands behind his back. "We originally came here intending to guide one branch of the native primate's evolution until they were physically indistinguishable from Olympians—to create a new Olympian race not only untainted by but immune to the Pthora Agent," he explained, referring to the adaptive biological weapon that had rendered our people irreversibly sterile.

"We had an incident before we could complete the mission." Hades glanced at me, one of the key players in said incident. "But the humans were ready. Their brain structure is similar enough to Olympians that they would make viable hosts for us now, if we needed it."

He didn't tell her we might not need the humans anymore, not with the deal he had struck with his sister and those hiding within their time dilation bubble for untainted Olympian embryos. Metanoia was our ally in this, but that didn't mean we trusted her. At least, not enough to share all our secrets.

Metanoia studied Hades for a long moment, no hint of her emotions crossing her face. "You made do with cloning technology," she pointed out, not understanding why the mode of reproduction mattered.

"It's not the same," Hades told her. "Biological reproduction introduces an element of random mutation that can't be mimicked through cloning. We are slowly dying from a myriad of conditions caused by the degradation and destabilization of our DNA and the limitations of our gene pool."

Metanoia eyed us both. "You two seem healthy enough."

Hades dipped his chin, acknowledging the validity of her observation. "I have been fortunate, and Cora—" He glanced at me. "Well, Cora experienced a beneficial RNA transfer from her human mother, who acted as a surrogate for her at the start of this lifetime."

Metanoia turned her full attention to me, and I imagined she was reflecting on all she had experienced in my mind. She had seen my whole life as Cora, both the lies I had grown up believing and the truths I had more recently uncovered. I wondered if she could understand the importance of reproduction better when she viewed it through the lens of the relationship I had with my mom, regardless of my mom and I not being genetically related.

"What my people did to you was inordinately cruel," Metanoia finally said, turning her attention back to Hades. "Genocide should never be an acceptable solution, and I appreciate your unconventional approach to ending this war. When this is all over, perhaps we can share information on how the Pthora Agent was created. Understanding its origins may help you formulate a way to eradicate it."

I looked from the Titan to Hades and back, a slow, disbelieving smile curving my lips. "That would be amazing," I said when Hades made no response, apparently at a complete loss for words.

Metanoia's focus grew distant for a few seconds, then refocused on Hades. "The first ships have emerged from FTL and are approaching the planet."

I licked my frozen lips, which only coated them in a fresh layer of frost, and glanced at the revenant cluster. It looked like little more than a strangely protruding hunk of ice. It wasn't time to activate it yet. But soon.

Hades and I pulled up our psychic hoods, while the Titan pushed hers back, exposing her white hair. She was no longer hiding from her people. She wanted them to find her. We did not, however, want them to know a couple of Olympians were down here with her.

I drained all the psychic energy from my hoplon suit, then activated my regulator, muting my psychic gifts until they, too, would be undetectable. The pervasive chill immediately seeped in through my powered-down armor, and I shivered, this time truly from the cold.

"There," Metanoia said, staring up at the overcast sky.

I squinted up at the gray cloud cover but saw no sign of a ship until, suddenly, something invisible dragged wispy white streaks out of the clouds. More such disturbances emerged, too many to keep track of or to count easily.

Metanoia raised her hand, and a sheet of crimson psychic energy burst from her palm, spreading out to cover the three of us and the revenant cluster in a nearly opaque shimmering red dome. I couldn't see much of anything beyond the barrier, but it was essential the gathering Tsakali force wouldn't be able to see *us*, either. Specifically, they couldn't see Hades and me. It meant that, for the moment, Hades and I were effectively blind, forced to rely on the Titan, our enemy turned ally, to keep us apprised of the situation beyond her barrier.

"Have they landed?" I asked, uselessly scanning the crimson sheet of psychic energy. I couldn't see a thing beyond it.

Metanoia closed her eyes, her face a mask of concentration. "Many of the ships, yes," she said. "More are still coming." She fell quiet for a moment. "Titans are unloading. I've never seen this many gathered together. There must be at least three hundred of them."

"And others?" I asked, imagining the horde of powerful psychics surrounding us. I reflexively reached out to grasp Hades' hand. His fingers were bulky through his armored gloves, but I held him tight, nonetheless.

"Yes," Metanoia said with a sharp nod. "The Titans are forming a perimeter around the dome. They're going to link up to break through my barrier. It won't take long with their numbers."

"How long?" I asked.

"Thirty seconds, if we're lucky."

I clenched and unclenched my jaw. "Will the Tsakali hold any of their force back in reserve?"

"No," she said definitively. "There's no need for a reserve force against a single Titan. They will throw everything they have at me."

I gulped down my rising nerves. "Are more ships still arriving?"

"Yes," she hissed, the sudden strain on her face telling me the Titans had started their assault on her shield.

Hades and I exchanged a worried look, and I swallowed roughly as a disturbing idea took shape in my mind. We needed to buy more time—enough time for all the ships to land. We couldn't risk them nuking the planet from orbit the instant they realized what we were up to.

"Will they be able to sense me through your barrier if I deactivate my regulator?" I asked in a rush, stepping closer to Metanoia. My hand pulled free from Hades' grasp.

"No," she said through gritted teeth.

Before I could talk myself out of it, I swept my fingertip around the stone in my regulator, unleashing my gifts, and pushed psychic energy into my hand. "Take what you need from me," I said, slapping my palm against Metanoia's lowered hand and curling my fingers around hers, holding on tight.

I dragged energy up from my psychic well and pumped it into the Titan through our linked hands, refilling her waning reserves until I scraped the bottom of mine. Breathing hard, I pulled my hand away, retaining just enough psychic energy to defend myself for a few seconds should the need arise. Electric-blue streaks appeared in the shimmering barrier shielding us, my psychic energy reinforcing hers.

"The last ship just touched down," she said breathlessly. "Prepare to activate the revenant cluster."

Heart hammering from the sudden influx of adrenaline, I sidestepped away from Metanoia and around Hades to press my gloved hand to the surface of the giant crystal. "Anastasis," I said, staring into the revenant cluster, waiting for the brilliant flash of light that would indicate the souls within were rousing.

But nothing happened. The revenant cluster remained dormant.

"Anastasis!" I repeated, shouting the word this time and pressing my palm harder against the rough surface of the crystal.

But still, nothing happened.

"Bare skin!" Metanoia called back to me. "The Pythian Revenants must *feel* your intent." She bared her teeth in a grimace. "And hurry!"

My eyes opened wider, and I looked at Hades, who appeared just as horrified. If I touched the revenant cluster with my bare hand, I would be infected. I would *crystallize*.

"Cora, no," Hades said, looking like he was going to be sick.

"I have to do it," I said, a quaver in my voice. My chin trembled at the pain in Hades' gaze. *I* had to do it—so *he* wouldn't.

47

I YANKED OFF MY glove and raised my trembling bare hand. Inhaling deeply, I prepared to sacrifice myself one last time for my people, then shakily released the breath and pushed forward.

Slender fingers curled around my wrist, stopping me from touching the revenant cluster with scant millimeters to spare. I whipped my head around to stare into Metanoia's glowing red eyes. Her other hand was still raised to produce the shield, her face a mask of fierce determination.

"Take over the shield," she ordered. Her hand burned with blue-streaked crimson psychic energy as she pushed some of what I had given her back into me. "I'll wake the Pythian Revenants." She grinned with wicked delight. "They can't hurt me."

My heart seemed to be lodged in my throat, and all I could do was nod. I *wouldn't* be crystallized after all. I still had a future—with Hades. *Because* of a Titan.

A little dazed by the near miss, I thrust my hand up into the air and replaced Metanoia's domed shield with my own, now crimson-streaked electric blue. I immediately felt the onslaught from the linked Titans outside. They weren't so much attempting to break through my barrier as sucking up the psychic energy I poured into the dome. Rushing blood roared in my ears. With every beat of my heart, I grew weaker while they grew stronger. I couldn't even use my connection with Meg to draw psychic energy through her and the Zari Amazons on board the *Elysium* as I had done on Othrys—Meg was too far away to allow for anything beyond basic communication. I had seconds until I was drained completely, and then it wouldn't matter if I had switched places with Metanoia. Crystallized or drained, I would be dead either way.

I gritted my teeth, attempting to balance the need to extend the life of the shield and to preserve my last reserves of psychic energy to keep me alive.

"Anastasis," Metanoia said, her hushed voice nearly drowned out by the roaring of my blood. By the pounding of my heart.

Light exploded out of the revenant cluster, the concussive force flinging me forward. I lost hold of the shield as I sprawled face-first on the slick, melting ice. I raised my head in time to see the shimmering barrier flicker, then vanish. My breath caught and my heart stuttered at the horrifying sight of all those Titans, backed up by twice as many armed Tsakali warriors.

There was a moment of stillness. A hush of terrifying anticipation. I watched, transfixed, as the enemy's collective attention shifted from us to the hulking crystal behind us, now pulsing with that heartbeat-like rhythm.

The first Titan stepped forward, her movements jerky, like she was trying to resist the lure of the revenant cluster. Another joined her, followed by two more, then others. Their steps started slow, resistant, but quickly smoothed out and sped up as the pull from the living crystal consumed them.

Suddenly, they were rushing toward the revenant cluster—toward us. My eyes widened, and I scrambled on my hands and knees to move closer to Hades, who watched the approaching horde with grim acceptance. Behind me, I sensed Metanoia crawling closer to us. I hadn't expected this. Hades and I would be trampled in this stampede of alien warriors. Such a ridiculous way to go, after everything.

After *everything*.

No. *No*. I refused to let either of us end like this. We would not have pointless deaths.

My fingers dug into the ice, and I scraped the bottom of my inner well for the last dregs of psychic energy. A smaller barrier would be far easier to maintain, especially if no Titans were actively draining it. We could huddle together under the shield. We could survive this.

But there was nothing within my well. Just the tiny amount of psychic energy I needed to stay alive. Just enough to keep my heart beating. Not that it would do me any good now.

Hades drew his laser pistol, but he didn't aim it at the incoming Titans. He adjusted a dial on the side of the gun and pressed the nozzle against the frozen ground, pulling back the trigger and holding it down. The ice beneath us lit up with the scattered glow from his weapon, quickly melting until the three of us huddled together in a three-foot-deep depression.

"Get down!" Metanoia shouted, and Hades and I did just that, laying on the slick ice and clinging to each other.

The first of the rushing Titans were mere steps away when Metanoia raised her hand, and a blue-streaked crimson barrier of psychic energy coalesced over our literal hole in the ground. I watched, breath held and eyes wide in horrified fascination, as Titan boots trampled over our hidey-hole.

I kept expecting them to stop. To look down. To see us there and to tear us apart. But the revenant cluster held them in its unbreakable grip. They hadn't even touched it yet, hadn't been infected with the Pythian Revenants yet, and were already lost.

We had already won.

By the time this was over, every Tsakali who had stepped foot on Antarctica would have a soul.

48

M ANY OF THE TSAKALI sat or kneeled on the ice, weeping, though they had no actual tears to shed, not even synthetic ones. Others walked aimlessly, the new moral compasses afforded to them by their Pythian souls spinning wildly as they reassessed everything they had ever done. I wondered if those other versions of Hades and me were out there, meshing with their new hosts. Or did they remain within the still pulsing revenant cluster, waiting for more Tsakali to come?

Hades and I watched the masses from a rise on the glacier. I had never seen so many of our ancient enemy, but for once, I was not afraid to be standing among the Tsakali. Rather, my blood vibrated with an anticipatory thrill. This was the start of a new era, not only for our people or for the Tsakali, but for the entire universe.

The war wasn't over yet. Far from it. But our part in the fighting had come to an end. These Tsakali, the changed ones, would carry our torch, first returning to Krystallos, then venturing out to spread the Pythian Revenants far and wide among their people.

Metanoia approached, climbing the steep, rocky hillside jutting up from the surface of the glacier. She held one hand up to shield her eyes from the sun rising behind us.

"How are they handling the *change*?" I asked the Titan as she reached the top.

Metanoia laughed dryly. "About as well as I did," she said, angling her body sideways so she wasn't staring directly into the sun. "They're coping. They'll get there."

"You'll help them," I said.

"Of course." She offered me a tight smile and dipped her chin.

"You didn't have to help us. To *save* us," I said, stepping closer and extending my hand to her. "We couldn't have done this without you. *Thank you*, Metanoia. We owe you *everything*."

She thrust out her hand and clasped my wrist, and I curled my fingers around her forearm. "You have given me back my people," she said earnestly. "There is no debt between us." We released arms, and she looked from me to Hades and back. "It was an honor to fight beside you both," she said and tucked her chin against her chest.

I pressed my fist to my heart and bowed my head in return. "What will you do now?" I asked her once our eyes locked again.

"After we spread the Pythian Revenants among our people?" Metanoia turned to gaze out at the Tsakali. "I think we'll return here," she said. "Do what we can to heal the damage we caused to this planet and to the native people—if they'll let us."

I let out a breathy laugh. "Good luck with that."

She peered at me quizzically.

"The humans will be extremely wary and justifiably resentful," I explained. "It will take *many* displays of goodwill and peaceful intentions to even begin to earn their trust."

Metanoia nodded. "If you have any advice, it would be most welcome."

"Be honest with them," I told her. "Tell them how you have changed. Explain why you want to help them. And if, after everything, they tell you to leave, then you must go. Leave them to their broken world. In time, they will adapt and overcome on their own. It's what humans do best."

"I truly hope it does not come to that," Metanoia said, once again surveying her people.

Hades' holoband beeped, and he raised his forearm, tapping the device to pull up the small floating holoscreen. "The *Charon* entered Earth's orbit," he said. "It will land in a few minutes."

I reached for his hand, giving it a squeeze. It felt surreal to be done with the fighting. Not just today, but possibly forever. This had been our purpose for so long. For my entire existence. I wasn't sure I knew how to *be* without the constant threat of attack from a mortal enemy.

"What will you two do now?" Metanoia asked, searching the overcast sky for our ship.

Hades and I exchanged a look, my small smile reflected on his lips. "Rejoin our people, for a time," I said. "Make sure they reach our new home safely, and then . . ." I shrugged. "I don't know. Ride off into the sunset, I guess."

Hades and Metanoia stared at me with twin expressions of confusion. Neither of them had ever seen a Western, let alone a movie, so their confusion was perfectly justified, but I didn't feel like explaining myself.

"It's just an Earth saying," I said and turned my face up to the sky.

The *Charon* burst out of the cloud cover and swooped down toward the ground, sunlight glinting off her silvery hull.

"Be well, Metanoia," Hades said, bowing his head.

I smiled at the Titan, sad to be saying goodbye to her even though I had been so afraid of her for most of our acquaintance. I looked at Hades, then turned toward the approaching ship. We walked hand in hand toward the future we hadn't been born into or inherited but had fought tooth and nail for. The one we had died for. The one we had chosen.

Together.

49

T EARS LEAKED FROM THE corners of my eyes as I spied on my other, fractured self, sharing a lively family dinner with my mom, Emi, and Raiden—and, if I wasn't mistaken, with Loki, the cat who had accompanied sim-Cora during the mission to rescue Fiona. I would never see them again, which was probably a blessing in disguise. I was only torturing myself with these *visits*.

We had been in cryosleep for sixty Earth years, only to be awakened after the last FTL jump. The next jump would be the *Elysium*'s final one, landing the ship on the outer edge of Terra's planetary system. Landing the ship, but not *us*. Hades, Tila, and I would be taking off in the *Charon* beforehand, riding off into the starlight—the universe's version of a sunset, I supposed.

Hades had already made contact with our people on Terra, living in what sounded like a burgeoning settlement. The Olympians who had been implanted into human hosts back in the Alpha site had had long enough to establish themselves on Terra while they waited for the *Elysium*.

They had already made the exchange with Artemis for untainted frozen Olympian embryos and were ready to begin gestating the first Terra-born generation as soon as the *Elysium* arrived with the waiting consciousnesses and stored human DNA profiles. The first generation born on Terra would be composed half of Olympians and half of humans. The individuals would be chosen specifically by Gertie based on their personalities and skill sets to provide the new hybrid Olympian-human civilization the best launchpad possible.

As I watched my counterpart laughing with my lost loved ones through the fisheye view of her consciousness orb, I wondered if they would be among that founding generation. I hoped so. I had always loved civilization builder games, and I knew sim-Cora would have a grand time applying her virtual experience to the real world.

Sensing Meg enter the Vault of Souls, I stepped away from sim-Cora's consciousness orb and hastily wiped under my eyes.

Meg rounded the corner and entered my corridor, wearing a hoplon suit like she had been born to be an Amazon. Her face was a mask of sympathy I felt echoed through our bond. The connection we shared was a slight comfort when I thought about all I would be leaving behind. I wouldn't be completely cut off from this place or these people because I would always have my bond with Meg.

"Everyone is gathered in the transport hangar," she said as she drew near. She glanced at the consciousness orb containing undulating electric-blue ribbons, then returned her attention to me. "There's no reason to rush, though, if you're not ready." She laughed under her breath. "Although Fiona would probably disagree."

I chuckled. "Is Hades still 'advising' her?"

"He is," Meg said, her eyes twinkling.

I shook my head. Knowing Hades, he had already recorded everything he needed to say to Fiona on a holodisk. But this was Hades we were talking about, and he was thorough in everything he did. And I meant *everything*.

"Let's go rescue her, shall we?" I said, linking arms with Meg and starting for the vault's exit.

M EG HADN'T BEEN KIDDING when she said that everyone had gathered in the transport hangar. Not merely the core group, but literally every living being on board the *Elysium*. Selene, Caly, Fiona, Hades, and Tila were joined by all the new Amazons. The crowd gathered near the *Charon*, creating a pleasant buzz of expectation in the cavernous space.

Selene stood with Caly near the bottom of the side hatch loading ramp, appearing to be barely suppressing her laughter while Hades stood nearby with Fiona, looking like a stern adult lecturing a petulant child as he *imparted his wisdom* on my petite friend. Tila broke through the crowd as we approached, her tail wagging enthusiastically and her mag boots clanking on the metal floor.

"Hey, little girl," I said, letting go of Meg's arm and scratching Tila's head in passing as the dog made a happy circuit around the two of us.

The crowd of Amazons parted to let us through, many touching my arms and wishing me luck or bidding me farewell as I passed. Fiona watched me with pleading eyes as I approached, and Selene's laughter finally broke free. Selene turned away, hiding her mouth behind a raised hand as she attempted to regain her composure.

"All right, all right," I said, taking hold of Hades' arm and pulling him away from Fiona mid-sentence. "Stop hogging the new captain." I stepped between them, shielding Fiona.

"Thank you," Fiona mouthed.

I grinned at her even as fresh tears welled in my eyes. "So, I guess this is it."

"Don't you dare say it," Fiona said in a rush. "This isn't goodbye. It's just us going back to the way we used to be—the best long-distance friends who ever lived."

My chin trembled. "Yeah," I said, my voice thicker than before. Except nothing was the way it used to be. Not even us.

Tears spilled over the brims of Fiona's eyelids, and she growled as she hastily swiped them away. "Stop it!" she laugh-cried. And then she threw her arms around me, hugging me tight.

I squeezed her back, amazed that an embrace could feel so easy, so necessary, when it would have been impossible before all the chaos started. "You'll look out for them?" I said when we parted, knowing the *them* I referred to needed no further definition. "When they're young? It can be confusing, growing up in a new body and coming to terms with who you used to be."

"Obvi," Fiona said with an eye roll before she wiped away a fresh string of tears. She made a shooing motion. "Now get out of here before I lose it completely."

Laughing so I wouldn't sob, I turned to Selene next, and she held out one hand to clasp forearms with me. "You will never be forgotten," she said, her eyes glassy.

I forced a shaky smile, but I couldn't manage any words. Instead, I pulled Selene in for a hug. She would be making her final backup before the next jump, as her current body had to be discarded before the *Elysium* reached Terra to prevent herself from sterilizing the new generation of Olympians with the Pthora Agent. Selene would be reborn, eventually. Hopefully, in the same generation as sim-Cora. I liked thinking there would be a member of the old guard of Amazons around sim-Cora, who knew exactly what that other version of me had been through—and knew that even if sim-Cora wasn't Peri, she was still capable of greatness.

When Selene and I parted, I turned to clasp Caly on the shoulder. "Your mom would be so proud of you," I told her, knowing the indomitable leader of the Zari psychics had always seen her daughter's potential, even when Caly had been blind to it herself.

Caly's throat bobbed, and she nodded, apparently at a loss for words.

I turned away from them both and locked eyes with Meg, standing in a break in the crowd, well out of arm's reach. She bowed her head, her emotions overflowing into me as mine spilled over into her. My chest convulsed, and I forced a deep inhale, collecting myself as best I could.

My heart swelled with pride as I scanned the faces of the gathered women. These warriors, without whom we would have failed miserably in our mission to usher all the souls on board the *Elysium* to Terra.

I swallowed my mounting sorrow at the coming farewell and cleared my throat, pressing my fist over my heart. "It's been an honor to serve with you all," I said, my chin held high.

The sound of their fists hitting their chests echoed throughout the hangar.

I turned away before my composure could break and started up the ramp to the side hatch, my dog at my side and Hades following behind me. I didn't stop in the open hatch. I didn't turn around to see them all one last time. If I did, I might never leave.

But there was no place for me here. Not anymore. Not with that other version of me waiting to be reborn.

I took slow, deep breaths as I crossed the cabin to the helm and sat. I fastened Tila into the squat doggy seat that the maintenance bots had added to the *Charon* while we slept in our cryopods, then buckled my own restraints. Beside me, Hades strapped himself in.

Unable to resist, I peeked around the back of my seat at the side hatch, but the door was already sealed shut. Sighing, I turned toward the viewscreen, displaying the inner airlock doors straight ahead of the ship.

"Have you thought about where you'd like to go first?" Hades asked, pulling up the holoscreen in front of him and opening a navigation chart.

Anywhere, so long as it was with him. But there *was* one place I had longed to visit since my very first lifetime.

I nodded and licked my lips. "Home," I said definitively.

"Back to Earth?" he asked.

When I looked at Hades, his brows were raised. I shook my head and flashed him a weak smile. "Not Earth."

I was actually thinking about a home I had never seen, a place I had never had a chance to defend, but that I had fought for after it had already fallen. Hades had always been so focused on me, on my wants and needs. Now, for once, I was thinking about *him*—about *his* home.

Olympus had supposedly been destroyed during the war, but I had done a little snooping through the navigation system back on the *Elysium*, and the planet itself was technically still there. At least, it showed up on the navigation charts, so I figured it was worth checking out.

Hades' brow furrowed, and his eyes narrowed.

I waited until awareness dawned on his features. "Let's go home," I told him. "To Olympus."

EPILOGUE
Sim-Cora

"**H**OLY SHIT!" I EXCLAIMED as I walked into the attic only to find Loki sitting primly in front of the standing mirror that acted as our access portal to the greater simulation, his blue-striped tail curled around his front paws, concealing his tiny black toes.

I hadn't seen the cheeky little Cheshire cat outside of Allworld Online for years, or maybe even for decades. It was easy to lose track of time when no time actually seemed to pass. The seasons changed as they normally would, but the years all blended together into one endless string of the same year. The year we left Earth. To those who weren't *aware*, memories faded at the one-year mark, enabling the simulation to trick their minds into believing far less time had passed than it actually had.

Raiden, my mom, Emi, and I all looked exactly the same as we had the day I was uploaded to the simulation, though we estimated about sixty years had passed out in the real world. It was hard to keep track when every journal or calendar slowly erased and reset. We had only our memories to rely on, thankfully excluded from the memory fade that Gertie forced upon all the humans not in the know.

The last time I saw Loki in our humble Earth construct had been to introduce me to Jane, an uploaded human woman Fiona had found who had the unique ability to see through the simulation's candy-coated exterior to the raw code at its core. Since then, Jane had moved into the growing community here on our part of Orcas Island composed of similarly unique people who we had come to call *codeseers*. Gertie and Fiona agreed it was essential to find every single person who developed the ability to truly *see* the simulation—to prevent their awareness of Truth from unraveling the whole thing around us.

Hand still on the doorknob, I narrowed my eyes at the cat who was far more than he appeared. "What is it?" I asked him. "Did you find another codeseer?"

"If only," Loki said, the tip of his tail twitching. "We found *her*."

My heart skipped a beat, then stumbled into a gallop. My grip on the polished brass doorknob tightened, and I forced myself to release it. "Demeter?" I asked, wiping my suddenly sweaty palm on my jeans.

Again, Loki's tail twitched. "The one and only," he said. "She has gathered a sizable force of her followers in an in-development portion of the simulation."

"Which part?" I asked, finally crossing the threshold and stepping into the attic. Fiona and Gertie were always expanding Allworld Online. It was impossible to keep up.

"Austentopia," Loki said. "Specifically, the *Pride and Prejudice* role playing game."

I crossed the attic floor and crouched down in front of Loki. "Do you want me to go in?" I asked. "I can put together a team."

Loki's tail whipped around for a moment before settling back around himself. "No," he said, blinking his eerie neon-blue eyes. "She'll be keeping an eye out for you." He raised one paw and licked it lazily. "We need someone she won't ever see coming. Someone who can sneak in under her nose and snoop around to figure out what she's planning."

"One of the codeseers, then?" I sat down, taking the strain off my knees, and leaned forward. "You already know who, don't you?"

Several names came to mind from the codeseers gathered on Orcas Island. Cain, the decorated Marine, or Sasha, the CIA field agent. Maybe Kareem, the revolutionary leader, or even Jin, the e-sports champion.

Loki set down his paw and looked at me, unblinking. "Olivia."

My eyes widened, and my mouth fell open. "The *teacher*?"

"The Jane Austen scholar," Loki corrected, his flat look a silent scolding for being unable to see past someone's occupation to their true potential.

I laughed under my breath. "Okay . . ." I shook my head, not fully on board with his choice. Even if Olivia had the relevant expertise for the construct, she would still have to face Demeter and her cronies, and that was another matter entirely. "If you've got this all figured out, why are you coming to me?"

"Because we need you to convince Olivia to take the mission," he said, blinking as he looked away. *We*. So, he had already been talking to Fiona and Gertie about this.

"Olivia doesn't want to do it?" I asked. No real surprise there. She was hardly qualified to take on the demented, power-hungry ex-leader of the Order of Amazons.

"She has nothing against entering the construct," Loki said. "But we need her to go in blind so Demeter can't sense her intent, and she's opposed to having the last forty-seven years of her simulation experience erased."

I assumed that meant her codeseer abilities had awakened forty-seven years ago. There were so many of them now that I couldn't remember when each had joined us.

"You want me to convince her to give up decades of her life? *Now*? Aren't we close to Terra?" I winced at the stabbing pain in my skull triggered by the question about *the outside*. But we had to be close. The trip had been projected to take sixty years, and that was about how much time we calculated had passed.

"One more jump, and we'll arrive," Loki said, confirming my suspicion. "But Gertie refuses to complete the trip with the threat of Demeter hanging over the simulation, and Fiona has been unable to override her. Gertie believes Demeter has the power to ruin everything for the colony on Terra, and her primary directive to preserve Olympian life cannot be overruled." He released a long, drawn-out sigh. "Gertie refuses to budge so long as there is even the slightest chance Demeter could sneak into a new body during the first round of resurrections."

I scoffed. "So, what—Gertie is holding us hostage in the sim until we take care of the Demeter situation?" That meant the *Elysium* wouldn't make the last jump to Terra until we had captured and contained Demeter in an isolated construct.

Loki's whiskers twitched, and he turned his eerie stare my way. "Precisely." He blinked lazily, responding to my thoughts as well as to my words. "So I suggest you get a move on and have a little chat with Olivia, or none of you will ever be reborn."

~~The end.~~

The beginning.

A note from the author:

THANK YOU SO MUCH for joining Cora on her grand adventure! You'll see more of Sim-Cora, Loki, and friends in book two of the spinoff series, Allworld Online. Book one, *Allworld Online: Pride & Prejudice* is currently available in my bookshop and all the places in ebook, audio, and paperback.

Be sure to sign up for my newsletter to stay apprised of updates relating to further books and series in the Legacies of Olympus world (including Atlantis Legacy, Allworld Online, and more to come!), as well as news about special editions and bonus scenes. Other great ways to stay in touch: join my Discord server and follow me on Instagram.

If you love my stories and want to go deeper with bonus content, artwork, and merch, check out my reader subscription on Ream!

Again, thank you so much for joining Cora (and me) on this journey! I have loved writing every page of Cora's adventure, and I can't wait to see her again in the simulation!

Happy reading!

Lindsey Sparks

About Lindsey Sparks

Lindsey Sparks lives her life with one foot in a book—so long as that book transports her to a magical world or bends the rules of science. Her novels, from Post-apocalyptic (writing as Lindsey Fairleigh) to Time Travel Romance, always offer up a hearty dose of unreality, along with plenty of history, intrigue, adventure, and romance.

When she's not working on her next novel, Lindsey spends her time hanging out with her two little boys, working in her garden, or playing board games with her husband. She lives in the Pacific Northwest with her family and their small pack of cats and dogs.

www.authorlindseysparks.com

SIGNED COPIES & MERCH:
lindseysparksbookshop.com

REAM (serials, bonus stories, and merch subscription):
https://reamstories.com/lindseysparks

MAIN SOCIAL MEDIA

Instagram: @authorlindseysparks

YouTube: Author Lindsey Sparks

Discord: discord.gg/smTeDHQBhT

www.authorlindseysparks.com/join-newsletter

9 781949 485332